Praise

"O'Nan's best novel yet . . . It's hea[   ] I found myself sobbing at certain, often unex[   ] illiance lies just as much in O'Nan's innate c[   ] Emily's self-imposed isolation from, and dis[   ] If O'Nan's earlier novels were influenced by Poe, the specter of Henry James hovers delicately above Emily's Grafton Street home, insinuating itself into O'Nan's spiraling, exact sentences and the beautiful, subtle symbolism that permeates the novel."
—*The New York Times Book Review*

"Emily is as authentic a character as any who ever walked the pages of a novel. She could be our grandmother, our mother, our next-door neighbor, our aunt. Our self . . . In a portrait filled with joy and rue, O'Nan does not wield a wide brush across a vast canvas but, rather, offers an exquisite miniature. Just as Emily prefers van Gogh's depiction of a branch of an almond tree over the more spectacular *Sunflowers*, so, too, do we readers appreciate an ordinary life made, by its quiet rendering, extraordinary. No matter her—and our—unavoidable end, Emily . . . teaches us that small moments not only count but also endure."
—Mameve Medwed, *The Boston Globe*

"It takes a deft hand to do justice to the ordinary . . . but, if the mundane matters to you, then Stewart O'Nan is your man. . . . O'Nan's glory as a writer is that he conveys the full force of the quotidian without playing it for slapstick or dressing it up as Profound. . . . *Emily, Alone* [is] moody, lightly comic, and absolutely captivating. . . . With economy, wit, and grace, O'Nan ushers us into the shrinking world of a pleasantly flawed, rather ordinary old woman and keeps us readers transfixed by the everyday miracles of monotony."
—Maureen Corrigan, *Fresh Air*

"To say that nothing happens in this [*Emily, Alone*] is like saying that there's nothing going on in that glorious room in Amsterdam's Rijksmuseum where Rembrandt's numerous portraits of his mother hang. . . . [O'Nan] is a seamless craftsman who specializes in the lives of ordinary people. In Emily Maxwell, O'Nan has created a sturdy everywoman, occasionally blemished by pettiness and disdain for common idiocy, but always striving for a moral equilibrium."
—*San Francisco Chronicle*

"As riveting as a fast-paced thriller, albeit one that delves into the life and psyche of an elderly woman."
—*The Miami Herald*

"Stewart O'Nan's books are not about poverty, life's crises, gross injustice, or family drama; in fact, there's very little drama in his works. He has become a spokesperson—in modern fiction—for the regular person, the working person, and now, the elderly. . . . This is a writer who illuminates moments like that one, moments you never even noticed. . . . O'Nan's thoroughness is like a skill from another time—a quieter time, when it was easier to listen." —*Los Angeles Times*

"O'Nan's storytelling is as patient and meticulous as his heroine. He illuminates the everyday with splendid precision. Readers who appreciate psychological nuance and fictional filigree will delight in *Emily, Alone*."
—Stephen Amidon, *The Globe and Mail* (Toronto)

"Emily stretches for a kind of rediscovery. Throughout she is lovable and heartbreaking and real. When this novel ends, in a moment of great hope and vigor, you'll find yourself missing her terribly." —*Entertainment Weekly* (Grade A)

"O'Nan gives each small experience an emotional heft, and he's supremely skilled at revealing Emily's emotional investment in every small change in her life. . . . [A] plainspoken but brassy, somber but straight-talking [tone] infuses this entire nervy, elegant book." —*Minneapolis Star Tribune*

"[O'Nan] is an author who would drive all around town to avoid running over a single cheap thrill. He subverts our desire for commotion and searches instead for drama in the quotidian motions of survivors. . . . [*Emily, Alone*] quietly shuffles in where few authors have dared to go. And it's so humane and so finely executed that I hope it finds those sensitive readers who will appreciate it."
—Ron Charles, *The Washington Post*

"*Emily, Alone* demonstrates that though the distance between an incredibly boring book and a fascinating one may seem small, it is actually miles wide. It takes a madly inventive writer to make a novel about an old woman's daily existence as absorbing as this one is." —*The Daily*

"Stewart O'Nan is a master of introspection." —*The Denver Post*

"O'Nan's book, with great poignancy and humor, offers a rare glimpse into the life of a woman whose life is nearing an end. . . . [Emily is] an irresistible character—funny, flawed, and thoroughly unsentimental about her inevitable fate. . . . In different hands, this might have been a morose book, but it's actually delightful. O'Nan's ability to deliver such a flawless portrait of a woman thirty years his senior speaks to his gifts as a writer." —*The Dallas Morning News*

"*Emily, Alone*, by Stewart O'Nan, is a book of quiet yet stunning beauty; steady and trim from the outside, like its protagonist, and, just like her, stirring inside with deep longings, intense observations, and a strong attachment to living."
—*The Huffington Post*

"O'Nan has the rare ability to make the ordinary seem unordinary in a way that is reminiscent of Updike."
—*The Daily Beast*

"Reading *Emily, Alone* made me think of Charles Dickens. This is somewhat incongruous, because Stewart O'Nan's novels are not crafted out of the complicated, multilayered plots that we associate with Dickens. But O'Nan does share a laserlike observational talent with the Victorian master—one that can shock the reader into a sense that the story is lifted out of one's own family or even oneself. . . . O'Nan is a true virtuoso. . . . [Emily] is quietly heroic."
—William Kist in *The Cleveland Plain Dealer*

"Mr. O'Nan skillfully and sensitively re-creates Emily's world, from the city streets she nervously navigates in the car to her fears of illness and death."
—*Pittsburgh Post-Gazette*

"Old age treads the thin line between melancholy and mirth in Stewart O'Nan's marvelous new novel, *Emily, Alone*."
—*Buffalo News*

"There's a calm, enveloping tone to the story that belies its unflinching exploration of a woman's chronically discontented heart. . . . Its chief pleasure comes from unraveling this little old lady's mess tangle of emotions."
—*BookPage*

"Stewart O'Nan may simply be genetically incapable of writing a bad book. His characters are written with precision, intelligence, and verisimilitude; they're so luminously alive that a reader can accurately guess about what they're eating for dinner or what brand toothpaste they use. . . . The fact that Stewart O'Nan can take an 'invisible woman'—someone we nod to pleasantly and hope she won't engage us in conversation too long—and explore her interior and exterior life is testimony to his skill. Mr. O'Nan writes about every woman . . . and shows that there is no life that can be defined as ordinary."
—*Mostly Fiction Book Reviews* (online)

"[*Emily, Alone*] is an elegant examination of aging, family, and identity with a fine balance of the surprising and the expected. It is at once optimistic and totally realistic, and every page is a joy to read. As a sequel or stand-alone title, *Emily, Alone* is an understated yet powerful character study from one of America's outstanding storytellers."
—Bookreporter.com

"[By reading *Emily, Alone*] it is possible that the reader could reach a deeper understanding of the stage of life or the ways that we visit the sins of our parents on our children or of the folly of holding on to outdated patterns of living. When it comes to showing us to ourselves, Stewart O'Nan is a master."

—*New York Journal of Books*

"A warmhearted, clear-eyed portrait of a woman in her dotage who understands that life is both awfully long and woefully short, much of it passed in waiting and regret, but never, heaven forbid, about just the past, since 'every day was another chance.'"
—*Barnes and Noble Review*

"This exquisite novel plumbs an interior landscape rarely explored in literature. . . . It's testament to O'Nan's talent than *Emily, Alone* is a page-turner suffused with vibrancy, humor, even hope."
—*Macleans*

"Utterly devastating, poignant, so subtle. It is unpardonable that O'Nan is not a household name."
—Edward Champion on Twitter

"Emily Maxwell, in Stewart O'Nan's terrif *Emily, Alone*, joins India Bridge & Olive Kitteridge as women characters whom you won't soon forget."
—Nancy Pearl on Twitter

"[A] bracingly unsentimental, ruefully humorous, and unsparingly candid novel about the emotional and physical travails of old age. . . . The closely observed Emily is a sort of contemporary Mrs. Bridge, and O'Nan's depiction of her attempts to sustain optimism and energy during the late stage of her life achieves a rare resonance."
—*Publishers Weekly* (starred review)

"O'Nan again proves himself to be the king of detail. What people eat, how they eat it, what they think and say in the midst of eating it—this novel represents an almost minute mapping of the lay of the domestic land as O'Nan the sociological cartographer views it."
—*Booklist* (starred review)

"With sympathy and compassion, O'Nan spotlights the plight of aging baby boomers, further enriching our understanding of the human condition."
—*Library Journal*

"Another quietly poignant character study from O'Nan . . . Rueful and autumnal, but very moving."
—*Kirkus Reviews*

PENGUIN BOOKS

EMILY, ALONE

Stewart O'Nan's many novels include *Snow Angels*, *A Prayer for the Dying*, and *Last Night at the Lobster*. He was born and raised and lives with his family in Pittsburgh.

Stewart O'Nan

EMILY, ALONE

PENGUIN BOOKS

PENGUIN BOOKS

Published by the Penguin Group

Penguin Group (USA) Inc., 375 Hudson Street, New York, New York 10014, U.S.A. • Penguin Group
(Canada), 90 Eglinton Avenue East, Suite 700, Toronto, Ontario, Canada M4P 2Y3 (a division of Pearson
Penguin Canada Inc.) • Penguin Books Ltd, 80 Strand, London WC2R 0RL, England • Penguin Ireland,
25 St. Stephen's Green, Dublin 2, Ireland (a division of Penguin Books Ltd) • Penguin Books Australia Ltd,
250 Camberwell Road, Camberwell, Victoria 3124, Australia (a division of Pearson Australia Group Pty
Ltd) • Penguin Books India Pvt Ltd, 11 Community Centre, Panchsheel Park, New Delhi – 110 017,
India • Penguin Group (NZ), 67 Apollo Drive, Rosedale, Auckland 0632, New Zealand (a division
of Pearson New Zealand Ltd) • Penguin Books (South Africa) (Pty) Ltd, 24 Sturdee Avenue,
Rosebank, Johannesburg 2196, South Africa

Penguin Books Ltd, Registered Offices: 80 Strand, London WC2R 0RL, England

First published in the United States of America by Viking Penguin,
a member of Penguin Group (USA) Inc. 2011
Published in Penguin Books 2011

10 9 8 7 6 5

Publisher's Note

This is a work of fiction. Names, characters, places, and incidents either are the product of the author's
imagination or are used fictitiously, and any resemblance to actual persons, living or dead, business
establishments, events, or locales is entirely coincidental.

THE LIBRARY OF CONGRESS HAS CATALOGED THE HARDCOVER EDITION AS FOLLOWS:
O'Nan, Stewart.
    Emily, alone : a novel / Stewart O'Nan.
        p. cm.
    Sequel to: Wish you were here.
    ISBN 978-0-670-02235-9 (hc.)
    ISBN 978-0-14-312049-0 (pbk.)
    1. Widows—Fiction.   2. Older women—Fiction.   3. Life change events—Fiction.   4. Domestic fiction.
    I. Title.
    PS3565.N316E65 2011
    813'.54—dc22   2010035333

Printed in the United States of America
Designed by Carla Bolte • Set in Granjon

For my mother,
who took me to the bookmobile

Could it be, even for elderly people, that this was life—
startling, unexpected, unknown?

—Virginia Woolf

Emily, Alone

TWO-FOR-ONE

Tuesdays, Emily Maxwell put what precious little remained of her life in God's and her sister-in-law Arlene's shaky hands and they drove together to Edgewood for Eat 'n Park's two-for-one breakfast buffet. The Sunday *Post-Gazette*, among its myriad other pleasures, had coupons. The rest of the week she might have nothing but melba toast and tea for breakfast, maybe peel herself a clementine for some vitamin C, but the deal was too good to pass up, and served as a built-in excuse to get out of the house. Dr. Sayid was always saying she needed to eat more.

It wasn't far—a few miles through East Liberty and Point Breeze and Regent Square on broad streets they knew like old friends—but the trip was a test of Emily's nerves. Arlene's eyes weren't the best, and her attention to the outside world was directly affected by whatever conversation they were engaged in. When she concentrated on a thought, she drove more slowly, making them the object of honking, and once, recently, from a middle-aged woman who looked surprisingly like Emily's daughter Margaret, the finger.

"Obviously I must have done something," Arlene had said.

"Obviously," Emily agreed, though she could have cited a whole list. It did no good to criticize Arlene after the fact, no matter how constructively. The best you could do was hold on and not gasp at the close calls.

In the beginning they'd taken turns, but, honestly, as atrocious as Arlene was, Emily trusted herself even less. Henry had always done the driving in the family. It was a point of pride with him. When he was dying, he insisted on driving to the hospital for his chemo himself. It was only on the way home, with Henry sick and silent beside her, bent over a plastic bowl in his lap, that Emily piloted his massive Olds down the corkscrewing ramps of the medical center's parking garage, terrified she'd scrape the sides against the scarred concrete walls. For several years she used the old boat to do her solitary errands, never venturing outside of the triangle described by the bank, the library and the Giant Eagle, but after a run-in with a fire hydrant, followed quickly by another with a Duquesne Light truck, she admitted—bitterly, since it went against her innate thriftiness—that maybe taking taxis was the better part of valor. Now the Olds sat out back in the garage with her rusty golf clubs as if decommissioned, the windshield dusty, the tires soft. She wasn't a fan of the bus, and Arlene had made a standing offer of her Taurus, itself a boxy if less grand antique. The joke among their circle was that she'd become Emily's chauffeur, though, as that circle shrank, fewer and fewer people knew their history, to the point where, having the same last name, they were sometimes introduced by the well-meaning young, at a University Club function or after one of Donald Wilkins's wonderful organ recitals at Calvary, as sisters, a notion Arlene though not Emily found wildly amusing.

Today, as always, Arlene was late. It was gray and raining, typical November weather for Pittsburgh, and Emily stood at the living room's bay window, leaning over the low radiator and holding the sheer curtain aside. The storm window was spotted and dirty. A few weekends ago, her next-door neighbor Jim Cole had generously hung them, but he'd failed to clean them properly, and now there was nothing to be done until the spring. She would spend a morning tending to them herself, the way her mother had taught her, with vinegar and water, wiping them streak-free with newsprint, but that was months off.

Outside, the trees and hedges along Grafton Street were bare and black, and the low sky made it feel like late afternoon instead of morning. The Millers' was still for sale. Their leaves hadn't been picked up yet, and lay smothering the yard, a dark, sodden mass. She wondered who would be looking to buy this time of year. The last she'd heard, Kay Miller was in an assisted living place over in Aspinwall, but that had been in August. Emily thought she should visit her, though in truth it was the last thing she wanted to do.

When she thought of fashionable, flighty Kay Miller in a place like the one in Aspinwall, she couldn't help but picture Louise Pickering's final hospital room. The oatmeal bareness, the mechanical bed, the plastic water pitcher with its bent straw on the rollaway table. Consciously, she knew those places could be very nice, just as homey as your own bedroom, or close to it, but the vision of Louise persisted, and the idea that she was at an age where all was stillness and waiting—not true, yet impossible to dismiss.

She was dying, yes, fine, they all were, by degrees. If Dr. Sayid expected her to be devastated by the idea, that only showed how young he was. There was no point in going into hysterics. It wasn't the end of the world, just the end of her, and lately she'd come to think that was natural, and possibly something to be desired, if it could be achieved with a modicum of dignity, not pointlessly drawn out, like Louise undergoing all those torturous last-ditch procedures because Timothy and Daniel refused to give up. She'd never wanted to be eighty. Practically, she'd never wanted to outlive Henry.

A stale, metallic heat rose from the radiator, baking her shins. With her car coat buttoned up to her neck and her scarf already tucked in, it was oppressive. She let go of the curtain and turned away.

On the front hall runner, Rufus sat at attention, staring at the door as if he might open it by sheer mind power.

"I told you," Emily said, "you're not going anywhere. Go lie down. *Go.*"

Reluctantly he padded to his spot at the bottom of the stairs and circled twice before collapsing with a huff on the rag rug, his snout pointed toward her.

"Yeah," she said, "I've got my eye on you too, mister. I don't want to find anything when I get home. You know what I'm talking about."

He looked up at her guiltily, as if he understood, and part of her argued that it wasn't his fault. Technically he was older than she was, ancient for a springer, and lately he'd taken to sleeping most of the day away, like Duchess before she died. He could also be bad—and he'd never been before—getting into the garbage or gnawing on a chair leg or peeing on the carpet right in front of her, as if he'd gone senile. "What am I going to do with you?" she asked, as she would a child, because there was no answer. She could only scold him and clean up the mess, and when she left him home alone like now, she worried.

She heard Arlene's car pull in before he did. Out front, through the gauzy curtains, a dark blob filled the driveway.

Rufus barked a warning, pushing himself up off the rug. "Thank you," she called as he trotted, barking, to the door. "We know this person."

He wouldn't stop, and she had to make him sit, jabbing a finger at him so that he flinched, and she felt bad.

"I'll be back," she said, pulling on her gloves. "You be good."

She'd just had her hair done yesterday, and cinched tight her see-through plastic rain hat before cracking the storm door, propping it with a hip as she popped open her umbrella. She pushed through, and the cold hit her— moist but not as raw as she'd thought. Lately the latch of the storm door had been sticking, hanging up on the frame, letting in a chilly draft that infiltrated the whole downstairs. For an extra second she paused on the stoop to make sure it clicked shut.

Arlene hadn't pulled up enough, and Emily had to deal with a treacherous slope of lawn and drop-off of curb while battling the passenger door. The reek of cigarettes that rose from the upholstery was immediate, as if Arlene had just finished one. Emily shook her umbrella before pulling it in after her, and still she dripped all over her coat.

"Taking no chances, I see," said Arlene, whose own hair was a deep henna she'd adopted a few years ago, and which, like Arlene's carmine lipstick, Emily considered garish, too young. Her own color, though not natural, was at least plausible, a mousy brown streaked with gray. At their age, there was just so much you could get away with, and only if you remained tasteful.

"For fifty dollars," Emily said, "this has to last me till Thanksgiving."

"Does Margaret know what she's doing yet?"

As Arlene backed out, Emily craned to see if anyone was coming. Grafton Street was steep here, and with the rain it would be hard to stop.

"You're fine on my side," Emily said. "She hasn't called since the last time we talked, but they can't afford to fly." She didn't say she wasn't even sure Margaret was working, or that she'd been sending her checks every month so she could make her mortgage payments.

"What about Kenneth?"

"They're going to Lisa's parents' place on Cape Cod."

"It's tough to compete with that."

"Tell me about it," Emily said. "I'd love to go to the Cape, but that's not a serious option."

"It's not."

"It would be if I were willing to spend nine hundred dollars on a plane ticket. It might have been possible if Lisa had let me know in advance, but that's not how she operates."

"That's a shame."

"It's nothing new."

"Well," Arlene said with dismay, as if it were some consolation.

They passed the Pickerings' house and reached the stop sign at Highland. Emily stayed silent while Arlene waited for a break in traffic. Nattering, barely audible, WQED played their usual rushed Vivaldi. Over the years Emily had seen her share of accidents here—or heard them, first the heart-stopping screech of tires, then the empty split-second delay before the crunch of impact. Highland was flat and wide and fast, and regularly, as she puttered about the house, dusting the plants or thinning the magazines, the wail of a police car or ambulance beckoned her to the front window to see what had happened now. The worst brought her neighbors out, all of them clumped on the sidewalk to watch the fire trucks and debate the idea of a stoplight (never, Doug and Louise said; it would destroy their property values).

There was a gap after a bus, but Arlene balked.

"Did you hear about the bus driver in Wilkinsburg?" Arlene asked, turning to her.

"No," Emily said, and pointed to the road.

There was another gap, and Arlene launched them across in plenty of time.

"It was on KDKA this morning. This driver, I don't know what he was thinking. He left his bus running outside a McDonald's, and someone took off with it. They found it on the North Side, right behind Heinz Field."

"Maybe it was one of the Steelers," Emily said, because they'd had some run-ins with the police.

"Can you imagine, coming out with your Egg McMuffin and your bus is gone?"

Emily was content to accept this as rhetorical, watching the stately brick homes lining Highland pass, their columned porticos and many chimneys a testament to the city's former wealth. They perched high, each with its swath of lawn and loop of drive, separated from the common street by wrought-iron gates and black granite walls worthy of a churchyard. As a young woman from a dumpy backwater like Kersey, she'd coveted these mansions, though compared to the Fricks' Clayton or the Mellon estate or the limestone monstrosities along Fifth Avenue, they were modest. Henry had always been practical in that regard. The house on Grafton had never seemed too big or too small for them. Even after the children left, they could still fill it.

She thought of Rufus curled up under the dining room table, or settling in beside the hot air register by the hutch. In the late morning the sun slanted through the French doors that opened on her garden, illuminating a wedge of rug approximately his size, rendering visible a slow galaxy of dust motes above his sleeping form. Sometimes she had to check to make sure he was breathing. She wished she could do that, just laze the day away. The gray sky, the trees, the street—the Pittsburgh winter promised another five months of this, and worse. She could see why people her age scuttled off to Florida.

"So it's just us chickens?" Arlene asked.

"It's just us chickens," Emily said.

"Did you want to go to the club or do something else?"

"Do you have any suggestions?"

"How soon do we need to make reservations?"

"Soon," Emily said, remembering one of Margaret's birthday dinners there. It must have been forty-five years ago, because Margaret was slim as a ballerina in her pinafore, curtsying to everyone for the fun of it. Emily's own parents were there, a rare occasion, her father gawking in his cheap brown suit, impressed by the high windows and the murals on the ballroom's ceiling, the white-gloved waiters circulating between tables to deliver iced pats of butter stamped with the club crest. Emily would have arranged for Margaret to have her favorite—yellow cake with chocolate frosting—and Henry would have paid by signing his name. Forty-five years.

She could not stop these visitations, even if she wanted to. They plagued her like migraines, left her helpless and dissatisfied, as if her life and the lives of all those she'd loved had come to nothing, merely because that time was gone, receding even in her own memory, to be replaced by this diminished present. If it seemed another world, that was because it was, and all her wishing could not bring it back.

As they neared East Liberty, block by block the houses deteriorated, porches sagging, windows boarded over, retaining walls spray-painted. Trash dotted the yards and sidewalks, and at every intersection huddled fairy rings of signs from last week's election, the winners and losers drenched alike by the rain. Arlene had the heater blasting. It stuttered, a leaf stuck in the fan, but she didn't seem to notice.

"Could we possibly turn the heat down?" Emily asked. "I'm roasting."

"Are you serious?" Arlene said. "I've been freezing all morning."

"You probably just need something to eat."

"I had my coffee. It didn't seem to do much good."

Arlene was a famous complainer about her low blood pressure, though to Emily she sometimes came across as unaccountably proud of her condition, as if it were special, affecting only the select. Rather than endure a lecture, Emily closed her vent, pinched off her gloves, untied her rain hat, popped her top button and unwound her scarf. As if in compromise, Arlene turned the fan down a notch.

"That better?" Arlene asked.

"Thank you."

They passed the modernized façade of Peabody High School, where Henry had gone when it was all white. Though it was past nine o'clock, a few bareheaded boys roughhoused beside a bus shelter, laughing and swinging their backpacks at one another. Emily wondered if their mothers knew they were skipping school.

"Do you have your lights on?" Emily asked, because traffic coming the other way did.

"Yes, I have my lights on."

"I was just asking."

"And I'm just telling you."

She could not get used to the ugly orange Home Depot that had taken the place of the ugly blue Sears. As a young mother, she'd taken the children there to shop for clothes and to pick out Christmas presents. Margaret was wild for the perfume samples and the jewelry counter, while Kenneth was fascinated by the escalators and the wall of tropical fish and the booth where they made keys. Henry bought all of his tools there. They were still neatly arrayed in the basement, his screwdrivers and wrenches and pliers lined up by size on pegboard, having fulfilled their lifetime guarantees. The Home Depot had been there for ten years, and she'd never once set foot in it. The neighborhood had changed. Not that it was dangerous, not during the day. She probably hadn't walked this stretch of Highland since . . . she literally couldn't remember.

"Look at that," Arlene said, gesturing to the SUV passing them on the right. The driver, a black teenager with a sparse beard and squashed afro, was talking on a cell phone. "And you think *I'm* bad."

"You are," Emily said.

"At least I'm not on the phone."

"Who would you call—me?"

"Yes," Arlene said. "I'd call you and tell you to find your own darn ride."

"Touché."

Then, as if to test her, Arlene slowed and entered Penn Circle, the most frightening part of the drive. In the late sixties, to bypass the pedestrian mall they'd carved from the heart of East Liberty, the city planners had designed a giant roundabout a half-mile in diameter and five lanes wide, which pulled in traffic from the major arteries and feeder streets that had once met there and centrifugally whipped it around and then, without benefit of a stoplight, off in the four principal directions. The endless curves were supposed to keep speeds reasonable, but the practical result was an unbanked racetrack, with drivers pushing their cars hard through the turns, then rocketing across at the last second to make their exits.

It was not a style of driving that suited Arlene, and rather than seamlessly joining the flow, she came to a dead stop at the yield sign and hesitated excruciatingly before entering, then poked along on the right as traffic flew past, whizzing like missiles, their tires misting her windshield so she had to set the wipers flipping madly. She hunched forward over the wheel, gripping it rigidly. For her part, Emily braced a hand on the dash, anticipating impact, though soon enough, going so slowly, they grew a tail of cars stuck and unable to enter the inner circle. A white van filled the rear window, flashing its brights.

"Pass me already then," Arlene said.

The honking started, a pushy chorus outdone by one long, sustained note. A Honda jockeyed past and purposely cut in front of them, making Arlene brake, before it shot off again.

"Idiot," Arlene said. "Five lanes, and you have to be in mine."

She drove as if she were wearing blinders, holding her position, focused solely on the road in front of her. As more cars overtook them, Emily kept her eyes straight ahead as well, afraid of what she might see. Finally the van passed. She hazarded a glance back. There was no one; they were alone. Arlene signaled early for their exit. The blinker tinked and tinked, and Emily wanted to reach over and stop it.

"That's always pleasant," Arlene said once they'd made it out onto Penn Avenue and into normal traffic again.

"You did better than I could have," Emily said.

"Are you still too hot?"

"No."

"Oh," Arlene said as they passed the old Nabisco plant, cleaned up and advertising condominiums, "have you heard how much they're asking for a one-bedroom?"

"How much?"

"A million two."

"That's highway robbery. Who would honestly pay that to live in East Liberty?"

"They're calling it Eastside now."

"Who's calling it that? No one I know. It's a boondoggle if I ever saw one."

Besides the greed factor, she didn't actually mind the condos. Better than leaving the building empty. The real shame was that, winter or summer, when the plant was running, as you drove by you could smell them baking, even with your windows closed. They made Ritz crackers, and the warm, buttery scent surrounded the place like a cloud. In the spring, when the Arts Center held their annual fundraiser in the formal gardens that topped Mellon Park, you could stand with your lemonade and look out over the long slope crisscrossed with paths and over Fifth Avenue and beyond the tennis bubble and the playground and the far green fields and see steam rising from the factory and practically taste the air. Like any Pittsburgher, Emily had been strangely proprietary about the place, and the crackers, as if she'd made them herself, and was sorry it was gone.

So much of the city was, though some of this nostalgia was just her. From the beginning, having come from the sticks, she'd loved her adopted home with an outsider's eye, appreciating landmarks a native like Henry took for granted or scorned as corny. Though she'd lived here nearly sixty years, and had spent most of her social life among the country club set, at heart she was still a hick. Pitt's gothic Cathedral of Learning still seemed impossibly tall, the oak-paneled, stone-fireplaced rooms palatial, too good for students like herself. When she took the grandchildren on the Incline, she was just as awestruck by the view of the Point as Ella or Sam were. She arranged for Sarah and Justin to ride the Gateway Clipper to and from the Pirates game not because it was the scenic, grandmotherly thing to do, or because she'd done it with Margaret and Kenneth when they were their age, but because, as the fake steamboat navigated the two-toned confluence of the Mon and Allegheny, Emily could imagine George Washington standing on the riverbank, the city behind him nothing but an earthen fort and virgin forest, her own history, like America's, as yet unwritten.

When she was young, the city was her new world. Now it seemed she was losing it piece by piece.

Each street was saturated with memory. They followed Penn as it straddled the red-line between Homewood and Point Breeze, passing Mr. Frick's beloved Clayton, inviolable behind its spiked fence. There was a café on the grounds where she and Louise had had lunch every so often, and a peaked greenhouse the caretakers opened to the public. Like Frick Park with its rustic woodland paths and quaint bowling greens, it was an oasis, as long as you didn't contemplate where the money had come from.

Penn to Braddock, then across Forbes and on past the baseball diamonds where Kenneth had played and into Regent Square, Arlene's neighborhood, suddenly desirable, with its mottled sycamores and brick side streets backed up on the hollows of the park. Retirees and spinsters on fixed incomes like Arlene hung on in duplexes and 1920s bungalows, but, unlike East Liberty, it had attracted a generation of young families who could no longer afford Point Breeze. The little commercial strip by the Edgewood line was thriving. The theater was showing a Bergman revival (Louise had been a nut for Bergman, Henry bored), and Arlene pointed out a new slow-food bistro where there used to be a card store.

"They only have eight tables."

"Sounds expensive," Emily said.

"It's supposed to be very good."

"I wonder if they're open for Thanksgiving."

"I could check," Arlene said.

"I'm kidding. There's nothing wrong with the club."

"I forget whose turn it is for Christmas."

"Margaret's, but there are no guarantees with her."

"I'm starving," Arlene said, because they were close now.

"So am I."

They dipped by the angled entrance ramp and then beneath the Parkway itself, the overpass momentarily blocking the rain so that when they stopped at the light on the far side, the wipers squeaked. The Eat 'n Park was just up the hill, its lot busy, its windows warm and welcoming.

When the light changed, Arlene pulled forward and signaled for the left turn but failed to move over enough to let anyone by. As she waited for the oncoming lane to clear, Emily inhaled and exhaled slowly through her nose, trying to empty her mind. *Go*, she commanded silently, a psychic. Twice Arlene could have made it but held off, playing it safe. *Go*, Emily wished, and this time it worked. Once they were across and into the lot, she didn't offer a comment, or after Arlene had parked. That her side was well over the white line was minor. It was relief enough to be out of the car, and then, as they picked their way through the puddles, she noticed Arlene was wearing the Totes rain boots Emily had given her for Christmas years and years ago, and regretted her impatience.

Beneath the overhang of the front doors, she shook out her umbrella. Inside, re-energized by the smell of coffee brewing and the jumble of a dozen conversations, she folded away her rain hat and removed her scarf, stuffing it into the armhole of her coat before hanging it up. The Eat 'n Park was notoriously cold. She'd purposely worn a sweater, as had Arlene. There was a line to be seated, and they lingered by the display case of baked goods, admiring the pies. They pointed, careful not to smudge the glass. It was a weekly exercise, choosing which looked the nicest, though, living alone, neither was wanton enough to buy one.

"I'm sure they'll have pumpkin at the club," Arlene said.

"I'm sure."

Rhonda, the uniformed and cornrowed greeter, knew them. "Mornin', ladies," she said, not bothering to pull them menus, and scanned the room, almost full.

"Someplace warm, please," Arlene asked, rubbing her palms together.

"As you can see, we're a little busy today. Do you mind sitting near the kitchen?" Meaning the restrooms.

"Actually," Arlene said, "in our case that might be convenient."

Rhonda led them through the other diners to a booth against the far wall, with a view, through the swinging doors, of the dishwasher. Emily would have preferred a window seat, but a booth was better than a table, and the buffet was right there, the combined aromas of French toast and bacon and maple syrup enticing. She was embarrassed to discover her mouth was watering.

"It's no wonder," Arlene said. "It's almost nine-thirty."

"First I'd like some coffee."

"Me too."

From her pocketbook, Emily produced her coupon so she'd have it ready when the waitress came. In the booths along the windows, in the flat light from outside, middle-aged couples sipped and chatted, in no hurry to start the day, and she wondered what they did for work.

"So," Arlene said, "I take it Kenneth and Lisa have Easter then."

"Who knows? I've asked him time and again and I still haven't gotten a straight answer."

"You'd think they'd want to get tickets as soon as possible."

"You'd think. Oh, here's our friend."

Sandy had been there longer than Rhonda. She was a fair, broad-shouldered Pole in her mid-fifties with a chipped tooth and a serious Pittsburgh accent. Through their limited exchanges, Emily knew bits of her history. Her husband had worked at Union Signal right up the hill until they closed; now he was a security guard at Gateway Center downtown. Their son had played basketball for Central Catholic, then gone to Providence College. Just now Emily couldn't recall where he was or what he did for a living, though Sandy had told her many times. Another hazard of growing old.

"And hah're you ladies doin' today?" Sandy asked, clanking down two mugs and pouring coffee for them without asking.

"Fine, thank you," Emily said, handing her the coupon, which Sandy slipped into her apron. "How's Stephen?"

"Stephen's doin' good, thanks."

"Is he coming home for Thanksgiving?"

"We're goin' dahn 'ere for the whole weekend," Sandy said, gesturing over her shoulder with her thumb, as if his place were right outside.

"That's nice," Arlene said.

"Yeah, it'll be nice to get away from this weather. Does either of yinz want orange juice?"

"No, thanks."

"Okay, go ahead and help yourself. You know the rules."

"We do," Emily said.

"I feel better now," Arlene said when she was gone. "The coffee helps. You know what I'd like to do when Sarah and Justin are here?"

"What's that?" Why couldn't she let it go? Emily had just told her there was no guarantee they were coming. Sarah was out of college and working now, and might not have time off.

"I'd like to take them skating in Panther Hollow. We always had such fun there."

"If it's frozen. It might not be by then."

"I hope it is."

It was like Arlene to prod her most sensitive spots—calling up not just the prospect of the grandchildren's visit, but those long-ago nights when Emily and Henry took to the ice with his fraternity brothers and their dates, and later sitting around the bonfire, sipping hot toddies, the bowl of the woods around them dark, the stars above pure and clear. The pond was still there, and the hollow, and the stars. Only Henry was gone.

"It looks like they have that nice corned beef hash," Arlene said.

"Oh, good."

They waited until there was no line. Occasionally the plates were burning hot, fetched fresh from the kitchen, but today they were room temperature. The one Emily lifted from the stack was still wet. Rather than leave it for someone to clean up, she tipped it so the drops ran and fell to the carpet. As always, Arlene took a salad plate, as if she weren't hungry.

Both sides of the buffet were identical, a line of twinned chafing dishes, beginning with cantaloupe and honeydew slices, bananas and halved oranges, canned pineapple chunks and cling peaches in their own heavy nectar, cottage cheese and applesauce, three pastel flavors of yogurt, a tray of muffins and Danishes, several different breads you could slice yourself and feed through a toaster like a conveyor belt, at the end of which waited tubs of butter and margarine and cream cheese, then bubbling vats of real oatmeal and Cream of Wheat, followed by miniature boxes of cold cereal and their attendant carafes of skim and 2 percent and whole milk, before the steaming heaps of Belgian waffles and pancakes and scrambled eggs and sausages and hash browns—and all of it endlessly replenished. If it wasn't exactly gourmet fare, that was fine with Emily. She could be a snob about many things—Lisa would say everything—but at this price, just not having to cook was a luxury.

"I may have to make two trips," Arlene said, on the other side of the peaked sneeze guard, her plate already piled high.

"I don't see why you can't just use a normal plate," Emily said.

"I don't waaaah uhhhhh laaah," Arlene said, as if mocking her, or as if Emily had suddenly gone hard of hearing. Emily looked up from the Danish she was mauling with a pair of tongs. Arlene was staring at her, alarmed, as if someone had planted a knife in her back. Her eyes bulged, fixed on something invisible. Her mouth hung open, stuck.

"Aaah waaah," she said. "Aaah laaah."

In the instant before she toppled forward, out of reflex Emily took a step back, as if giving her room to fall, except the buffet was between them. Arlene fell, still clutching her plate, her face banging the sneeze guard.

Only then did Emily react, throwing her own plate aside and ducking around the buffet. Arlene was on the floor, the carpet around her littered with fruit. She lay curled on her side, still trying to speak, blood running from a cut above one eye.

The people in the window booths sat there staring at them.

"For God's sake," Emily shouted, from her hands and knees, "somebody help us!"

JUST VISITING

It was just one of her spells, Arlene insisted. She had them whenever her blood pressure dipped too low. She didn't seem surprised. She was more upset about the gash on her forehead, a rucked line of stitches holding the livid edges together. The confession made Emily picture her fainting in her apartment, or, more frightening, behind the wheel. Arlene didn't know what all the fuss was about. It was her own fault. She should have eaten something.

The doctors weren't convinced, and kept her for more testing, moving her to a semiprivate room that overlooked the row houses of Bloomfield. Here, at least, they were given a window. Clouds drifted above the bridge that arched across the valley to meet Bigelow Boulevard. Five stories down, the rainy blocks were gray, the stoplights on Liberty Avenue the only color.

When the EMTs had wheeled Arlene out of the Eat 'n Park, Emily asked if she could go with them. No, it was against regulations, but she could follow them, and so she'd dug through Arlene's pocketbook for her keys and braved the slick streets. She hadn't been scared, fueled, she suspected, by adrenaline. Now when the nurse recommended she retrieve a few things from Arlene's place to make her stay more comfortable, Emily wanted to say that was a onetime deal, and not repeatable. They could tow the car. She'd take a taxi home.

"Will you make sure my purse is safe?" Arlene asked.

"Of course I will," Emily said.

"You'll probably want your robe and slippers," the nurse prompted. "Most people like their own PJs better than ours."

"If you could bring my book. It should be on my nightstand. Either there or on the end table by the loveseat. And would you mind feeding the fish? They only need three pinches of the dry stuff. You'll see it by the tank."

Emily left with a list and a clear mission. She would drop the Taurus there, pick up Arlene's stuff and take a taxi back. The hard part would be parking on the street. She hoped there would be a long, empty stretch of curb so she could just coast into a spot. It didn't have to be right in front of her door. She had no qualms about leaving it half a block away. Personally she didn't consider the neighborhood the safest, a buffer between Wilkinsburg and Swissvale, but Arlene left the car out every night.

She took the easiest route, through Shadyside, avoiding Penn Circle. It was drizzling, misty. Maybe the rain had kept people in, because Fifth Avenue wasn't bad. As she passed the Arts Center and the green expanse of Mellon Park, she thought she was lucky. She kept up with traffic, watching for the flare of taillights ahead, braking when she was supposed to brake. No one rode her bumper, no one honked. It had been so long since she'd driven, and yet, after this morning, she found she was much less fearful behind the wheel than riding beside Arlene.

She'd been worried for nothing. This time of day Arlene's street was deserted. She angled the Taurus toward the spot at the bottom of Arlene's stairs and rolled up as close to the curb as she dared. *There*, she thought, turning the car off, but when she tried to pull the key out, it wouldn't come.

She pushed it in, knowing on some cars you had to, but it did nothing. She'd canceled her triple-A, and she could see herself being stuck here and having to call a garage.

She twisted the key, as if to switch the car on again. Nothing. That didn't make any sense, and she checked the gearshift. The stubby Day-Glo arrow pointed to D.

"For Pete's sake." That's what she got for being so pleased with herself.

With Arlene's things, she didn't have a hand for an umbrella. She cinched tight her rain hat, ducked her head and trundled up the stairs. On the porch she had to set everything on a lawn chair so she could fit the key in the lock, then gather it all in her arms and haul it up another flight. She was winded, and thought that Arlene was lucky she hadn't passed out here and broken her neck.

At the top, the stairwell turned and there was another door, unlocked, that opened on a narrow hallway that led to the apartment proper. The place was laid out strangely, having been fashioned from what must have once been a spacious home. The whole idea of a duplex went against Emily's nature. She couldn't imagine living above someone, her every footstep registered. She appreciated her neighbors, she could even say she'd loved Louise and Doug, and Ginny and Gene Alford, and Isabel and Ev Conroy, Dotty and Fred Engelmann, the whole old gang, but she didn't want them listening to every move she and Henry made. It was just one more aspect of Arlene she would never understand.

Inside, the apartment was dark and smelt of old smoke. The only light came from the windows, and, glowing a lurid undersea green beside Henry's mother's Baldwin upright, boxy as a coffin, the humming aquarium. On the walls, mercifully obscured by the gloom, hung the awkward, misbegotten still lifes Arlene had painted for her adult ed classes—painstakingly shaded apples and pears and wine bottles that, instead of taking on volume, remained flat as cave drawings. She and Henry had one themselves, a group of pockmarked, foreshortened oranges relegated to Henry's office. While Emily spent more time with Arlene than with anyone else, their social life was a public one, made up of dates, occasions and entertainments. It was rare that they encroached on each other's privacy, and creeping alone through her sanctuary felt like trespassing. She wondered if Arlene's neighbor was downstairs, silently marking her progress.

She used the kitchen as a base, dropping the stuff on the table and draping her rain hat over the spigot, then went through the rooms, flicking on lights. The place was tidy as a hotel suite, every surface cleared off and polished, and Betty wasn't scheduled till Friday. As someone who waged her own never-ending war against clutter, Emily was envious, and at the same time suspected this level of neatness was excessive and possibly neurotic, a by-product, like her own, of not having enough to do.

The bedroom was a museum, each piece of furniture an heirloom. On the cherry dresser, in heavy silver frames, as if they were hers, leaned the familiar senior portraits of Margaret and Kenneth wearing the shaggy hairstyles of the seventies. Arrayed before them like pawns were smaller pictures of the grandchildren, and, unframed, the most recent Christmas photo from each family, though not a single shot, Emily noticed, of her.

She found Arlene's book on her nightstand—a British whodunit Emily had lent her. It sat squarely atop a compact leatherette Bible with gilt-edged pages, a kinked silk ribbon holding Arlene's place. For a second Emily thought the Bible was Henry's, which she kept by her own bedside for those stormy nights she couldn't sleep, but no, there was Arlene's name embossed on the cover. Arlene had given similar Bibles to Margaret and Kenneth on their confirmations, and then the grandchildren, extending the tradition into the new century, though, as gifts, they never elicited the proper gratitude. Emily considered bringing Arlene's along with her mystery, but she might think it presumptuous of her, and anyway, it would be safer here. Emily had heard horror stories of things disappearing in hospitals.

She plumbed Arlene's dresser drawers for a bra and underwear and a pair of socks. Her robe and slippers were in the closet, along with dozens of hatboxes from decades past, and while Emily was tempted to snoop, she knew how upset she would be if Arlene pawed through her things, and shut the door. In the bathroom she gathered her toiletries, zipping them into a monogrammed Dopp kit.

Feeding the fish was simple. She lifted the lid, dropped in three pinches of vile-smelling flakes and watched them spread atop the water.

"Eat up," she said, because at first the fish weren't interested. It was only after she'd closed the lid and backed away that they rose to kiss the surface. As the flakes absorbed moisture and sank, the fish darted to intercept and suck them in.

Arlene gave her fish names and spoke of them as if they had distinct personalities. Emily couldn't tell them apart. The catfish were catfish, the angelfish, angelfish; the rest were whatever they were. She'd always thought Arlene would enjoy a real pet like a cat, but whenever she brought it up, Arlene said she couldn't stand the hair and dander, not to mention the

problem of the litter box. Emily saw her strict neatnik's need for total control as limiting. She was missing all the fun. Pets were meant to be affectionate and messy, like Rufus, someone to love who loved you back
regardless of your shortcomings. The best Emily could say of the fish was
that they were decorative, pleasant enough to look at but not the most
heartwarming companions.

Her job done, she called a cab. "Five minutes," dispatch said. She turned
out the lights, leaving the apartment exactly as she'd found it.

Rather than stand in the cold, she waited inside the front door. After fifteen
minutes she climbed the stairs and called to see what the holdup was.

"He's on his way," they promised.

"I could have been there by now," Emily said, because it was true.

She also wanted to get Arlene some flowers, and the hospital gift shop
would be punitively more expensive than the Giant Eagle. She thought—
not seriously—of canceling the cab and driving herself, but then she might
have to come back in the dark, and she didn't want to risk that.

Arlene would be all right. She'd seemed fine, yet Emily kept seeing her
mouth moving, trying to form words—"waaah luuhh wuuh"—just before
she pitched forward. There were no warning signs that Emily could remember, not like Henry with his coughing fits. She was afraid it was a
stroke, that Arlene would end up talking out of one side of her mouth like
Louise, or wheelchair-bound like Cat Osborn, but at the hospital she was
her old self, joking—only partly in apology—that she must have given
Emily quite a fright.

The Taurus sat at the curb. The keys were in her bag. She could stop at
home and let Rufus out and make sure he had water.

"This is silly," she said to the wet sycamores.

She was still dithering when the taxi appeared at the end of the street,
making the decision for her.

On the way over, she noticed that the cabbie drove no better than she
did. She resented the meter, and though the man offered to help with Arlene's things, she declined his offer, tipping him the minimum 10
percent.

"You're a lifesaver," Arlene gushed, as if she'd crossed the Sahara. She was propped up, watching the same soap opera as her neighbor, her lunch tray pushed to one side, the Jell-O untouched. They were going to take her for some sort of scan in about ten minutes.

"You must be starving," Arlene said. "You should get something from the cafeteria."

It was her way of asking Emily to stay, as if she'd just popped in to drop off her things. Emily hung up her coat to show her she wasn't going anywhere. She helped her with her robe, then moved the chair so they could both watch TV.

Her positioning was strategic. From where she sat, she couldn't see the gash on Arlene's forehead. More than anything, the sheer size of it disturbed her. She could picture it healing, but not without leaving a disfiguring scar, and again she thought of Louise, the long days they reminisced, laughing in that blank room, until visiting hours ended, both of them knowing she would never come home. She wondered if Arlene's insurance would cover plastic surgery, or whether, at her age, they wouldn't even bother.

"Do you have any idea who these people are?" Arlene asked, pointing at the TV.

"They all seem to wear a lot of makeup," Emily said. "Especially the men."

She was hungry, but waited until the nurse came for Arlene before taking the elevator down to the ground floor, and then was disgusted by her gummy grilled cheese and lukewarm tomato soup. The flowers at the gift shop were preposterous, and had seen better days. Somehow she'd make it to the Giant Eagle tomorrow.

Upstairs, Arlene wasn't back from her scan. Emily stood at the window, looking down on her kingdom. It was nearly four, and the sky was beginning to deepen. Rufus had probably knocked over the garbage to communicate his disapproval. She went back to her chair and watched CNN until it repeated. Worried that something might have happened, she searched out the nurses' station, but they couldn't tell her anything. She went back to her chair, then the window, then the chair again, this time for the local news, though by now her mind was running through the awful possibilities and she could hardly concentrate.

When they finally rolled Arlene in, she was groggy from the sedative.

"We're going to let her sleep now," the nurse said, pulling the curtain closed.

Visiting hours ended at eight. She recommended that Emily go home and come back in the morning. "I'd say you've both had a long day of it."

She wanted to stay so she would be there when Arlene woke up, but the woman was right, she was worn out. She took a cab, sitting downcast in the back, and tipped the driver begrudgingly.

The house was dark, the front walk puddled. The storm door stuck, frustrating. By the glow of the streetlight she fitted her key into the lock, setting off Rufus. When she opened the door, he spun and spun on the runner, growling a needy greeting, prancing, frantic for her attention.

"Yes," she said. "Yes. It's very exciting."

MYSTERIES OF THE BRAIN

The doctors couldn't find what was wrong with her. It wasn't something as obvious and catastrophic as a stroke or a brain tumor. For lack of anything better, they were calling it an episode, as if there might be a whole series of them. At her age, as Emily updated Margaret over the phone, relaying what Arlene had told her, it was likely a combination of several smaller problems. For a start, she was probably dehydrated, which was common in the morning. They also thought she was suffering from low blood sugar. Emily herself felt faint and headachy when she didn't eat, and, like her, Arlene had a habit of skipping meals, substituting coffee or sweets. It was one of the great dangers of living alone.

"She did look thinner this summer," Margaret said.

"Plus who knows how much damage the smoking's done. You know she used to smoke the unfiltered ones. Those were the real coffin nails, those old Pall Malls. It's a miracle she's lasted this long. Your father smoked the same brand. He stopped around the time I was pregnant with you because I literally couldn't stomach the smell, but he must have smoked a good fifteen years. I'm sure that had something to do with what happened to him."

"She's in good spirits, though?"

"You know Arlene, she acts like everything's peachy. She doesn't see why she has to be there. She can't smoke, that's her big complaint. Speaking for myself, I'd be terrified. I'm sure she'd appreciate a call."

"I'll try her when we're done. How are you holding up? Do you need me to come down and help out?"

For weeks Margaret had stonewalled her about their plans for Thanksgiving. Now she was ready to drop everything, and Emily was unaccountably jealous. More out of pride than spite, she promised herself not to broach the subject.

"That's kind of you to offer, but I don't think it's necessary. We're hoping she'll be home by the weekend. They've got her on fluids. You should see her, she's hooked up to more monitors. I'm sure it's costing a fortune."

"You let me know if you need me."

"I'm fine, just a little shaken, naturally. You should have seen the look on her face. For a second I honestly thought she was dead. I'm lucky I didn't have a heart attack myself. They sent a very nice bouquet, the Eat 'n Park."

"That was nice of them."

"We're very loyal customers."

This wasn't meant as a prompt, but Margaret dutifully asked for Arlene's room number.

"So," Emily said, "that's all the excitement on this end. What's going on in your neck of the woods?"

"Not a whole lot."

It was her standard answer when she didn't want to talk. Too often she acted as if Emily's calls were an inconvenience, as if she were keeping her from urgent business. As a teenager she'd been distant and secretive, then for years as an alcoholic, hiding her sickness from everyone. Emily expected her to change after rehab, for the two of them to admit their mistakes and become closer, yet she still held Emily off, mistrustful, as if her own mother's interest in her life was suspect.

"How's Sarah?"

"Good, I guess. I haven't talked to her in a while."

"What's a while?"

"She was supposed to call on Sunday. She's not always good about that. Okay, I know what you're going to say."

"I wasn't going to say anything."

"Anyway," Margaret said, "she's fine. She and her roommate are volunteering for Obama, so they're never around."

"Does he really need the help in Chicago?"

"This is at his headquarters, so it's national. She's very excited."

"She should be careful not to exhaust herself. How's Justin?"

"Good. He's got midterms this week, so he's keeping busy."

"How about you?"

"I'm hanging in there. Thank you for the check, by the way."

"You're welcome," Emily said automatically. She wanted to ask about her job prospects, had the question formulated and cued up in her mind—*Any movement on the job front?*— but at the last second decided this wasn't the time. Instead, she asked, "Have you decided what you're doing for Thanksgiving?"

She hadn't meant to, not at all, and now it was too late to take it back. Her intent wasn't to force a confession from her, but the initial silence which met her words let Emily know they were unwelcome.

"Sarah's break's so short we can't really go anywhere, even if we could afford to. We're going to have a nice, quiet dinner here at home, just the three of us. You're welcome to join us, you and Arlene. We've got room, that's not a problem."

"That's all right," Emily said, because it wasn't a proper offer, just a sop, and once she'd said, "I love you," and gotten off, she wondered why she'd brought this insult upon herself. For a while she sat in Henry's chair, pinching her lips between her thumb and forefinger, pondering what perverse urge made her ask Margaret the one question she'd specifically forbidden herself. Flopped at her feet, Rufus raised his head to look at her, then let it drop back to the carpet. In the corner, the grandfather clock ticked off another minute, its brass pendulum swinging back and forth behind the glass.

"Very interesting," she said.

THE VIEW FROM THE FIFTH FLOOR

With Arlene in the hospital, Emily's days assumed a new shape. In the mornings she still woke at dawn and read the *Post-Gazette* with her tea and toast so she would know what was going on in the world, but now instead of folding the comics and working on the crossword while QED played their Handel and the blue jays and nuthatches skirmished at the feeder, she rinsed her cup and saucer and gathered her things and drove the Taurus to Bloomfield to be with Arlene.

If she wanted, she could stop at the Giant Eagle on the way for some cranberry muffins, or the Rite Aid for Arlene's quince hand lotion. She could drop her books off at the library instead of waiting to make a special trip. The possibilities were limitless. She still wished the car were smaller, especially at the narrow entrance of the visitors' lot, where she had to undo her belt and open her door to press the button and pluck the ticket so the gate rose, and parking was always a precarious exercise, but she was careful and didn't let the few tight spots intimidate her.

The visitors' lot, apparently by design, was the least convenient of the many parking fields, so far from the rear of the hospital that Emily counted the walk as exercise, something she didn't get enough of at home. In bad weather it could be challenging. The wind came blasting across the flat, open space, snatching at her umbrella and tangling her hair, pulling tears from her eyes. All she could do was duck her head and keep moving. She was grateful when the doors automatically parted for her, relieved to finally be inside where it was warm.

She was among a small group of regulars who haunted the lobby and the cafeteria until the official beginning of visiting hours. Most were like her, solitary older women, though there was one tall gentleman who carried a plaid thermos along with his folded *Post-Gazette*, as if he were going off to work. She nodded to them in the halls or on the elevator, and though they never exchanged names or stories, they shared a muted camaraderie. She hadn't noticed the phenomenon when Henry was sick, or Louise, possibly because she was so caught up in their suffering and her own terror that she couldn't acknowledge anyone else's. Looking back, she was probably in shock. Now it was good to know she wasn't alone, and she sought out their faces, giving them, if only briefly, her most serious, reassuring smile.

Upstairs, she knew the nurses, and Arlene's roommate Thalia and her friend Jean, and the orderlies who delivered their meals. At home, Emily frequently went for whole days without speaking to another person, at most talking to herself or Rufus. Here there was a constant stream of people recapping last night's TV shows, or helping them solve the crossword, or discussing which new movies looked good, or sizing up the Steelers' opponent this Sunday. None of it meant anything to Emily, but just the easy give-and-take excited her, the way driving made her feel surprisingly alive, part of something larger again.

The halls were constantly busy. Like a ship, the hospital operated by its own rigid clockwork, which meant there was always something to look forward to. Morning meds, the coffee cart, vital signs—every interruption was precisely scheduled, checked against a chart.

Lunch arrived in time for the noon news. Like the staff, Emily now disdained the cafeteria, slipping around the corner to a sandwich place that made its own soups. Their sandwiches were so big that she and Arlene could share one. Sometimes she had to wrap what was left of her half in a napkin and take it home rather than let it go to waste.

After lunch, they watched Arlene's soap operas, or Arlene watched while Emily read beside her, from time to time looking up from her book and falling into the scene on-screen until she realized it had hijacked her attention. The effect wasn't unpleasant, just confusing, as the two stories blended until neither made sense. Arlene, fully engaged, talked back to the actors. "Don't do it," she said. "She's lying." It reminded Emily of Henry holding conversations with his baseball games, instructing the Pirates' manager to put on a bunt or change pitchers. She'd never been a vocal fan, content to sit back and watch without comment, but now, for the sheer fun of it, she seconded Arlene, or threw in her own two cents, though she was often wrong, not knowing the whole convoluted backstory.

"I don't like him."

"Who?"

"Him, with the mustache."

"He's one of the good guys."

"Are you sure? I don't like the way he looks."

"He used to be a bad guy, but he's changed."

"So he could still be a bad guy underneath."

"No. Now shush. I want to hear this."

All My Children, The Guiding Light, One Life to Live. The people all seemed the same to Emily, artfully coiffed and dentally blessed, an entirely different species from the ones on the grotesque talk shows that followed.

Through the window, clouds settled over the bridge and Herron Hill beyond, over the whole city. Cars were driving with their lights on, their wipers working. It was that gray time of day just before the school buses rolled when Emily most keenly felt her own inertia, her life no longer an urgent or necessary business. At home she would be sitting in Henry's chair with her feet up, reading her book and listening to the stereo on low, and feel sleep overtake her. She might make herself a cup of tea and nibble a cookie for some energy, or, giving in to the dreariness, switch off the music and move upstairs. Rufus anticipated her, nestling into his bed by the fireplace before she slipped off her shoes and got under the covers. It was warmer upstairs, and the reading lamp on the wall behind her shed a cozy yellow glow over the pages. Rufus soughed. The radio on her night table was tuned to QED as well, so that as she inevitably drifted off, Corelli or Telemann galloped melodically alongside her, which made her return to the world only more confusing, waking up to the blather of the news, the windows gone dark.

Now she used the dregs of her afternoons to fit in her outstanding errands. She made sure Arlene had everything she needed, then bade her and Thalia and Jean and the girls at the nurses' station goodbye and braved the gusty walk to the car, already plotting her stops. Arlene was low on fish food, so she had to detour through Squirrel Hill. She was still unclear on their names, but she'd come to enjoy watching them dart and swoop to catch the flakes before they hit bottom. She didn't linger in the apartment, though occasionally, charged by Arlene to retrieve something, she found herself leafing through the scrapbooks Arlene had amassed to follow her students' progress. She'd taught at the same city school for thirty years, through dire and violent changes, the neighborhood deteriorating, growing more and more dangerous. Twice she'd been attacked, yet she never considered quitting or asking for a transfer. Like Henry, she had a superhuman patience and an unwavering dedication to her profession that Emily envied more than understood. Along with her class pictures, among the browning clippings celebrating graduations and weddings, service promotions and births, were obituaries, decades old now, of boys still in their teens. These were her children, yet Emily knew nothing of them, and the discovery lent Arlene—whose life, with its lack of attachments, had seemed so simple—an air of mystery.

By the time she locked up the apartment, the day was almost over. Now it was a race to make it to the Giant Eagle or the Rite Aid and back home before dusk blinded her. Traffic was heavier, and sometimes rather than battle it, she put off the trip till the next day, with the result that, as the week progressed, she always had somewhere to go.

Rufus was justifiably unhappy with her new schedule, though that was no excuse for pulling her used tissues out of the trash and shredding them all over the bath mat. She scolded him, then after dinner, to make up for her absence, took him for a walk around the block. It was chilly and damp, and the weak streetlights embellished their breath. Generally she didn't go outside at night, and as they trod the darkness cast by the Coles' hedges, she felt adventurous and daring, as if they were trespassing.

With all the walking and running around and just the effort of being out in public, she was frazzled, and caught herself yawning in front of the TV. When *Jeopardy* ended, she called Arlene to see if she needed anything for tomorrow, put Rufus out one last time, then went upstairs and turned on her electric blanket to preheat the bed.

She undressed and put on her robe and settled in to read a bit, surprised by how few pages she'd gotten through at the hospital. QED's evening music was too lush, big noisy concert recordings of warhorses she could happily live the rest of her life without hearing again, when a simple prelude and fugue by Buxtehude or one of Purcell's anthems would have been perfect, yet she kept it on, softly, each cough from the audience recalling the many performances she and Henry had endured at Heinz Hall as longtime subscribers, listening to the symphony meander through the same schmaltzy Schumann and Brahms and Berlioz.

Every night she tried to read, but her mouth tasted of toothpaste and her mind was restless, snagging on all the chores and errands she hadn't gotten done. She needed to buy tea bags, she had to pay the gas bill, she'd wanted to air out the car and spray the seats with Febreze—and knowing she'd forget if she didn't write them down, she opened the drawer of her night table and found her pen and pad and made a list so in the morning she'd have a jump on the day ahead.

The hope was that Arlene would be discharged by Friday at the latest. When the doctor said they wanted to monitor her over the weekend, Arlene was upset.

"I just want to sleep in my own bed," she said tearily.

"It's only two more days," Emily said, patting her hand, but she understood. Of all people, she knew how easily one's world could be taken away.

CLOSE TO NORMAL

They brought Arlene down in a wheelchair, over her flimsy protests. It didn't mean anything, it was just hospital policy, a hedge against lawsuits. Emily swung the car around and got out to help, but Arlene was already up and headed for her, skirting the hood. With her scarf and Jackie O glasses, Arlene looked like a faded star trying to sneak away incognito. The doctor had chosen to cover her gash with an eye-catching white bandage that hinted at brain surgery.

"I can drive," she said.

"Don't be ridiculous," Emily said, blocking her progress. "You need to rest."

"I'm tired of resting," Arlene said, but retreated to the passenger seat.

"Take care now, you two," Sue the nurse said. "I don't want to see you troublemakers back here."

They both thanked her, and they were off, into midmorning traffic. All along Liberty Avenue, trucks were double-parked and unloading in front of restaurants. Emily drove as if she were being tested.

"What's that I smell?" Arlene asked, sniffing. "It's like those fabric softener sheets."

"Sorry. I spilled some coffee. I used Resolve on it." Emily pointed vaguely toward the floor below the radio, and Arlene inspected the carpet.

"You can't even tell."

"No, it worked very nicely."

"Except for the smell," Arlene said.

"I'm sure it will go away."

"I hope so."

"You're feeling better."

"I never really felt that bad," Arlene said. "Once they sewed me up, I was fine. It was just being there I was upset about. They've been poking and prodding me for a week and still don't have a clue."

"They were just being careful."

"The worst place for someone our age is in the hospital."

"I don't know if that's true," Emily said.

"The infection rate's higher, for one thing." Arlene thumbed her window down an inch. "Do you mind terribly if I have a cigarette?"

"I thought the doctor told you to quit."

"I am. He's got me on the patch." She pulled back the sleeve of her jacket to show Emily a flesh-toned square, then lit up. "If it's going to happen, it's not going to happen overnight. He knows that."

"But you're going to try?"

"I'm going to try," Arlene said.

"That's very brave of you."

"I expect it's going to be unpleasant for everyone involved."

"It'll be worth it."

"You say that now. Just wait."

"If there's anything I can do to help."

"Thank you," Arlene said. "I would like to ask one thing of you, if that's possible."

"Anything."

"Please don't be too disappointed in me if I can't."

"I won't," Emily said, though she thought that was the wrong attitude to begin with.

They cruised along Fifth Avenue, past the crumbling robber baron mansions and the sooty spire of the Presbyterian church and the red-brick postwar apartment complexes and the bare trees of Mellon Park and into Point Breeze. The hospital pharmacy had filled Arlene's prescriptions, and over the weekend Emily had restocked Arlene's fridge, so there was no need to stop. Emily offered anyway.

"I think I'm fine, thanks," Arlene said. "I was going to tell you before, I'm impressed you're driving again—and doing very well, I must say. That, to me, is brave."

"It made more sense than paying for a cab every time I had to go somewhere."

"I appreciate you taking care of everything."

"You'd do the same for me."

"Still, I appreciate it. I'm sure it wasn't easy."

"You know what tomorrow is?" Emily asked.

"Tuesday."

"How do you feel about breakfast? I bet Rhonda and Sandy would love to see you."

Emily knew it was a risk. She worried that it might be too early, or that Arlene would be leery about returning to the scene of the crime. She didn't mean to rush her.

"On one condition," Arlene said. "I drive."

"That's fair. Just make sure you eat something before you get going."

And like that, they were back to their old schedule, as if nothing had happened.

She pulled up in front of Arlene's, expertly angling the Taurus for the curb, then hustled around to take Arlene's bag full of stuff. Arlene was slow going up the stairs, hauling herself along by the railing. Though it hadn't rained in days, she was wearing her Totes boots. Emily stayed behind her, shifting the bag to keep a hand free, as if she could catch her. It was only when they were on the porch and Emily was searching for the key that Arlene asked, "How are you going to get home?"

THE RESURRECTION

Arlene seemed fine driving, no more or less terrifying than before, yet Emily didn't trust her. For years Arlene had been frail and distracted, that was just how she was. She'd always been too thin, practically concave, waistless. She was the finicky eater in the family, where Henry was the bear, a lusty plunderer of seconds and leftovers. Her hands shook, her lips trembled. She coughed and coughed, racked, as if she were dredging something up. Often she searched for words, trailing off in midsentence, then waving away the incomplete thought, one hand flapping. Now, without her cigarettes, she was worse, frustrated with herself and the world, as if it were taking all of her patience not to explode. That didn't bother Emily. She was prone to her own fits and rages (like Margaret, and, from what Margaret said, Sarah), and Arlene's even temper bugged her. A little irrational anger made Arlene less schoolmarmish, more human. The problem now was that Emily couldn't stop seeing Arlene talking nonsense to her across the sneeze guard, the moment replaying like a nightmare.

The fall wasn't the awful part. It was Arlene's mouth moving, her tongue unable to decode her brain's scrambled message. *Waah laah wuhh.* The doctors hadn't been able to pinpoint the source of the problem, so what was to stop it from happening again?

It was just her own fear, Emily realized. Arlene was taking her medication and making a conscious effort to change—not easy at their age. Emily gave her credit, and yet the moment came again and again like a premonition. Both Margaret and Kenneth said it was natural something that traumatic would stay with her. Emily didn't want to hear it was normal. She wanted to know how to get rid of it.

She was extra vigilant now when she and Arlene were together, watching closely as if she might anticipate and thereby prevent the next episode. Listening to Arlene intently instead of just nodding along, Emily was surprised by how much of her conversation was plucked straight from the newspaper or the radio. Like the local media, she was particularly fixated on the Steelers, a topic Emily cared little for but could vaguely discuss by recycling what she'd absorbed over breakfast. Arlene went further, weighing the strengths and weaknesses of their opponents as if she'd personally scouted them. She knew the names of the players the way Henry or Kenneth would, whereas the only one Emily knew, from endless repetition, was Ben Roethlisberger. To her, these details were meaningless—the Steelers either won or lost—but to Arlene they comprised an entire universe she felt free to share with anyone they met, and, this being Pittsburgh, she regularly engaged waitresses and cashiers and random people in line, trading long, involved speculations Emily couldn't fathom—more proof that Arlene was not doddering and confused but open to the larger world and possibly more with it than Emily herself was.

And still, unbidden, Arlene spoke to her across the sneeze guard, and she was afraid.

At the same time, Emily was secretly pleased she'd been able to help Arlene, as if this proved she was the stronger of the two, and pledged she would be ready the next time. Discovering she could be relied on in an emergency—and that she might be needed again—gave her the courage, one bright, dry morning after breakfast, to tug on her gloves and follow Rufus out the back and take the branching flagstone path Henry had laid forty years ago to the side door of the garage.

Rufus heard the keys and raced ahead.

"Don't get too excited. We're just looking."

When she got the door open, he pushed past her, his nails scrabbling on the concrete.

"Well, pardon me."

Inside, the air was colder, and damp, the dark, closed box a natural refrigerator. The Olds sat in the dimness, filling the single bay, the far window throwing precise, elongated panes of sunlight across the roof, tattooed with the tracks of the Coles' cat, Buster. How he got in was a mystery, but, as with his occasional murder of her friendly visitors, the birds (or her hated enemies, the voles), she'd long ceased trying to curb what was obviously a force of nature. Still, did he have to pee on everything?

She pressed the button and the sectioned door rumbled up, the steel wheels creaking, letting in the day. Rufus escaped to the courtyard between their garage and the Coles', sniffing at the grated drain in the middle, which for years had served as the tip-off circle for Kenneth and his friends' basketball games.

Aside from the silt of dust and the cobwebs decorating the antenna, the car was pristine. After her last accident, her insurance had paid for a new grille and front bumper. She'd carefully driven home from the dealer, then left the Olds out front with the hazards on while she asked Jim Cole to put it in the garage for her. It hadn't moved since.

She'd taken the necessary precautions mothballing it—literally, dosing the glove box and seats and carpet as she would an old suit before storing it in a closet. She'd disconnected the battery as Henry did with the motorboat every winter, though she suspected it was dead from disuse. A jump and it would be as good as new.

Like the house, the garage had been built in the twenties, and was designed for nothing larger than a Model T. The gap between the Olds and the wall was so narrow that Emily had to sidle along the car as if she were inching across a ledge. The door was locked against thieves. At the sound of her key popping the knob, Rufus came dashing back in as if he might be left behind.

"Fine," she said, and he squeezed by and jumped into the front seat, taking his place as her passenger. She leaned down and reached under the dash until she felt the latch of the hood release, pulled it with a clunk, then shut him in.

She'd misremembered. The battery wasn't disconnected. It was gone.

"Curiouser and curiouser."

The only place it could be was downstairs, under Henry's workbench. That was exactly where she and Rufus found it, identified by a note in her own hand. She or possibly Jim Cole had had the foresight to bring it inside so it wouldn't freeze. It might even be good, but it was far too heavy for her to carry upstairs, let alone across the backyard. It was Tuesday—Jim was teaching. She was stymied, unless Marcia was at home.

Her Honda hybrid was out front, so Emily crossed the driveway and rang the bell. The Coles were the most accommodating of their new neighbors—the only ones she could count on now that the old crowd was gone—and she tried not to impose on them too often. When Marcia answered the door in her sweats and slippers, her hair mussed as if she were sick, Emily felt compelled to apologize even before she explained her situation.

"I'm sorry. I've turned into such a weakling."

"It's no trouble, honestly," Marcia said, pointing her bare toes into her hiking boots. "I was just doing my yoga."

She added a fleece jacket and a Steelers baseball cap. It was an outfit Emily wouldn't dare go outside in, and less than flattering to Marcia, who was Margaret's age and, as Emily's own mother had liked to say, pleasingly plump.

Emily led her across the lawn and inside, shooing Rufus, who knew Marcia but sniffed at her crotch anyway. "Watch your head," she said on the stairs, not sure if Marcia had ever seen Henry's workshop. Normally it was Jim who helped her.

Marcia squatted and, with effort, lifted the battery and set it on the workbench. "It's heavy."

"Last year it wouldn't have been a problem for me," Emily said. "I just don't have that kind of strength anymore."

"And we're taking it to the garage?"

"If you can manage it."

"I can try."

At the top of the stairs Marcia had to set it down, and then at the edge of the back porch, and just before the door of the garage. "If nothing else, it's good exercise."

"Thank you," Emily apologized.

Inside, she thought it would be rude to point out Buster's tracks, though they were everywhere. Likewise, there was no need to comment on the smell.

When Marcia finally hefted the battery up and in, the leads didn't reach the terminals.

"I think it goes the other way," Emily suggested, and then there was the trip to the basement to find the proper wrench. She brought back a handful.

Marcia stood clear as if she feared being electrocuted. "After all this, it better work."

"We'll find out. It may need a jump anyway."

Again, Rufus took his seat beside her, convinced they were going somewhere.

"You really think so?" Emily said, and turned the key.

Nothing but a clicking.

"Try it again."

Click-click-click-click.

"I figured as much," Emily said. "I've got cables in the trunk."

"I don't know if you can jump it from my battery. It's a completely different system."

"It should say in the manual. Or I could just call triple-A."

"Let me look," Marcia said, and went trotting off down the drive.

Emily opened the trunk—bare as Henry's workbench—and took out the zippered plastic pouch that contained the jumper cables, a Christmas gift from Arlene, then stood there waiting, considering the chromed bulk of the Olds. It had been his, and she loved it for that, but it was far too large. She worried that she would tear the mirrors off trying to back out. She couldn't ask Jim or Marcia for help every time she had to put the car away. The registration was valid, but the inspection sticker had lapsed. She had no doubt it would pass. It would have been easier if it were falling apart. It was typical of Henry, with his engineer's love of the indestructible. He'd been so proud of the mileage, celebrating each showy turn of the odometer. "Every time we drive this car," he said, "we're making money," which made sense to Emily, their shared thriftiness both a source of easy comedy to their friends and a touchstone of their marriage. Her father had been the same way, hanging on to his Bible-black Plymouth with its Keystone Kops running boards and bug-eyed headlights until her high school friends teased her. Now, out of necessity—or was it convenience?—she had to overcome all of that history and do something she wasn't sure Henry or her father would understand.

Marcia's hybrid was so quiet it startled Rufus from his vigil at the drain as she pulled into the courtyard. She turned for the far garage, then backed up.

The battery was in the trunk, a regular twelve-volt model. Emily stretched the cables as far as they'd go.

"You've done this before, obviously," Marcia commented.

"When you have teenagers, you learn," Emily said, then regretted it. The Coles were childless, and while they'd never discussed the issue, Emily gathered that it was not by choice. Occasionally, when they were relaxing on their back deck, or when Emily lingered on the stair landing to peek through their living room window, she'd see Marcia or Jim pick up Buster and cradle him like a baby.

Emily shuttled between the two batteries, sidling along the wall, using both hands to open the clamps. When she clipped the ground to a flange on the Olds' engine block, a spark crackled.

"Is it supposed to do that?" Marcia asked.

"It means we've got a good connection. Now we sit and let it charge a little."

The wait gave Emily the chance to inspect Marcia's car. Next to the Olds it looked sleek and futuristic, a tidy white space capsule. The inside was surprisingly roomy. Marcia said it didn't use a key, just push a button and it started. The controls were all in a small clump on the dashboard, including the shifter.

"That's different," Emily said.

"It's strange at first, but you get used to it."

"How is it on the highway?"

"It's just like a regular car. It's not going to go a hundred miles an hour, but it can do eighty, no problem, and you never have to stop for gas."

"Never?"

"Almost never. I think, highway, it's rated around seventy. What does yours get?"

"Not seventy," Emily said.

Getting back in the Olds was like time-travel. The couchlike bench seat, the olive upholstery, the fake wood accents of the dash, the chrome knobs of the radio—it all belonged to an era she and Henry had passed through but could not properly call theirs. It was an '82, meaning Henry had just turned fifty-three—still young. It was the largest Olds they made, a long, solid car befitting a department head at Westinghouse, and utterly impractical. The children were gone, it was just the two of them, but Emily understood: this was his reward. Arlene made fun of it, calling it Henry's Braddock Cadillac, after the rusted sixties monstrosities that crisscrossed the poorer sections of the East End, and while Emily never laughed at the jab, privately she thought Arlene wasn't so far off. Driving the biggest car made a statement. Unlike Arlene, she didn't think advertising one's status was bad, especially if you'd worked hard for it, and no one worked harder than Henry.

She fitted the key in the ignition. "Here goes nothing," she told Rufus, and twisted her wrist.

The starter chugged, juddering, spewing a blue-white cloud over Marcia's car, then sputtered, coughed and died.

It caught on the second try, running rough before settling to a steady idle. She revved the engine a few times to make sure, then stepped out and unhooked the cables in the reverse order.

"While I've got you here," she asked Marcia, "I hope you don't mind if I press you into service," and had her spot her as she backed out of the garage.

All she needed to do was keep her wheels straight. She knew this, yet she was tentative, unable to gauge the true bounds of the fenders.

"You're good," Marcia called, craning and waving her on, until, halfway out, Emily eased up on the brake and, on faith alone, let the Olds slide—too fast—backward into the courtyard. That she cleared both sides she attributed to luck as much as fear.

Marcia clapped for her. "Well done."

"Thank you. There's no way I could have done that by myself."

"Looks like someone paid you a visit." Marcia pointed to the paw prints on the hood.

"That's all right, I need to wash it anyway."

"I wonder if it was that big tortoiseshell that's been hanging around. Have you heard him serenading his lady friend?"

"Is that what that was?"

"He and Buster had a run-in last week. Now I just keep him inside at night. It's not worth a trip to the vet."

"No," Emily agreed, then thanked her again.

Marcia walked ahead of her down the driveway, turned backward, motioning Emily left to keep her from bumping their fence. Emily didn't need any help, but followed at a crawl, waving as Marcia climbed the porch stairs and stood there watching.

Before pulling onto Grafton, Emily paused. She needed to drive around awhile to recharge the battery. She'd thought resuscitating the car—and before lunch—was a major accomplishment, but now she realized she had nowhere to go. Out of habit, she turned downhill, toward Highland. Once they were moving, Rufus lay down and curled up on the seat as if he were cold. She should take it to a garage and have it looked at, but for that she'd need an appointment. She could drive through the park, up past the AquaZoo, where the roads were wide and empty this time of day. As she pictured the school buses lining the winding curves, she had the terrible feeling that she'd left the back door of the house unlocked. Too late now. At the corner she signaled left, headed for East Liberty—but really, what was the sense in pretending?—for Regent Square and Arlene's. It was the route she'd be taking the most, and as her first, looping turn confirmed, she needed the practice.

PILGRIMS

Kenneth called in the middle of the afternoon, practically shouting over the clash of voices in the background. "Everyone's watching the game," he explained, and she could hear the beer in his voice. Emily turned down her own stereo, as if that might help. She'd been having a quiet day until then, listening to Britten's War Requiem as she leafed through her basket of catalogs, dog-earing possible Christmas gifts for the grandchildren.

Kenneth had caught her daydreaming of Coventry, the music calling up the solemn awe she'd felt as she and Henry walked the stones of the bombed cathedral, its lacework arches open to the blue sky. The new cathedral Emily thought less than successful, unnecessarily modern (now, just forty years later, it seemed dated, plainly ugly), but the ruins more than compensated. Henry must have spent five rolls of film trying to capture the warm orange the setting sun brought out of the stone. Everything was a picture. St. Michael and the Devil. The cross of charred beams by the altar with FATHER FORGIVE in gilt on the wall. The stained glass of the baptistry. She wished he would put down the camera, but she knew, too, that they'd never be back again, and, like her, he wanted to keep it. At night, from the window of their dingy inn, after a heavy dinner downstairs topped off with a syrupy port, they could see the spire, lit against the dark sky, and she imagined the planes leaving their bases in Germany and climbing into the freezing air. She'd listened to the radio dispatches from London as a child, safe in the endless hills of central Pennsylvania, and had thought, naively, of what she would do if the Nazis blitzed Kersey. As silly as that sounded now, it wasn't an idle game. Her fear was real, and to finally be there, where people had survived and carried on with grace and good humor, was both humbling and inspiring. The trip had been Henry's birthday present to her, the fulfillment of a long-ago promise, a dream of hers, and revisiting it filled her with a wistful satisfaction. The phone had broken the spell. She wasn't surprised that it was Kenneth. He'd always had bad timing. Though part of her resentment—petty, she recognized—was that he'd chosen Lisa's family over his own.

"So?" she asked. "How is everyone?"

"We're all going out at halftime to play football on the beach. You should see the waves."

"Isn't it cold?"

"It's a tradition."

"Be careful," Emily said. "You're not a teenager anymore."

"Thanks. Now I'm sure to break something."

Behind him, the room cheered.

"Who all's there?"

"The usual crew, plus Ella's friend Suzanne."

"I don't think I know her. Is she new?"

"They've been together a while now. I don't think you've ever met her."

"Is she nice?"

"Very nice, for a Cowboys fan."

"I must be missing something," Emily said, suddenly impatient with him.

"The Cowboys are playing. Badly."

He broke off to respond to a heckler, leaving her speechless. He was doing his duty, and she supposed she should be grateful, but as she waited, noting the sun warming her plants in the bay window, she remembered how busy Thanksgiving used to be, the house and kitchen overrun, every shelf of the fridge crowded, the street bumper-to-bumper with parked cars. She didn't miss the chaos or the mess, she just wished there were a way she could see the children.

"Sorry," he said. "You know how Texans are."

"Not to bring up an unpleasant subject, but have people started working on their Christmas lists?"

"One holiday at a time is all I can handle."

"It's coming whether you like it or not."

"What do *you* want?" he asked.

"I want us all to be together as a family. That's my Christmas present this year."

"Meg's going to be there."

She hesitated for only a second, as if her disappointment were fleeting, easily swallowed. "Honestly, at this point I'm trying to get rid of stuff, not add new things I don't need."

"Okay, but if you think of anything."

"I'm serious. But, please, sweetheart, you really need to let me know what Ella and Sam want. I'd rather avoid cutting things close like last year if at all possible."

"I'll do my best," he said, echoing Henry—always fending off her worries with his noncommittal optimism—and she thought how lately she'd been seeing more and more of him in Kenneth, when before she'd found little resemblance.

"One more thing I wanted to run by you," she said.

"Shoot."

"Your father's car. Are you interested in it?"

"Oh, wow," he said.

"It's just too much for me, and it's so old I wouldn't get anything for it as a trade-in."

"A trade-in."

"I've talked to a few people, and they say it's not worth it. I figured you always liked it."

"I do," he said. "I'm just not sure where I'd put it."

"It runs fine."

"I'm sure it does, but . . . You're actually going to buy a car."

"Would you rather have your old mother take the bus?"

"No."

"I still need to get around. I'm thinking something small, maybe a little hybrid like Marcia's."

"Have you ever bought a car before?"

"So far I've been spared that pleasure. Believe me, I've been doing my homework."

"I'm sure you have."

"Any tips?"

"Try Cars-dot-com. That's where we found the Mazda."

She asked him whether it made more sense, for her own peace of mind, to buy new. She could tell he wasn't thrilled with the idea that she was driving again, but she could count on him, as she'd counted on Henry, to advise her in practical matters. And while he wouldn't give her a definite yes on the Olds, she knew that eventually he'd take it. He wouldn't be able not to.

Rufus, driven upstairs by the music, came down to investigate and sat at her knee, lifting his chin so she could scratch under his collar.

"All righty," Kenneth finally said, a signal that he was done.

"I know what that means."

"Have fun at the club, and please give our best to Arlene."

"I shall. Give my best to the Sanners."

After she'd gotten off, she put Rufus out and restarted the disc from the beginning. Rufus crunched his treat into pieces, took a sloshing drink of water and waddled back upstairs. Beneath the murky opening theme, church bells tolled, and she pictured the cathedral, the bare yews reaching over the chancel, the spire rising into the sky. Somewhere downstairs there were albums filled with Henry's pictures of that day, and the next, when it had rained and the pub Louise had recommended was closed. As the horns and then the chorus entered, Emily looked up from her Lands' End catalog, squinting, as if trying to remember something elusive, but the music was just music now, recorded voices and tympani booming from the stereo. There was nothing she wanted to buy. The models all seemed too pleased with themselves, as if they'd discovered an easier way of life. She flipped through the pages, wondering when Margaret would call, if at all.

THE BELLE OF THE BALL

Getting dressed for the club, Emily struggled with her jade necklace. She bent forward toward her vanity, chin tucked to her chest, arms curled behind her ducked head, blindly trying to pinch open the clasp and marry it to the tiny eyelet. With every miss she let out her held breath like a sigh. She'd get it eventually—she'd never failed yet. It was the contorted position as much as the clumsiness of her efforts that was humiliating. Over the years she and Henry had made a ceremony of the moment. There was no need to ask him. On formal occasions like tonight he would stand behind her like a valet, waiting for her to finish her makeup. She'd find him admiring her in the mirror, and while she discounted his adoration of her beauty—based, as it was, on a much younger woman—she also relied on it, and as time passed she was grateful for the restorative powers of his memory. No one else saw her the way he did. He knew the eighteen-year-old lifeguard she used to be, and the fashionable grad student, the coltish young mother. When he solved the clasp, he'd watch her regally settle the necklace on her chest, and then, with his hands on her shoulders, bend down and kiss the side of her neck, making her close her eyes.

"Stop," she'd say.

"Stop what?"

"Stop what you're doing."

"What am I doing?"

"You're making us late, that's what you're doing."

"I'm ready to go."

"I can tell."

Now when she finally succeeded and straightened up again, she nearly expected him to be there. She fixed the necklace so that it sat evenly, then, glancing upward, stopped and appraised her own face as if it were strange and captivating.

The glow from the vanity was unforgiving. The hollows beneath her eyes had gone crepey, almost transparent, showing a bruiselike purple. Her mouth was deeply creased, her skin mottled with beige patches, the effect of too much sun. A downy fuzz fringed not just her upper lip but—in the glare of the bare bulbs—her cheeks and chin. She caught herself frowning out of reflex and looked away before clicking the light off.

The image stuck with her as she gathered her lipstick and tissues for her clasp purse. Her hair was thin and stiff, kept presentable only by frequent visits to the salon. Her body—once her glory—had sagged and flattened long ago. Even her perfect posture was gone, her very bones and sinews unreliable. If nothing else, she could still dress well. Downstairs, she verified it in the front hall mirror, avoiding her face.

"What do you think?" she asked Rufus. "Am I going to be the belle of the ball?"

He looked up at her, worried. His eyes were rheumy, and she plucked a tissue and wiped the goo from the corners.

"I know, it's no fun getting old. At least you don't have to go parade around in front of people."

She was still mulling the idea when Arlene picked her up. Even in the darkness of the car, Arlene's lipstick seemed too stark, a stab at a glamour that Emily could not imagine was the fashion with anyone below the age of seventy—a vampirelike, Joan Crawford effect. Her perfume was fruity, and hurt Emily's sinuses.

"Don't you look nice," Arlene said.

"So do you," Emily said.

Arlene had trouble enough seeing during the day, and the drive to Oakland, though less than a mile, took a good fifteen minutes. As they pulled into the club behind a familiar Cadillac, Emily was relieved to see a team of valets waiting for them beneath the porte cochère.

Inside, under the glittering chandeliers, Arlene's lipstick didn't seem so noticeable, if only because Emily's attention lit immediately on her forehead. The gash was still livid, the stitches visible. If Emily were her, she would have worn a scarf or a turban, as Louise had after her chemo, but Arlene was either brazen or blissfully unaware. She'd had her hair done, and was wearing her favorite diamond chips and the matching pendant from Henry's mother. As they crossed the lobby to the grand staircase that swept upward along the far wall, they passed fellow members gathered in conversation, cocktails in hand. Emily's instinct was to shield Arlene from them, but the sheer number rendered that impractical, and then Arlene was waving to Lorraine Havermeyer and Edie Buchanan as if she wanted to call attention to herself.

Lorraine and Edie were best friends, spry, ninetyish widows who lived in the old Webster Hall apartments a few blocks up Fifth Avenue from the club. Shrunken and hunched, they were fixtures on the scene, inseparable, present for every lecture or opening at the Carnegie and the Scaife, every first night at the Benedum Center. Arlene made straight for them, dragging Emily in her wake. They all traded Happy Thanksgivings, asking after one another's families.

"We heard what happened," Lorraine said, pointing at the gash.

Rather than minimize it, Arlene dipped her head to give them a better look.

They both craned forward, inspecting the doctor's work like rival surgeons.

"It must have been terrifying," Edie said.

"I wouldn't know," Arlene said. "I was out like a light. Emily's the one who had to deal with everything."

"It looks like it hurt," Edie asked.

"It did at first, but the doctor gave me these great painkillers. For a while I had no idea where I was, and I didn't particularly care either."

"It could have been much worse," Emily said.

Oh, she'd been lucky, they agreed.

The talk turned to falls, a favorite topic, and timely, with winter coming on, ice their mortal enemy. Jean Daly had slipped in her kitchen and broken her hip, and now her children were trying to move her to a home. The horror with which Lorraine delivered the story annoyed Emily. It was the ultimate cautionary tale, the moral being *Don't fall*, as if they were made of glass. In a sense they were—their fragility was irrefutable, medically proven—and yet Emily detested the inevitable rundown of accidents and tragedies, the more fortunate clucking their tongues and counting their blessings, all the while knowing it was just a matter of time. She didn't need to be reminded that she was a single misstep from disaster, especially here, without Henry, surrounded by the survivors of their earlier life.

She was aware that it was just her frame of mind, that she'd had a bad day and was feeling sorry for herself. Usually the club was a comfort, unchanging, a bastion of middle-class civility and permanence, like the church. The Doric columns and flocked wallpaper, the potted rubber plants and wing chairs, the trophy cases and herringbone floors—they had all been here to greet her sixty years ago, the first time Henry ushered her into the Maxwells' world. In Kersey she'd waited tables at the Clarion Hotel, but she was unprepared for the scale of the dining room, easily a hundred tables set with crystal goblets, gilt-edged china and heavy, monogrammed silver. By chance, that first night, one of their servers was a fellow student from her economics class. Dressed like a cadet in an immaculate white jacket with gold buttons, he silently poured their water and moved on, never betraying their secret. It would be decades before Emily felt she belonged, as if she'd had to earn the right through long years of service. Now, by default (and the trustees' rigid bylaws), the club had become hers, Henry's membership passing to her so that Arlene was forever her guest, though she'd been coming here since she was born.

If nothing else, the club gave them a place to go. These seasonal gatherings were tribal, a means of renewing one's allegiance and catching up on the fortunes of one's fellow members. As much as Emily might protest or wish otherwise, she was just as curious to hear the hottest gossip.

"Did you hear about Bibi Urquhart?" Lorraine asked, already shocked.

They hadn't.

"She's moving—you'll never guess where."

"Fort Lauderdale," Emily said.

"Try again."

"West Palm," Arlene obliged.

"Butler."

They both looked to Edie to see if it was a joke.

She nodded, shrugging at the kookiness of the idea.

"I don't get it," Arlene said. "She doesn't have family there, does she?"

"She wanted out of the city," Edie said. "She found this cute little place by the country club, very reasonable. It has a pond and woods. It sounds idyllic."

"The taxes are cheaper," Lorraine said.

"They can't be *that* much cheaper," Arlene said.

"I wouldn't mind a place in the country," Edie said. "As long as I didn't have to live there."

"A summer place," Arlene said, meaning their old cottage at Chautauqua, which Emily had had to sell after Henry died, and for which Arlene would never forgive her.

"That gets expensive," Emily said. "Especially if you're only there a couple weeks a year."

"She's serious," Lorraine said. "She's putting her house on the market."

"And it's such a lovely house," Arlene said, covering her mouth as if it had been leveled.

"It's gorgeous," Edie said. "But for one person living alone . . ."

"It's just too much," Lorraine finished.

They speculated in low tones about the asking price, which led to a review of how Squirrel Hill was doing, and what other neighborhoods were losing value, and how the schools were failing and the tax base dwindling—an argument *against* leaving the city, Emily tried to mention, but quickly they were on to the elections, and the presidential race, and the larger issue of how the Republican Party they knew was gone, hijacked by the right, leaving them no one to vote for, a lament Emily had heard time and again, and which, like most of the world's problems, would not be solved by any amount of small talk.

Lorraine and Edie said they were going to take the elevator up to the dining room. Arlene said she and Emily would brave the stairs. They'd see them up there.

They tarried to make sure they wouldn't. Arlene took the opportunity to step outside for a smoke. As Emily waited, surveying the lobby, she thought that maybe Bibi was right, that solitude might be a more suitable life for a woman their age. And yet she couldn't shake off the question of what one would do out there in the middle of nowhere, especially in the winter. She had no illusions about the country. It was where she'd come from. She knew the terrible boredom and insularity firsthand, the paralyzing sense of being stranded hundreds of miles from real life. Only a city person would see it as freeing.

She hadn't had much of a lunch, and was glad when Arlene returned. As Arlene navigated the room, skirting the many social circles, people glanced away from their conversations to follow her, gawking as if she had a knife sticking from her head. She kept on, beaming at Emily, looking pleased, as if she were carrying some gleeful secret.

"I just saw Claude Penman outside, with Liz?" She laid a hand on Emily's forearm and leaned in close to deliver her scoop, her eyes shining. "She's in a wheelchair. You should see her. She looks *awful*."

THE DAY OF REST

Sunday Emily drove the Olds to church. Both she and Arlene preferred the early service, and it was a pleasure to guide the long car through the gray, empty streets, knowing the *Times* would be waiting for her when she returned.

The congregation was all regulars, mostly older, so small they took up just the first few rows. Calvary was grand, a mock-Gothic pile, and to save energy, only the lamps that hung directly above them shone, the wings and rear pews lost in the gloom. The night before had been freezing, and the stone held the cold, the space beneath the soaring vault too vast to heat. The Altar Guild had decorated the sanctuary with fresh pine boughs, scenting the chilly air. Emily kept her coat buttoned and watched the tapers waver and smoke. As a child she'd loved the pageantry of Advent, the delicious month of buildup to Christmas. Now, having outgrown most of her earthly desires, she thought she understood the longing for Christ's arrival.

O come, O come, Emmanuel,
and ransom captive Israel.

"I am the Alpha and the Omega," Father Lewis intoned, letting the meaning settle, when there was no need with this crowd, naturally drawn to last things. Emily saw the words as a promise. From beginning to end, her life was safely contained in Him, as was Henry's, and the children's. In this way she could believe in eternity, even as she imagined death as an endless darkness.

Each week she came to be renewed by the music and the simple eloquence of the liturgy. With Arlene she processed to the rail and crossed one palm atop the other to receive the body and the blood, and afterward knelt at her seat, eyes closed, her forehead resting on her clasped hands, at peace. The recessional was boisterous, the organ triumphant, the bass vibrating the air. She shook Father Lewis's hand and tugged her gloves on.

Outside, the world was bright and cold, and as she drove Arlene home, the spell dissipated, and she was left with the day. She would start on the crossword. Margaret would call. She needed to take the chicken out of the freezer. It all seemed so meager that she thought, fleetingly, of dropping Arlene off and coming back for the eleven o'clock.

At home she put on Bach's Christmas Oratorio and brewed a pot of tea before going through the *Post-Gazette*. Rufus aligned himself with the radiator so he could keep an eye on her. She separated the glossy flyers from the news, making a neat pile at her feet, then slid out the classifieds and real estate sections. She clipped her coupons and set them safely aside before taking the pile into the kitchen and adding it to the recycling.

Stripped of its advertising, the *Post-Gazette* was criminally thin. While she relied on their local coverage, and still loved the funnies, she was glad she had the *Times* to keep her company. The Arts section or Book Review alone could rescue an afternoon. Rationed correctly, the puzzle would last her all week. She and Louise used to compare their progress, or lack thereof, commiserating or crying foul when the editor asked too much of them. Even now, when she caught on to the pun that unlocked a puzzle, she wondered if Louise had gotten it, when of course Louise was beyond the reach of home delivery.

The news was old. A bomb had gone off near a mosque in Baghdad. A teenager had been stabbed at a party in Garfield. Alcoa—which Henry and now she owned a fair amount of—was cutting jobs. The Steelers were playing Cleveland. It was supposed to snow tomorrow, just a dusting. She made her usual survey of the obituaries, and was relieved to find no one she knew. She noted those close to her age and younger, but refused to brood on them. She didn't want to be one of those old ladies obsessed with death, hearing it in every tick of the clock and creak of the floorboards, as if it were prowling around the house like a burglar. There was no need to hurry things. She would be among their number soon enough.

She dispatched with the *Post-Gazette* and pressed on through the *Times*, pouring herself another cup of tea. Rufus lobbied her to go outside and then did nothing but stand there like a cow and sniff the air. She gave him a treat anyway. She let the CD repeat, and then, when she'd wrapped her legs in an afghan and taken up her lucky pen, let it repeat again.

Starting was always hard, but rewarding too, completing the easy clichés and catchphrases before decoding the coyer clues. She was pleased that she could still retrieve the names of poets and rivers and films, and was nimble enough to hold the competing possibilities of intersection in her mind until the right combination fit. "Nigeria's neighbor" was GABON. "Steakhouse shunner" was VEGAN.

"'Capacious canine,'" she asked Rufus, "who does that sound like?"

When the grandfather clock chimed one, she stopped for lunch—Lipton chicken noodle soup and a turkey sandwich. She put on Schütz's *Story of the Nativity* and ate in the breakfast nook, looking out on the backyard. The weatherman was a day late. Wisps of snow floated down like ash. The birdfeeders were low, and when she'd had enough of her sandwich, she took her crusts outside and scattered them on the window ledge, then sat with a cup of coffee and some Nilla wafers and watched a pair of chickadees feast.

That Margaret hadn't called nagged at her—really, that she hadn't bothered to call on Thanksgiving—but Emily resisted the urge to pick up the phone. All Margaret had to say was that she'd booked her flights. Was that too much to ask? *Behold the handmaid of the Lord*, the chorus rejoiced in the living room, but, as she sat there with the dregs of her cup, a napkin crumpled in one hand, a feeling of inertia took her. The day was half over and she'd gotten nothing done.

Running the dishes didn't count, or refilling the feeders, taking the single chicken breast from the freezer and baring it to the air. They were just ways of procrastinating, putting off the tedious job of writing her Christmas cards. She was using a picture Kenneth had taken of the grandchildren at Sam's high school graduation, Sam in his gown, the other three smiling in their spring best. It was a tradition, each grandchild getting a chance to be the center of attention. He was the last, the baby of the group.

Next year she'd have to find a different shot. Friday she'd made a special trip to the post office to buy holiday stamps, so there was no excuse, and still she roamed about the downstairs, distracted, as if she'd forgotten something.

Everything she needed was in her secretary. She gathered her address book and the stamps, the bag with the cards and a pair of permanent markers she'd bought strictly for this purpose, and established herself at the dining room table, setting out her materials left to right in an assembly line.

She did the grandchildren's first, adding, *All my love, Grandma*, to the printed greeting, and was immediately dismayed by her handwriting. Since winning a plaster of Paris bust of Shakespeare for penmanship in the sixth grade, she'd prided herself on her cursive. In the last few years it had deteriorated, become shaky, her hand tremulous, as if she suffered from a nervous disease. It may have been the day, the exalted promise of the morning spoiled, but she saw her squiggly letters as more proof that she was bound to lose everything, at least in this world.

Her address book confirmed it, the pages inhabited equally by the living and the dead. Helen Alford had been gone ten years now, yet Emily could bring back the ratty Swarthmore sweatshirt Helen wore to play touch football with Bud and the children Sundays in the park. George and Doris Ballard, who used to carpool to the symphony with them. Conrad and Hilde Barr, who moved to Roanoke. Ida Blair. Judy Burke. Each name called up raucous dinner parties and gin-and-tonics on sunny patios, lazy Saturday afternoons at the swim club, station wagons filled with noisy boys in polyester baseball uniforms. The temptation was to mourn those days, when they were young and busy and alive. As much as Emily missed them, she understood the reason that era seemed so rich—partly, at least—was because it was past, memorialized, the task they'd set themselves of raising families accomplished. The thought of Margaret was enough to remind her that not all of their times had been happy, that, in truth, much of it had been a struggle, one that was far from over, if that was in fact possible. No, probably not. Even after she herself was dead, Margaret would still be battling her, just as, occasionally, Emily still fought with her own mother, both guiltily and, being eternally wronged, self-righteously. Though everything faded, nothing was ever done.

Based on last year's tally, she'd ordered a hundred cards and envelopes. So far she'd completed twelve. In the living room, her puzzle waited, and the book review, the arts section. She could put on Bach's Mass in B minor, pull the afghan over her and sink deep into Henry's chair. Falling asleep while the sky outside colored and then dimmed appealed to her. It was Sunday, after all.

The notion, like the temptation to give in to nostalgia, was fleeting, and impractical. If she quit, the cards would just be waiting for her tomorrow, ruining two days instead of one. It was her job. No elves would magically sneak in overnight and do them for her. It would take her hours, and they'd probably look awful, but, honestly, what else did she have to do? She took an envelope from the stack, found the next living person in her address book and kept going, pressing down hard so the words would be legible.

KINDRED SPIRITS

E very other Wednesday, Betty came to help her keep the worst of the house at bay. As fastidious as Emily was, she could no longer get down on her knees and scrub the tubs, or wash the shower curtains, or give the floors an honest mopping. For years Arlene had sung Betty's praises, and though Emily had regarded the idea of hiring someone to do her housework as a badge of laziness and privilege—in the sixties most of her friends had had cleaning women—now she couldn't imagine how she'd ever done without her.

Tuesday night, Emily primed the rooms, gathering Rufus's toys and straightening magazines. She lightly went over the stove and sink, polishing the water-spotted tap so it shone, and set out a new S.O.S. pad. It was all she could do not to empty the garbage.

In the morning she counted down the minutes till eight, when Betty pulled up in her little silver Nissan, the back plastered with stickers supporting the troops, the Steelers and the unions. Emily lurked behind the curtains while she unloaded her vacuum and gym bag and bucket full of supplies. She was stocky and close-cropped in a puffy down coat, sporty warm-up pants and bright white running shoes, and at fifty possessed a briskness Emily envied. She was from Butler originally, and retained its broad, flat accent. With her bad teeth and disdain for makeup, there was something real and unspoiled about her. Not a lack of sophistication but an honesty and common sense that reminded Emily of her mother's circle in Kersey, a small-town directness that put her at ease.

Before she reached the porch, Emily had the door open for her. Rufus, who was losing his eyesight, lowered his head and growled as if he didn't know her.

"Don't be rude," Emily scolded.

"Aw, it's all right. I know, Roof, you're just doing your job. He's like Bongo. Anyone comes to the house, he's got to check him out first. That's right, boy, you protect your master."

Emily took Betty's coat as if she were a guest, hanging it in the closet next to her own. She asked after her husband Jesse, whose back had been acting up, and her daughter Toni, stationed in Norfolk with the Navy.

"She's talking about wanting to buy a house down there 'cause they're so cheap, with all the foreclosures going on. I wouldn't want to buy a house that way, I don't know. It's hard when you're just starting out. Arlene tells me you're thinking about getting a new car. Is that right?"

"I'm just starting to look."

"Good for you, Emily," Betty said, knotting her smock behind her.

"I'm afraid you're the only one who thinks so."

"You're lyin'. No, I'm sorry, you can't live without a car nowadays, especially if you're by yourself."

"Thank you," Emily said.

"You can't be any worse than Arlene, right? I'm just kiddin'."

"No you're not."

"No, but yeah, you've had that Olds how long now?"

She had to subtract. "Twenty-five years this year."

"So it's officially an antique. How's it handle in the snow?"

"It doesn't."

"There you go," Betty said. "What are you looking at?"

"I'm thinking something small. But safe, like a Subaru, or maybe a hybrid like Marcia's."

"Those are supposed to be nice."

They were standing at the foot of the stairs. Betty had her rubber gloves on and her bucket in one hand, and Emily didn't want to hold her up.

"Anything special today?" Betty asked.

"We should probably start getting the kids' rooms ready so we don't have to do them all at once."

"Gotcha."

Having someone else moving about the house was always strange. From the kitchen, Emily monitored her progress. By upbringing as much as inclination, she was incapable of sitting around while someone else was working, and as Betty attacked the master bath, running water in the tub, Emily pulled on her own pair of rubber gloves and took the opportunity to polish the silver she planned to use at Christmas, envisioning Margaret and the children arrayed around the table, happily passing dishes.

They spent the morning working separately, as if they'd agreed to stay out of each other's way. Upstairs, the handle of Betty's bucket clanked. A squirt bottle squirted—*fssh, fssh, fssh*. A toilet flushed. A vacuum roared back and forth, bumping furniture. Emily listened with satisfaction, knowing that with each passing minute, the two of them were getting the house ready.

Just before noon, she went up to let Betty know what was available for lunch. Having lived alone for so long, Emily took pleasure in feeding her, as if she were company. She'd planned on their favorite grilled cheese sandwiches, and yesterday she'd picked up some of the nice tomato basil soup they both liked from the Crockery.

"I don't think that's on my diet," Betty joked.

"What would you like to drink? I bought some Diet Pepsis for you."

"A Diet Pepsi would be great, thanks."

Emily set the table in the breakfast nook, and then, when Betty was ready, served them, pouring herself a cup of tea. She'd almost sat down when she remembered: pickles.

"I hope it's all right."

"It's wonderful, Emily. Thank you."

"I find I need something substantial on a day like this, otherwise I get chills."

"That's 'cause you don't have any meat on your bones—you and Arlene."

"Arlene doesn't eat, she just eats sweets. I eat all the time, I just can't seem to keep up my weight."

"I wish I had your problem."

"No you don't," Emily said. "I try to tell Dr. Sayid and he thinks I'm lying. He wants to give me this supplement that's like baby formula."

"Ensure. Lots of people use it."

"I can't think of anything more unappealing."

"Y'ever try it?"

"No, have you?"

Betty laughed at the idea. "I would if my doctor told me to."

"Okay, you've made your point."

"After what happened with Arlene, I don't want to have to worry about you too."

"You don't," Emily assured her.

"Just try and stop me. Oh, I forgot to tell you. Edgar died."

"Edgar?" For a second she couldn't place the name, and feared she was losing her memory.

"Arlene's Edgar."

"Ah." A fish.

"It was very sad. We had a burial at sea." She swirled a finger downward.

"I'm surprised she didn't call me."

"I'm sure you'll hear about it."

"I'm sure."

"Now, tell me," Betty said, "who thinks you shouldn't be buying a car?"

It was rare that Emily had the chance to explain herself to someone who knew her situation—it was rare that anyone would be interested—and she eagerly framed Margaret's and Kenneth's reservations versus her needs as if pleading the case to a neutral observer. There was no need. A friend, Betty had already found in her favor.

"They're just worried about you. They don't want you to hurt yourself."

"Or anyone else, yes, I get it. I could say the same about Margaret but I won't." When Margaret was drinking, she'd been in several accidents, and at one point had her license taken away.

"Come on, Emily, that's not fair."

"No, you're right. They don't trust me. That's what hurts the most."

"It's probably a shock to them. You stopped for a long time."

"Because the Olds was too big for me. They don't even make cars that size anymore."

"It *is* humongous."

What a luxury it was to have someone who listened instead of contesting every point. Betty's visits reminded her of how starved she was for conversation, and counsel. For so long Louise had been her sounding board, the one person she could go to when she and Henry disagreed, as they often did, about the children or Arlene. Betty served the same purpose, but with the extra advantage of knowing what Arlene was up to—a kind of double agent—and yet Emily for the most part spoke openly with her, secure in her belief that Betty wasn't spreading her secrets around town. She was well aware that now and then Betty might leak word to Arlene, being a direct conduit between them, but that was different. She depended on Betty to return the favor, maintaining a constant low-level intrigue that kept things interesting and, in a strange way, brought them all closer.

For dessert they indulged in a plate of mint Milanos, and then, too soon, it was time for Betty to get back to work. As always, over Betty's protests, Emily cleared the table and did the dishes.

In the afternoon they changed places. Rufus turned circles on his bed as if fluffing it, then folded himself down. The whole upstairs smelled tartly of lemon and ammonia. Betty had left the lights on, as if encouraging Emily to inspect her work. The water in the toilets was foggy. In the master bath Emily rearranged the pain relievers on the shelf above the sink, and the brushes on her vanity, putting everything back exactly the way she liked it.

She spent the rest of the day in Henry's office, sitting at his computer with her credit card on the freshly polished desk, ordering Christmas gifts. The shipping was outrageous, but at this point what choice did she have? She crossed off her lists, keeping a tally of how much she'd spent on each grandchild, trying to be fair-handed, which was difficult, since she had so many ideas for Ella and Sarah and so few for Sam and Justin. She would not buy them video games. There was too much mindless, hateful entertainment as it was. If Arlene wanted to, that was her business, but she would not be party to it. She'd hoped they would have outgrown them by now—they were in college, for God's sake—but their wish lists were nearly identical: *Assassin's Creed*, *Call of Duty 4: Modern Warfare*. At the risk of further solidifying her reputation as a fuddy-duddy, she bought them clothes they could wear to the club.

The mail was late, and contained a glittery card from Nicky Ouellette in Hilton Head, whom Emily hadn't heard from in ages and had therefore dropped from her list. She immediately retaliated, sharing her irritation with Betty as she penned an overjoyed note. *So good to hear from you!*

"You know what I hate," Betty said. "The ones that come from out of nowhere right before Christmas."

"And there's nothing you can do about them."

"I haven't even started mine, so you're way ahead of me."

"You'd better get going."

"I know. I'm gonna have to do them this weekend, along with everything else."

"It's just a bad time of year," Emily agreed.

"Are you doing a tree this year?"

"Are you kidding me? I'd never hear the end of it if I didn't. I'll let them help me with it. That's something we can all do together."

"There you go, put 'em to work."

"Don't laugh. You know who's going to end up taking it down—the two of us."

"That's all right," Betty said. "I like a tree. It's not Christmas without one."

"It's true," Emily said. "There's something about the smell."

"And the lights at night."

Just fond small talk, yet it meant so much to her. She wanted to stay and chat, but Betty had finished the dining room and was moving on to the kitchen, and Emily retreated upstairs to write her a check. That reminded her: she'd have to stop at the bank next week and pick up Betty's bonus— five crisp twenties in an envelope with an oval cut to show Andrew Jackson's face. She wrote it down so she wouldn't forget.

After mopping the kitchen floor, the last thing Betty did was take out the garbage. Emily heard the back door open and close, and then, seconds later, the rumble of the big wheeled drum. Tomorrow was garbage day, and though at first Emily had insisted she was perfectly capable, Betty had taken upon herself the job of rolling the container, with the heavy recycling bin perched on top, down the driveway to the curb. Emily waited for her to come back in the front and summon her, calling up the stairs, "Okay, Emily, I'm all done."

Emily fetched Betty's coat from the closet. In the front hall she thanked her and handed her the check. "Please give my best to Jesse."

"Say hey to the family for me," Betty said.

Emily saw her off, waving from the bay window as she ducked into the little Nissan and then headed down Grafton Street, stopping at the stop sign. She signaled, turned into a gap in traffic and was gone. For practical reasons, Emily had kept the stereo off, and now, without her music, the living room was silent. After having company all day, the place felt empty, yet at the same time Emily was relieved to be alone again, and pleased to have a clean house. She crossed to the front hall and made sure the storm door was shut tight, then gently shot the deadbolt, sealing herself in. Rufus knew that meant dinnertime, and barked once to prod her.

"Yes, yes," Emily said. "Just hold your horses, Mr. Fatty."

FAMILY PICTURES

Emily thought it was not morbid but absolutely natural that as she grew closer to her own end, she became more and more interested in her origins, and wanted to pass that knowledge on to her children. Her mother and father had come from clans whose roots traced the valleys of north-central Pennsylvania, linking towns like Kersey and Ridgway and Saint Marys. The Waite and Benton men were farmers and loggers and miners at first, and only later tradesmen and merchants, the women generally housewives, along with a few unmarried Sunday school teachers and missionary aunts. Her own father had worked as a building inspector for the county, while her mother taught kindergarten and first grade. They had struggled to achieve and maintain their middle-class respectability in the face of a depression and a world war, a feat Emily thought was lost on her own children, accustomed to an affluence that must have seemed their birthright as much as it had been Henry's and Arlene's, born to fortune.

As if to remind them of her own humble beginnings, every Christmas Emily gave Margaret and Kenneth a framed picture of another forgotten branch of the family, and if these gifts were initially met with indifference, that was fine. Emily had conceived of this as a long-term project, one that might take their entire lives to finally resonate, as it had with her. She'd come to appreciate her Kersey upbringing only well after she'd fled the town and made the long-wished-for transformation into a fashionable city dweller. Not that her teenaged estimation of the place had been wrong—it was even worse now, a dying Appalachian backwater—but, looking back, she saw that, like Margaret, she'd been an ungrateful child, stubborn and arrogant to no real purpose beyond her own vanity.

At the dining room table, as she scavenged through her mother's loose black-and-white snapshots with their quaintly pinked edges, the month and year neatly machine-stamped in all four margins, she found photos of herself standing with her arms crossed on a dock or leaning against the fender of the Plymouth or sitting on their back steps eating an apple, always with a slightly fiery scowl, as if she'd specifically asked not to have her picture taken. As a child she'd been emotional, a crier, a brooder, a showy thrower of tantrums. Once she'd begun, she could not be appeased. Why, her mother pleaded, did she have to be that way? There was no good answer. It was just the way she was. Difficult. Touchy. Mean. Her relatives blamed it on her being an only child, spoiled from too much attention. Her father tried to turn it into a joke. Little Miss Moody Patootie. Don't look at her cross-eyed. Wait till you have kids of your own, her mother threatened, as if Emily would pass her temper on like a disease of the blood, until, inevitably, she did, and oh, it was rich, there was no end of the I-told-you-so's. She remembered, many times, trying to coax Margaret and Kenneth to smile—Kenneth, who had Henry's sweet nature but followed his big sister's lead—so as not to ruin a group portrait (so as not to embarrass her). Those were here as well, the prime of their family life carefully documented in album after album, an editing job put off until the children had left, then attacked with commemorative devotion. The patent falseness of so many shots staged to mark an occasion only deepened the mystery of the past, its unhappiness dressed up, hidden, invisible to the camera.

Often, as she leafed through the sticky, plastic-coated pages, spotting herself with a frizzy perm or wearing a loud, printed blouse, she was struck by how long life was, and how much time had passed, and she wished she could go back and apologize to those closest to her, explain that she understood now. Impossible, and yet the urge to return and be a different person never lessened, grew only more acute. Yes, Henry was a saint—a martyr at his most passive—but how did her mother and father ever put up with her? How did she not throttle Margaret?

It was easier to revisit people she didn't remember. Her mother had done the hard part, tracking down the names and writing them on the back, along with a date, where available, and a note making clear their relation. To cover as much ground as possible, Emily chose only those pictures that showed a whole family. Last Christmas she'd given them her Great-Great-Grandfather and -Grandmother Benton and their four children squinting in front of a ramshackle farmhouse, along with their hired man, all of them in their Sunday best, the men with hats in hand. Following her scheme, this year's would be a studio portrait of her Great-Great-Grandfather and -Grandmother Waite and their three girls from 1872. The flash bleached the girls' dresses, their faces pasty and shadowless, the baby, Lily, turned to the side, unsure. The Waite branch of the family was the more prosperous, which was obvious from the fact that they could afford this portrait, but of them individually Emily knew little. John William Waite was a cooper. Kathleen Gamble Waite would outlive him and two of their children, leaving only the middle girl, Helen, to mourn her. Emily tried to imagine inhabiting their world, and as she peered into their faces, straining to feel some connection, she wondered at how, a hundred years from now, some descendant of hers would search her face, hoping to intuit her life and times, and realized the futility of her mission. Why should Margaret and Kenneth care about these strangers? They were all doomed to be mere emblems to those who didn't know them. And to those who did?

The question of how she would be remembered was not one she wanted to contemplate. Her life had been happy, for the most part, her disappointments mild, common, yet when she recalled herself, she did so with a mix of self-righteousness and shame, holding up her worst moments against her best intentions. She would never forget the names she'd flung at Henry in her rages, or the times she'd made her mother cry. She came from a place and a generation that didn't believe, as Margaret and Kenneth's did, that you could—or should—forgive your own sins.

She'd already found the picture she wanted, and as if to cut off her thoughts, she boxed up the rest and lugged them back down to their place in the basement. Here, in the dingy corner behind the furnace, where seepage darkened the wall of the foundation, rested their history. She'd spent countless hours sorting the pictures and mementos into stackable Rubbermaid bins, each neatly labeled, and still there was so much more to do. She pulled the string of the bare bulb, and it all disappeared.

Rufus was waiting for her at the top of the stairs. "Who wants to go for a car ride?" she asked, making him twirl, but even after dropping the photo off to be copied at the Rite Aid, she couldn't shake her mood.

She ended up going to bed early, reading Henry's Bible while the Chicago Symphony mauled Shostakovich. She marked her place and listened in the dark for a while, the Coles' Christmas lights blinking, tinting the ceiling. It was ridiculous how, with no one's help, she'd worked herself into a perfect state. There was no reason either. The past was the past. Better to work on the present instead of wallowing, and yet the one comforting thought was also the most infuriating. Time, which had her on the rack, would just as effortlessly rescue her. This funk was temporary. Tomorrow she would be fine.

ALL-WHEEL DRIVE

The first real snow was always a surprise. It began after lunch on a gray day, just a few fat flakes sifting through the trees and telephone wires, but as she was changing Margaret's sheets, the air was suddenly flocked with white, the wind streaking wild currents sideways down the street. That morning the radio had predicted scattered flurries. She expected this was one of them, and enjoyed the spectacle for a moment before getting back to work.

Doing Kenneth's bed, she noticed the snow was still falling steadily, beginning to accumulate in patches on the backyard, if not the tarred garage roof or driveway. By the time she took the armful of dirty sheets downstairs and got the washer going, the grass was frosted. In the dining room, Rufus sat at attention by the French doors, following the birds' crisscrossing sorties to the feeders, or so she thought. When she came closer, she could see, mere feet away on the concrete slab of the porch, hogging the spilled sunflower seeds, a beady-eyed squirrel.

She wasn't sure if this was the same one she'd battled last winter—a sneaky suet thief—but that didn't matter. All squirrels were her enemy.

"What is it? What do you see?"

As she reached for the lock, Rufus stood up.

"Git him," she whispered, slowly turning the door handle. "Git that squirrel."

"Woosh," she said, and flung the door wide. He bolted out, swerving as the squirrel shot across the yard. He was too old, his back legs moving in unison, the same way he sometimes hopped down the stairs. Lagging badly, he chased it to the base of the cherry tree and then stood there looking up into the tangle of branches, though by now the squirrel had leapt to the garage roof and tightroped across the stockade fence at the rear of the courtyard, disappearing behind the Coles' garage. Rufus lifted his leg and marked the trunk, leaving a warning.

"Good boy," Emily said, welcoming him inside with a treat. "You almost had him."

After a long, sloppy drink of water, he returned to his post, flopping down and watching the yard. She gathered her calendar and her cookbooks and set up shop at the breakfast table, putting together her menus for Christmas. Margaret and the children would be there for five nights. Saturday they'd be tired from traveling and she could do something easy like her lasagna. Sunday they'd have dinner at the club, after *The Nutcracker*. She needed to plan lunches, and buy breakfast food, a separate list. In the living room, a brass choir played Gabrieli's sacred motets. Outside, the snow flew, gathering on the flagstones of the path and the branches of the cherry tree, the scene as peaceful as a Hiroshige print. She wanted to prolong the feeling, and, like a child, hoped the snow wouldn't stop. Every time she looked up, she thought she'd gotten lucky.

By late afternoon, as the light died and gray invaded the dining room, the caps topping the fence posts had to be four inches tall. The yard was pristine, only the sunken bowls of the flagstones mapping the paths to the garage door and the gate. When she let Rufus out after feeding him, she stood on the back porch with her arms folded against the cold, soaking in the quiet. It was funny how nature restored order to the world and made it easier to believe in grace. She could see how earlier people had worshipped the seasons.

A snowblower racketed around the front, a rude intrusion. It proved to be Jim Cole, doing her walk first. She waved to him from the bay window, making a note to set aside some cookies for them tomorrow. Darkness was coming on, and up and down the street, Christmas lights played over the sculpted lawns and hedges. She couldn't remember when the neighborhood had looked so pretty, and took it as an invitation. She tugged her boots on and jiggled Rufus's leash to get him going.

Stepping outside in her knit hat and scarf, she felt intrepid. Jim had cleared the walk, but there were untouched stretches above and below them. She decided to head uphill to Sheridan, where it was level. At the corner, as Rufus was christening the hedges, the streetlight above them flickered to life, silver at first, then a wan, coppery orange. The snow was falling straight down now, gently. Grafton hadn't been plowed yet, the center packed and slick, and she remembered Henry and Cal Miller sledding with the children on a night like this—could it be?—forty years ago. More, because that was the night six-year-old Daniel Pickering ran his shiny new aluminum flying saucer into the bumper of the Alfords' Lincoln and lost his front teeth. They had watched Timothy and Rachel, made hot chocolate and played Monopoly while Louise and Doug took Daniel to the emergency room.

She would end up there if she wasn't careful. No one on Sheridan had shoveled, though someone had taken the time to build an adult-sized snowman, complete with a Steelers tassel hat and ski gloves. Emily paused before it to admire the construction while Rufus sniffed at its base. Across the street, a gigantic blow-up Santa glowed beside a coach light. She thought it was not so much garish as generic, a store-bought joy. Another trend she didn't get were the icicle fringes people hung from their gutters. An old fogey, she preferred the classics: all-white or multicolored strings of bulbs, a fresh-cut pine wreath on one's front—but not garage—door. And yet, as they strolled through the electric carnival, passing staid and then blinking displays—even one that crawled and danced like the border of a movie marquee—she was grateful for the sheer silly exuberance of her neighbors' decorations. The exterior, like the lawn, had been Henry's job, and though Jim would have happily hung their old outside lights, she had never liked them much, and learned to make do with a simple wreath from the School for the Deaf, adding her own bow. This year she hadn't even done that yet, using Margaret as an excuse, when all she had to do was drive over to Wilkinsburg.

She decided she would, tomorrow. Right now the Olds was useless, but by then the roads would be clear. She could drop by Arlene's and surprise her with one—and maybe some boughs for the mantel, yes, and a few to surround her mother's crèche. By the time she reached the dead end of Sheridan, she had her plan for the morning.

Coming back down Grafton, she had to take baby steps, one hand out for balance, as if she might slip and grab the hedge. Knowing he'd get a treat, Rufus strained at the leash. She unhooked him, and he bounded free, romping across the yard.

Jim, bless him, had salted the walk. The Olds still sat under a sparkling coat of snow, white as a bar of soap. Henry never would have left his baby at the mercy of the elements, but instead of feeling guilty, once again Emily marveled at the gross impracticality of the old boat. Marcia's hybrid was front-wheel drive. Emily wondered if that was enough for Pittsburgh. The Subaru wagons she'd been looking at online were all-wheel-drive, maybe a smarter choice, living on a hill.

Was it just the beauty of the snow that buoyed her, the novelty of the world transformed? Inside, still inspired, she put on some of Bach's chorale preludes and laid a fire. She ate her soup and toast in the rocker by the hearth, Rufus at her side, alert for crumbs. He smelled like wet dog, though she would never hold that against him. His nose was running, and out of reflex his tongue flicked up and licked it.

"Please," Emily said, "I'm eating," and dabbed at his snout with a paper napkin she tossed into the flames. "I hope you're not getting sick."

All evening she found herself drawn to the windows. As she readied herself for bed, she peeked out a last time and was pleased to see it was still floating down, the Coles' lights coloring the yard a tropical, cough-drop aqua. In bed she read a little with the radio, then turned in. The day had been an adventure, and she expected to sleep well.

Sometime in the night, she woke to a thunderous concussion and glass shattering, as if a bomb had gone off downstairs. Rufus was up and barking a warning. In her groggy state she thought someone was breaking in, and after hooking on her glasses, rolled over and reached for the heavy flashlight Henry kept by his side of the bed, only to find the batteries had died. It was still the best weapon she had, and once she got her robe and slippers on, she brandished it head-high like a club.

She stomped across the floor as if the sound of a larger person might frighten the intruder. Rufus clamored at the bedroom door, ready to fly down the stairs and protect the house, when, outside, a car revved, then revved again, louder, like one of Margaret's delinquent boyfriends calling her to her window.

She was just in time to see a massive old station wagon slalom down the hill, the bright fan of its headlights swinging wildly until it straightened out on the flat and then, barely braking, fishtailed wide onto Highland. Below, the Olds sat cockeyed across the driveway, its front wheels on the Coles' lawn. Dark shards littered its parking spot.

"For Christ's sake," Emily said. "Of all the goddamned things."

The clock on her nightstand said half-past three. She set aside the flashlight, turned on her reading lamp and sat down on her bed to call the police. They seemed disappointed that she hadn't been able to catch the license plate, as if the accident were her fault.

When she'd hung up, she thought they were partly right. She shouldn't have left the car on the street in this weather. She could have tucked it into the driveway, or had Jim stick it in the garage. She'd wanted Kenneth to come and get it, but, as always, he'd put her off, too busy, and now it was too late. It was useless to think this way, and with a sigh she stood and went to the hamper and exchanged her robe for her dirty clothes so she could go out and assess the damage.

HIGHWAY ROBBERY

The mess would take some time to clean up. The whole process of filing a claim seemed hopelessly old-fashioned, submitting forms and photos, arranging for the police to send in their report and then waiting for an adjuster to venture out from the local home office. When, after the first week, Emily called and was put on hold for twenty minutes, the representative she finally spoke to told her the storm had created a huge backlog. They were doing everything they could.

Meanwhile, the garage that had towed the Olds was charging her twenty dollars a day for storage.

"They should have left it there," she told Arlene, a bitter jest she repeated to Betty when she came, and over the phone to both Margaret and Kenneth.

While she was outraged at the jackass who'd hit her, and always would be, that at least had been an accident. Practically, it didn't matter that he'd left the scene. Even if he'd stopped and apologized, with the state's no-fault policy she'd be in the same pickle.

She reserved her worst fury for the people who, by lawful contract, were supposed to help her. For years they'd taken her money in exchange for a promise, and woe to her if she was late with a payment. Now, when she needed them the most, they were nowhere to be found. It reminded her of getting Henry's ridiculous hospital bill a month after the funeral and the hoops they made her jump through to take care of it. What was truly galling was that this evasion of responsibility was their business model, and the politicians did nothing to stop it.

"How is this different from the last time?" Kenneth asked, as if he were trying to get her goat.

"Last time I was able to drive my car until the check came through."

"They can't give you a loaner?"

"How would I know? I call and all I get is some customer service person God-knows-where who won't tell me anything."

His view was that she should hope it was totaled. That way she'd get a check and the company would take the car off her hands, rather than her having to deal with getting it fixed and then negotiating a trade-in, always a losing proposition.

"But I thought you wanted it," she asked.

"I did, because you were getting rid of it. Now it might work out that you don't have to, and that's fine. We don't have room for it here anyway."

Privately she'd cultivated the idea that the car represented an unspoken bond between him and Henry. She didn't understand how he could give up on it so easily, unless he was just trying to appease her—always possible. He was his father's son.

Margaret thought it was a sign. Since her last rehab she was a great believer in things happening for a reason, seeing fate in the random, as if a cosmic predestination were the only benign explanation for how her life had turned out. While it was true that the accident had cleared a spot in the garage for a new car, Emily held a more rigorous view of free will.

Regardless of these grandiose speculations, the immediate result was that Arlene had to drive her everywhere, a nightmare, with all of their errands. Christmas was nine days away, and Emily felt time running out. She would need a car while Margaret and the children were in town, if only to pick them up at the airport. Renting was akin to throwing money away, and so, motivated by what she hoped were practical reasons, she had Arlene chauffeur her one last time to Baierl Subaru off McKnight Road and paid the year-end clearance price for a cobalt-blue '07 Outback wagon. She'd done her homework, but still, she was aware the odds were good that the car would outlast her. She wasn't sure Henry would understand.

Certainly her parents wouldn't. The sales tax alone was more than his trusty Plymouth had cost her father. It was the largest check she'd ever written, and as she tore it off and handed it to the salesman and then logged the obscene figure in her ledger, she feared she was making a grave mistake.

KLEENEX

As she plucked the tissue, the box lifted with it off the top of the toilet tank, then, when they separated, dropped back empty. She blew her nose, regarding the gray cardboard bottom through the plastic slit, annoyed at the extra task. With some effort, she tore the box apart so it would take up less space in the wastebasket. She'd bought a three-pack last week, saving a dollar, as always, with a coupon. As she pulled it from the linen closet, running her thumbnail along a seam between the boxes until the shrink-wrap split, she noticed she was out of sixty-watt bulbs. She'd have to put them on the list.

She took the new box downstairs and swapped it for the half-full one by Henry's chair, then went around weighing the open ones until she found the lightest—on the kitchen counter—and switched them. She put the light one in Henry's office, beside his computer, took the nearly full one that had been there upstairs and centered it on the toilet tank.

She could have stopped there, but, carried by her own momentum, she checked the rest of the upstairs boxes. She moved the fullest to her nightstand, the second fullest to the children's bathroom, and the fuller of the last two to Margaret's room, where Margaret would be sleeping. Only then, with order restored, could she go on with her day.

A few nights later, while she was reading in bed, her lamp burned out, and with a twinge she remembered that she'd forgotten all about the bulbs. Honestly, her mind was a sieve. Rather than wait till morning, she got up and went downstairs in her robe and slippers and wrote it on the list, with a 2 for two two-packs. Next time she'd be prepared.

EXTRAVAGANCE

Maybe Margaret was right, because the car was a godsend. Instead of having to follow Arlene's schedule, now she could set out anytime she liked. The Subaru was several generations removed from the Olds in all respects, the interior a rich-smelling black leather with amenities Emily at first considered frivolous but found she used every day, like the seat warmers. The ride was amazingly quiet, and the sound system was better than her home stereo, boasting a dozen speakers and a six-disc changer—all standard equipment. Coming home from the Giant Eagle, she glided through East Liberty, Byrd's Gloria lending the drab blocks a melancholy gravity. In the way-back, a thoughtfully designed mesh net kept her groceries from sliding around.

The car was small, but had some giddyup to it, and handled easily. Snow was no problem, even coming down Grafton. Between the traction control and the antilock brakes, she couldn't put it into a skid if she tried. Best of all, it fit in the garage with room to spare.

The biggest difference was the gas mileage. She suspected the estimates on the sticker were inflated, and made a point of checking the first time she filled up. Though she'd yet to take it out on the highway, the car was getting almost thirty miles to the gallon, three times what the Olds got.

Arlene fawned over the map lights and the makeup mirror in the visor, and joked that she was jealous. Emily believed her. Beyond the fact that Arlene didn't have the means to replace her Taurus, the Subaru had shifted the balance of power. Now when they went somewhere together, they took Emily's car, and Emily, citing Arlene's doctor, refused to let her smoke in it.

She also refused to let Rufus destroy her new leather seats, banishing him to the way-back, the carpet there protected by a rubber mat. This restriction proved harder to enforce. He was unhappy being exiled, despite her laying down one of his favorite blankets, and regularly jumped over the backseat and squirmed his way through to the front, taking his accustomed place as copilot, his nails digging in, leaving scuffs and scratches. Emily grew tired of scolding him and installed an expensive set of adjustable bars that made it look like she'd caged him for safe transport.

"I don't blame you," Betty said. "You want to keep it nice."

It was Wednesday and Emily had taken her out to the garage after lunch to show off what she called "my present to myself."

"It looks fast, with the hood thingy," Betty said. "What do they call it—the Fast and the Furious."

"It's not too much, is it? I don't want to be like one of those middle-aged men who buys a Porsche."

"I don't think you have to worry about that."

"Not that I qualify as middle-aged anymore."

"It's nice, it's just different."

"Not what you expected."

"No, you said you were looking at them. I don't know. Maybe it's the color."

"Too bright."

"Maybe."

Emily understood. She had trouble believing this sleek, nimble machine was hers as well. There was something incongruous, if not outright ironic, in the mismatch of car and driver. She felt decrepit, while it was brand-new, and at no time in her life, even as a long-legged teen, had she been sporty.

"I can wipe this off if you want," Betty said, pointing to the roof, spotted with faint cat tracks.

"Honest to God," Emily said, taking the rag from her and doing it herself. "I've only had the thing a week."

"You think that matters to him?"

"Oh, he knows exactly what he's doing. That's the way cats are, very calculating."

"I think you're giving him too much credit."

"I'm sure they wouldn't be happy if I let Rufus walk all over their cars."

Betty chuckled to let her know she was being ridiculous. "That I'd like to see. Seriously, though, Emily, it's a beautiful car. Toni would completely approve."

"Thank you," Emily said, but back inside, as they tended to their separate tasks, she worried that Betty, whose little Nissan was rusting, might think she'd been extravagant.

She was hanging the guest towels in the children's bathroom when a truck rumbled down Grafton and squealed to a stop out front. She knew the putter of the mail van; this was larger, possibly FedEx or UPS. Belatedly, Rufus barked and struggled up from his spot beside her bed. He stood at the top of the stairs and looked at her as if waiting for permission, then, when the doorbell rang, charged down, frantic.

She had a number of items from Eddie Bauer on back order, including Margaret's big gift, a goose-down comforter, and had been fretting that they wouldn't arrive in time. She tried not to be too hopeful.

The bell rang again.

"You got it?" Betty called.

"I'm getting it."

Rufus was still sounding the alarm, as if no one else could hear.

"Move," Emily said, blocking him as she cracked the door.

The deliveryman held a poinsettia, the pot wrapped in gold foil—Kenneth and Lisa's traditional gift, a polite, not quite personal offering, accepted by Emily in the same spirit.

"Mrs. Maxwell?"

"That would be me. Just ignore him, he's harmless."

There was nothing to sign. The man wished her happy holidays, hustled back to his step van and was off before she could set the pot on the front hall table and close the storm door.

There was a miniature red envelope taped to the foil. The card was bordered with jaunty holly. In the florist's careless hand, the message read:

MERRY CHRISTMAS WITH LOVE FROM THE MAXWELLS.

Emily wondered how much it cost, and whether Lisa had phoned in her order or gone online. Not that it mattered.

The plant itself was flawless, the leaves a brilliant vermillion, the delicate flowers in the center just beginning to bud, the result of a long, involved hothouse process, keeping it in the dark much of the day so it would bloom at just the right time. Twice in the past Emily had tried to transplant them outside, but they weren't hardy enough. Like the others, this one would have its few weeks of glory in the front window and then linger on in Kenneth's room, another thing to remember, slowly dropping its leaves, its stems drying to twigs as the winter months passed, until she would have to throw it, pot and all, in the trash. Over the years she'd mentioned the waste of it to Lisa several times, not to complain—she wasn't ungrateful or trying to be unkind—but to suggest more practical and affordable choices, yet every Christmas another perfect poinsettia arrived.

She pushed her geraniums and African violets aside to make room. In the sun, the leaves were even brighter.

"Wow," Betty said. "That's a nice one."

"Isn't it," Emily said.

CHRISTMAS CHEER

With Margaret coming, the question was what to do with the booze. Out of respect for her sobriety, Emily's instinct was to stow it in the basement—not locked away but boxed and out of sight—except Margaret might take the empty liquor cabinet as an insult. Would it be better to pretend everything was fine? She'd tried that the last time. Fool me once, except Margaret hadn't fooled anyone in years, not even herself. Emily felt equally helpless. Either way, Margaret could fault her, and after much agonizing, she decided to go with her first instinct.

Until she filled two heavy boxes and lugged them downstairs, barely making a dent, she hadn't realized how much there was—not just Henry's collection of scotches and the normal Episcopalian assortment of hard stuff but the brandies and ports and sherries and different liqueurs they'd amassed over the years, many of them presents, some, like the cone-shaped bottle of Poire William and the dark rum from Kenneth and Lisa's Caribbean trip, untouched. The bottom shelf was like their basement, packed with forgotten odds and ends. They had two open bottles of Drambuie, and two of her favorite Grand Marnier left over from the days when they used to entertain. Cointreau, Armagnac, amaretto, B&B, Calvados, Courvoisier, Rémy Martin.

Though recently she'd apologized for blaming others for her own personal choices, in the past Margaret often said it was no wonder she drank, given her role models. Emily had never taken this accusation to heart, since neither she nor Henry were what she would consider heavy drinkers. Yes, they drank socially when they were younger, but when Emily recalled their parties, she remembered the backyard flickering with tiki torches and Henry tending the barbecue, card tables laden with baked beans and potato salad and slices of watermelon and brownies, the whole neighborhood gathered—kids and adults—for a good time. There would be croquet and horseshoes, and the boys would organize a wiffleball game in the courtyard, drafting Henry to pitch. Maybe later Kay Miller would get out of hand and topple her lawn chair, or Gene Alford would break into song so that Ginny had to clamp a hand over his mouth, but by then the children were in bed. It was possible that Margaret watched them from her window, her nose pressed against the screen, but what she would have seen wasn't some depraved bacchanal, just a circle of friends trading stories and laughing, glad to have one another's easy company at the end of the night. It wasn't until Margaret was a teenager that they started having problems with kids stealing beers from coolers, and it was to Emily's eternal shame that, under her relentless questioning, Kenneth confessed that Margaret was one of the culprits.

Emily hadn't let her off easy, though it was the late sixties and there were far worse things girls her age were into. No one could say Emily had ignored the problem. If anything, she was too vigilant, and this was just the beginning. From then on the two of them waged a daily struggle over clothes and boys and grades and smoking until, to the relief of everyone, Margaret went off to college, leaving the much easier, eager-to-please Kenneth, whose vices and desires were transparent. They'd had their flare-ups, yet at their very worst, which had not been often, she'd felt disdain from him, never hatred.

She'd thought about this a great deal, having directed, at the same age, that same obliterating anger toward her own mother. At some point—maybe when she'd fled Kersey and left that stultifying world behind, or when she began a family of her own—she'd been able to put it aside. She feared that Margaret hadn't, and that that—that she, through no fault of her own besides her existence—was somehow behind all of her problems. Louise said she would drive herself crazy trying to figure out why Margaret was the way she was, knowing it wasn't in Emily's nature to let even the smallest matter drop.

She had tried. She had compromised, listened, waited, prayed. She'd lent her money—tens of thousands—foolishly, perhaps, though she could rationalize it, saying she'd done it for the children. Looking back, it was hard to say if her efforts had succeeded. Was Sarah happy on her own in Chicago, as Margaret claimed? Was Justin really enjoying school? Emily had no way of knowing. She couldn't even be sure Margaret was sober, though that was the assumption they were operating under.

After all this work, Emily thought, filling yet another box, she'd better be. Was she being uncharitable? Overwrought? Why did the mere idea of Margaret's arrival set her off? Shouldn't she just be happy she was coming?

The shame of it was that this was the best time of year to linger at the table after dessert and savor a wee dram, as Henry put it. Christmas meant the foamy, sweet kick of eggnog, and her Grandmother Waite's breathtaking rum balls. She would have liked to offer Sarah wine with dinner, now that she was of age, but that too was ruined.

She didn't bother with the mixers or the glasses. The last box was a grab bag of half-pints and miniatures and Henry's many flasks, all of which, to her dismay, needed polishing. She lugged it down, careful on the stairs, and set it atop the others beside his bench. She couldn't resist counting them—eight full boxes of liquor. Stacked like seized evidence, they seemed to support Margaret's case, but Emily knew better. This accumulation had taken decades, and while she still enjoyed an occasional nip, most of these bottles would survive her. Not that that was any great loss. Henry would want Kenneth to have his scotch. The rest held no such sentimental value.

In the top box rested a curved hip flask she'd given Henry for Christmas years ago, engraved with his initials. She lifted it out and angled it toward the light to admire the filigree. Slim as a cigarette case, it fit perfectly in the back pocket of his favorite corduroys. He carried it on their fall walks in the park, and while he tinkered in the garage at Chautauqua. Winter nights in Panther Hollow, as they sat by the bonfire of broken-down pallets and watched the children skating where they'd once courted, he handed it to her first and then pretended to disinfect the mouth with his sleeve. Weekends and vacations, at the end of the day he set it with his Hamilton on his dresser, another elegant accessory. That was what alcohol was to her, an extra, civilized pleasure, part of the sophisticated life she'd always wanted. She understood that Margaret had a disease. What she couldn't figure out was why.

She unscrewed the cap and passed the threaded stem under her nose, taking in the scent of old smoke, knowing she shouldn't, then tipped it to her lips. The scotch was dank and peppery, with a sting of iodine. She held the sip, letting it puddle on her tongue a moment before swallowing, monitoring its progress down her throat to her stomach. The warmth rose from her core straight to her face, a flush like the first stirrings of a hot flash. Just a taste, that was all she wanted. She capped the flask, returned it to the box and closed the flaps. After a brief search, she covered the stack with a dropcloth, topping it with a paint tray and an old roller—still too conspicuous but the best she could do. Was it enough? Probably not, but if Margaret wanted a drink that bad, at least she'd have to look for it.

Later, her back hurt, and she had to lie down with a heating pad. She set her glasses on her nightstand, slung one arm over her eyes and, as she expected, drifted off to sleep. When she woke up, it was dark and she was sweating. Some obnoxious Rachmaninoff was playing, meaning QED was into their evening schedule. She swung her legs off the bed and sat on the edge for a second, rubbing her face, and then laughed, thinking: *The things you do for your children*.

THE BUSIEST DAY OF THE YEAR

Emily had just finished putting the lasagna together when Margaret called. She was on her cell phone, her voice warped and ragged with static, cutting in and out, then suddenly gone, as if she'd been kidnapped.

"Hello?" Emily tried. "Hello!"

A minute later Margaret called back. The reception was better, though she gave no explanation.

They were going to be late. The storm coming up the East Coast had grounded everything. Sarah's flight out of Chicago was delayed as well. The airline wasn't telling them much, but the planes were still sitting on the ground in Charlotte.

Outside, as if to refute her, the sky was blue.

"How's the weather there?" Emily asked.

"Here? Fine. If we were flying direct, it'd be no problem. It's the stupid hub thing—whoever thought that up was a genius. My worry is that we'll miss our connection and end up spending the night there, which would not be fun, as much as I love the Charlotte airport. This weekend's so busy, if we wait till tomorrow to go out, we might not get there at all, so it's not like we have a choice."

"I'll just sit tight till I hear from you."

"It could be a while."

"I'm not going anywhere," Emily said.

"Neither are we," Margaret said.

She called Arlene to let her know. She was supposed to come over at two so they could go meet them at the baggage claim.

"How's she doing?"

"About how you'd expect."

"Oh my."

"Yes," Emily said, "oh my."

"What does that mean for our dinner plans?"

"Everything's on hold for now."

"I should probably hold off on my garlic bread then."

"I think that's wise," Emily said.

Their departure time came and went, and still she waited, as she said she would, resisting the urge to call Margaret's cell. The Met was broadcasting Prokofiev's War and Peace, a rare offering, but she couldn't enjoy it. The plan had been for them to fly in around midafternoon. That would give them time to get settled while she baked the lasagna. It took fifty minutes to get to the airport, another twenty to park and wait for their bags. As Napoleon drove deep into Russia, she pushed dinner further and further back. Society dines late, Henry's mother loved to say, but anything beyond eight o'clock was absurd.

She kept thinking they wouldn't be having this problem if Margaret had just taken a half day yesterday as Emily originally suggested. So she didn't have any vacation days left. What about sick days, or personal days? Couldn't she talk to her boss? Margaret acted like it was an impossible request, as if Emily didn't understand her position. This might be their last Christmas together, Emily was tempted to say, but didn't, knowing that Margaret would see it—correctly—as blackmail, and so they had both come away frustrated.

It was no one's fault, just the weather, and the airlines' idiotic system that hadn't saved them from going bankrupt and then asking for a government bailout every few years. She knew she shouldn't let it upset her, but she'd been anticipating this visit for so long. On the phone Margaret had sounded harassed and testy, and though Emily knew better, she'd taken it personally. They were both just having a bad day.

Rufus was helping her set out candy dishes of red and green M&Ms when Margaret called.

"Right now they've got us leaving at two-twenty, which would get us into Charlotte around four-fifteen. We miss our connection, but they say they can get us on the five o'clock, so if everything goes right we should be there around six-thirty."

"That's not bad." This way Emily could cook the lasagna ahead of time and then reheat it. All they'd have to do was warm Arlene's garlic bread and put together the salad.

"We'll see if it actually happens," Margaret said.

"Hang in there."

Arlene was following the storm on the Weather Channel and didn't think it was likely. They had Charlotte experiencing four-hour delays.

Emily wanted her to be more positive. "We'll just plan on leaving here at five-thirty unless we hear something different. I'm going to go ahead and put my lasagna in regardless."

Preheating the oven took longer than she'd thought, but maybe part of that lag was her impatience. Everything was going slowly today. She was already dressed for the airport, and tied on her apron to protect her outfit. The pan was heavy and cold from the fridge, and she almost dropped it, one end banging the rack. She set the timer and went back to the living room, where the French were in full retreat. The house was ready, each room tidied as if she were opening her doors to the public. She'd moved Henry's chair so they could put the tree in the front window. In the dining room the table was set, complete with a rambling holly centerpiece and brand-new candles. Her mother's crèche stood on the sideboard, un-adorned, Joseph and Mary kneeling beside the chipped Baby Jesus, humble under his blanket of brown corduroy. Downstairs, a dozen flimsy boxes of old ornaments rested on Henry's workbench, along with the inside lights. There was nothing left to do but wait.

The lasagna had been in for about a half hour when Margaret called again. Sarah's plane had arrived in Chicago, but their flight had been pushed back another forty-five minutes, meaning the five-thirty was out of the question. The next flight to Pittsburgh was at six-ten, but it was overbooked, and they couldn't get on standby until they were all in Charlotte. She'd looked into trying another airline, but they'd already checked their bags.

"It really shouldn't be this hard. I'm seriously thinking of just turning around and going home."

"Don't do that," Emily said.

"I know, they'll charge us anyway, but at this point I'm so fed up I just want to leave. The thing that pisses me off is that no one cares. Not a single person here is taking any responsibility for what's happening. It's not their problem—that's their attitude. And then they wonder why everyone hates them."

"How's Justin?"

"Tired of listening to me bitch. He's watching a movie on his laptop. He's like Dad—he just shuts it all out."

"It's a talent."

"I suppose it is, in this case. So we have no idea when we'll be there."

"That's fine," Emily said. "Just let us know if anything changes."

"That's what I figured," Arlene said. "So are we still having dinner or should I plan on fixing something for myself?"

"Let's see what happens," Emily said. "There's still a chance they could make it."

"I think you're being optimistic."

"Of course I'm being optimistic. I want them to get here."

As the grandfather clock marked each passing quarter hour, the odds grew longer. Still, when Margaret called around four-thirty and said they were boarding and had confirmed seats on the eight-forty-five, Emily was as disappointed as she was relieved. What was she going to do with all that lasagna?

"I'll stick it in my freezer and have it for lunch," Arlene said. "I'm not proud."

Emily could do that too. That wasn't the point.

"What time do you want me to come over?" Arlene asked.

"I don't care. Whenever you're hungry."

"Is it too early? Actually I'm getting a little peckish."

"That's fine," Emily said, giving up.

The light was dying, night filling in the bare trees, closing around the house. War and Peace gave way to the news, and she turned off the stereo, the silence forcing her back upon herself. She should have been glad they were going to make it, but it was too late, her hopes for the day had soured.

She left the good china on the table and set the breakfast nook with her everyday dishes.

"Isn't this cozy," Arlene said, an attempt to cheer her that Emily let pass.

"I hope it's all right. I haven't tasted it."

It was fine, but she ate without appetite. Once the pan had cooled, she divvied it up into two Tupperware containers. The tiramisu from Prantl's she'd save for another day.

Their flight wasn't due till ten, a good half hour past her bedtime. She'd gotten up early that morning to get everything ready, and needed a cup of coffee to keep going. She had to remind herself to use the bathroom before they left.

"Good idea," Arlene said.

The airport was farther than she'd driven in years, and though there was no traffic, it was dark. They skirted downtown along the Mon wharf, the Parkway feeding them through a chute, up a sweeping ramp and into the flow of the Fort Pitt Bridge.

"Watch," Arlene said, of a Hummer looming up behind them.

"I see him," Emily said.

The view of the Point tempted her—the Hilton would be lit for Christmas, the rivers black and glittering—but she needed to concentrate on the road, and then, that quickly, they were into the bright, tile-lined tunnel, the lanes so narrow she was afraid of bumping the Hummer, passing on the right. Once they were through, she found an opening and moved over to the slow lane, where she was content to stay, keeping pace past the vacant office parks and discount furniture outlets, the towering mercury-vapor lamps tinting everything a hazy copper until the I-79 interchange, beyond which lay a spacelike blackness broken only by floating taillights. She slowed and flicked on her high beams, revealing the shoulder and a speeding strip of hillside. There were deer out here. Even if she glimpsed one entering her headlights, she wouldn't be able to stop in time. It didn't avail her to dwell on the fact, and she focused on Margaret and the children, her sole reason for being there.

Margaret and Justin had come for the week at Chautauqua, but Emily hadn't seen Sarah since last Thanksgiving. She was doing something with computers for a commodities brokerage right there in the Loop and sharing an apartment with a college friend, the way Emily had her first year out of school with Jocelyn, waiting tables to pay the rent. She imagined being young and free again, the whole city opening to her—Grant Park, and the Art Institute, taking the El to work in the mornings. She hadn't been to Chicago in nearly forty years, yet that made it seem only more romantic. Margaret said there was a boyfriend. Emily wanted stories.

Margaret had a new beau as well—a man-friend, she called him, as if their arrangement were casual and adult rather than passionate. With her looks, she would never lack for suitors, as long as she paid attention to her weight. Emily couldn't imagine anyone brave or patient enough to take on all of her problems, though some men, she knew, would be drawn by the idea of rescuing her.

Of Justin she'd heard little beyond his major—astrophysics—and his grades, straight A's. Like most boys his age, he struck Emily as unformed. He'd been a timid child, bright but quiet, oddly impersonal, always watching, and she wondered if, away from his mother, he might find himself. Like Henry, he had a scientist's mind. Henry had been soft-spoken, and could seem easily swayed, but on points that mattered to him he was adamant, his silence effectively the last word. She hoped Justin was tending the same inner strength.

Her sole wish, now, was to be closer to them. It was hard to follow their lives from a distance, to send out cards and letters and presents, to call week after week and then receive in return only the barest of news, grudgingly given and heavily censored. Since Jeff had left, their lives seemed precarious. She worried for each of them individually and for the family as a whole. She fretted especially about Sarah and Justin, how they would turn out, and thought it unfair that she would probably not be around to witness it. She'd watched her own children grow up, maybe that was enough—as if one were allowed to see only so much of life, the future, like the past, necessarily hidden and mysterious.

A cluster of taillights veered off, and their exit appeared, the sign floating out of the night.

"You said US Air?"

"Yes," Emily said, though where they were going, it didn't matter.

They parked in the short-term garage and walked through the echoing lower level in the cold. Ahead, across the concrete island reserved for shuttle buses, the curbside pick-up was a madhouse, taxis and vans and limos jostling for position, cars double-parked with their trunks popped, blocking others in, while a single state trooper blew his whistle and pointed to drivers trying to find a spot, waving them through. Travelers with bags lined the sidewalk, searching for their rides. As she and Arlene crossed, traffic had to stop, snarling things further, and Emily wondered who in their right mind had designed this system.

Inside, the newly arrived milled like penned cattle around the baggage carousels. The sheer number of people made her eager to leave. She checked a monitor but couldn't find their flight.

"Are we too early?" Arlene asked.

"Maybe I've got the wrong number." Because there were three from Charlotte.

The number she had was right. According to the big board they'd been delayed. They weren't due till eleven.

"Why didn't she call me?"

"Maybe they were already on the plane," Arlene guessed, though at that moment no explanation could have consoled Emily.

Upstairs, most of US Air's ticket agents had been replaced by electronic kiosks, and the few who remained acted as if Emily was bothering them. "I'm sorry, ma'am, we don't have any other information here." Then what were the computers for? She remembered Margaret's tirade over the phone. At the time she'd thought she was being unreasonable. Now she totally agreed with her.

"I think I need to sit down," Arlene said as they rode the escalator, and when Emily reacted with alarm, patted her arm. "I'm fine, I just need to get off of my feet."

With the crush, seats were at a premium. She installed Arlene in an alcove between the rental car desks, and after making sure she was okay, went in search of a Hershey bar to tide her over. In the little newsstand she winced at the price, thinking this could have been avoided if she'd just served the tiramisu. But why should any of her plans work today?

She'd lost faith, or lost the energy for it. Sitting beside Arlene, she was overcome by the urge to surrender, to lie down across the filthy seats and go to sleep. She hadn't brought a book—as her grandmother had wisely counseled—and her mind spun empty, juggling the letters of signs (BUD-GET: BUD, GET, BET, DEBT), reading the people in line.

"Want a piece?" Arlene asked, offering the bar, and Emily broke one off.

The mystery of chemistry. For a second the chocolate dissolving on her tongue made her feel better.

"I really didn't think it would be like this."

"Please," Arlene said. "It's not your fault."

"I wish she would have called."

As they waited, watching the escalator, Emily thought of all they would do tomorrow. After church they were supposed to get their tree. They had tickets to the matinee of *The Nutcracker* at the Benedum, then dinner reservations at the club. She was hoping they could stop at the Carnegie afterward and see the trees of the world (the paper said there was a carol sing-along), but now she was afraid she'd conk out.

"What time have you got?" Arlene said, as if she couldn't trust her watch.

The last ten minutes were interminable. At eleven sharp the monitor said their flight had arrived, and Emily and Arlene took their places among the other families and hired drivers at the foot of the escalator.

"I feel like we should be holding a sign," Arlene joked.

Above them, a girl with Sarah's red hair appeared, wearing a pair of felt antlers, but it wasn't her. A soldier in desert camouflage said no, this flight was from Atlanta.

"They sure are taking their sweet time," Arlene said.

"It's a big plane," Emily said. "Then they have to walk a ways and wait for the train."

They'll get here when they get here, her mother used to say, and now that they were almost upon them, Emily worried that, as in the past, the visit would not go smoothly. On top of all her holiday plans, she had serious matters to discuss with Margaret—last things, if that wasn't being too melodramatic. She didn't expect them to suddenly come to a deeper understanding, let alone acceptance, of each other. She just wanted to make known her final wishes, and for Margaret to honor them as she trusted Kenneth would. The money was the least of it.

"Is that them?" Arlene asked. "I can't see."

"I don't think so," Emily said, because the pretty girl standing beside the shaggy, dark-haired boy who resembled Justin was a blonde. It was only as they descended, revealing Margaret behind them, that she realized the girl was Sarah.

"What did she do to her hair?" Arlene said.

"What do you do to yours?"

"I know, but . . . I don't like it."

"I think I do," Emily said as if surprised, and waved to get their attention.

They held themselves back, trying not to block the other people, letting Sarah and Justin come to them. Sarah smelled sweetly of tangerine, Justin strongly of body spray. Behind them, smiling tiredly, Margaret waited her turn. She looked surprisingly good. She wasn't as thin as she'd been that summer, when Emily worried she was starving herself, indulging in exercise the way she'd turned to food as a child, or drugs as a teenager, or alcohol as an adult. Her cheeks were fuller, and while Emily took it as a good sign, she knew from long and painful experience that, just as a relapse was part of the process of recovery, everything with Margaret was temporary and beyond her control, even—maybe ultimately—her happiness.

Emily reached out and took her in her arms.

"You made it."

"Barely," Margaret said.

PRESS FOR ASSISTANCE

"This is us," Emily said, and thumbed the remote twice to open the doors, the locks clicking, the hazard lights blinking orange.

"*Nice*, Gram," Justin said, nodding hearty approval.

"I love the color," Sarah said.

Margaret took charge of the bags, arranging them in the way-back.

"Why don't you sit in front, with your long legs," Emily told Justin.

As the rest of them piled in, she showed him how to scoot the seat forward. Behind him, Margaret leaned her head back and crooked one arm over her eyes like a sleeping mask.

"Everyone have enough room back there?" Emily asked.

"We're good," Sarah answered.

So far Margaret hadn't said a word about the car, and Emily wondered if, with all of her money troubles, she resented it, then dismissed the idea. Why was it important that she say anything? And still it bothered Emily.

The place was a maze. She followed the signs up a curving ramp and then at the booth had to switch on her map light to find the ticket.

She fed it into the machine. The machine spat it back.

She tried again.

There was another car behind her.

"What am I doing wrong? Anyone?"

"The arrow goes on top," Margaret finally said, flatly, as if it were obvious. "You have to line up the stripes."

She was right, and they were free.

"I guess you're an old pro at those things." Emily flicked her eyes to the rearview mirror.

Margaret still had her arm over her face. "No. The arrow always goes on top."

"Thank you," Emily said. "I'll have to remember that."

THE HOSTESS WITH THE MOSTEST

The next morning Margaret went with them to the eleven o'clock service, leaving the children to sleep in. Sarah was fighting a cold, and Justin was wiped out from his finals. Emily wasn't sure why Margaret felt compelled to make excuses for them. They weren't regular churchgoers, and hadn't been for years, a fact that confused and saddened Emily. She didn't want them to feel obligated, but it would have been nice if they'd made an effort. It had been a late night for everyone.

Normally she would have stopped in at coffee hour to show Margaret off, but they needed to eat lunch before they went out tree-shopping. When they got home, the water was running upstairs, and the *Post-Gazette* was strewn across the living room. In the kitchen, the cutting board was covered with crumbs. A jam-smeared saucer and a glass with a ring of milk at the bottom sat congealing in the sink. Justin was holed up in Henry's office, wild-haired, in a T-shirt and sweatpants, e-mailing on his laptop. Sarah had beaten him into the shower, he confessed, shrugging as if he were powerless.

"You can use mine," Emily said. "Come on, time's a-wastin', Pokey Joe."

"Just let me close this."

By the time he did, the water had stopped. He unplugged his adapter and wound the cord around it, tucked the laptop under his arm and slumped upstairs.

"Can he move any slower?" Emily asked.

"They're in vacation mode," Margaret said.

"Is that it?"

"I don't think either of them gets enough sleep."

Emily had to laugh. "They certainly did this morning."

When Sarah came downstairs, pink-eyed and sneezing fitfully, Emily relented. Having battled migraines her entire life, she forgave illness. She plied her with soup and coffee, setting a box of Kleenex next to her place. It was all right if she'd rather stay home than go pick out a tree, but to Emily's relief, she was game.

Emily had saved the process of buying a tree not simply because she needed help but because she thought it would be a fun thing to do as a family. She'd envisioned them tramping through the rows of fragrant Scotch pines and blue spruces in the snow, choosing their favorites and then voting, as the children had when they were little, except it was sunny and close to fifty, and they'd waited too long. The trees the School for the Deaf had left fit into one corner of the basketball court. The survivors leaned against the fence, scraggly, misshapen rejects not worth half the asking price. Even the best had massive holes. The question wasn't which one to choose, but whether choosing any of them made sense, and though she cast about for rescue, as the leader of this misconceived expedition, the decision fell to her.

"Justin, honey, can you hold that one up? Thank you, that's it. What do you think? Maybe if we put that side in the corner?"

"It's not going in the window?" Margaret said with disappointment.

"I don't think there's anything here that could go in the window. I think this is the best we're going to do."

For a moment no one spoke, their passivity total, as if Emily was the sole motive force. Why had they bothered coming? Was it just to humor her?

Finally Arlene stepped forward and ruffled the branches. "It's a little uneven, but I suppose it could work."

Justin stood with his head down, bored.

"Sarah?"

"It could be like a Charlie Brown tree."

That was enough of a consensus for Emily. She was done trying to encourage them. She paid the attendant, asked for a fresh cut of the trunk and then helped him center the blanket she'd brought so the branches wouldn't scratch her roof.

At home there was only time to get it into the stand on the back porch before they had to change for *The Nutcracker*, leaving her with the feeling—as she sat in the darkened Benedum Center—of a job left undone. The matinee was packed with families, which was as it should be, but one had made the mistake of bringing a baby, and compounded their error by not removing the child when it first started squalling. Several times it subsided only to begin again, a near-comedic form of torture Emily couldn't believe the ushers condoned.

With the unseasonable warmth, the theater was stuffy, a chronic problem. Midway through the second act, Justin reached across Margaret, tapped Emily on the arm and pointed to Arlene. She was unconscious, her face slack, hands upturned and limp in her lap, and a shock seized Emily, remembering the Eat 'n Park, until she realized Arlene was just snoozing, lulled by the heat and the ballet's glacial pace. Rather than let her remain an object of fun, Emily had Justin nudge her. Arlene woke and looked down the row, and Emily nodded like a proctor.

On her right, Sarah cleared her throat over and over, mashing tissues to her nose, and Emily thought that maybe she should have stayed home. They'd seen this same clunky production a dozen times. Justin wasn't interested, if he'd ever been. While she was no fan of Tchaikovsky, Emily couldn't imagine Christmas without *The Nutcracker*, just as she counted on the trees at the Carnegie and the Messiah sing-along, but, sitting there, barely following the plot, she decided that this might be their last year.

In the car, the children thanked her, though Emily suspected Margaret had prompted them.

"Yes, thank you, it was lovely," Arlene said. "What I saw of it."

"I was fading in and out there a little too," Margaret said.

They could have all done with a nap, but Emily had budgeted only enough time to freshen up and feed and water Rufus before they had to hop in the car again and head off to the club. She was actually glad they'd made the early seating, especially after last night. Sarah didn't look like she had much left.

Under the crystal chandeliers they took their places, Justin conspicuously the only male. He slouched, hiding behind his hair as Kenneth had when he was a teenager, shifting to the side to let the busboy fill their water glasses. He so obviously didn't want to be there that Emily couldn't resist prodding him about school.

"It's good," he said, as if that might satisfy her.

"What was your favorite course this semester?" Arlene asked.

"I don't know. Quantum mechanics was okay."

"Are there any girls in your classes?"

"Not ones you'd want to go out with."

"None?"

"None that want to go out with me."

"A different matter altogether."

In the middle of this interrogation, a waitress with her hair gathered in a saggy bun arrived to take their drink order, looking to Emily and Arlene to start.

"Go ahead," Margaret said with a flip of her hand. "Get what you usually get."

"Are you sure?" Arlene asked.

"I'm driving," Emily said, "so I'll stick with water."

"I'll just have water too," Arlene said.

"Club soda with a lime, please," Margaret said.

Sarah had green tea, Justin a Sprite. Conversation resumed, yet for Emily the question lingered. Would it really not bother Margaret if she ordered a glass of Chablis? Around them, people were tipping martinis and Manhattans, but they were strangers. To watch those who knew how hard and constantly she'd fought her disease raise a glass seemed a needless test, just as there was something unfair to all of them in her offer, though Emily couldn't see another alternative besides silence, of which they'd had enough. She thought her worry was perverse. Here, again, she was second-guessing Margaret when she should have been giving her credit.

"So, Sarah," Arlene said, "how are you liking the City of Big Shoulders?"

"I like it."

"It beats Silver Hills, I imagine."

"Your job sounds interesting," Emily said.

"Not really. It's pretty basic. It's just setting up network stuff."

"I'm not even sure what that is."

"Virtual conferencing. I make sure people from the different offices can talk online. It's not really new."

"It's beyond me," Emily said. "Now, I've heard rumors that there's a gentleman in the picture, is that right? Or is your mother making him up?"

Sarah gave Margaret a put-upon look.

"Does he have big shoulders?" Arlene asked, and Justin laughed.

"I can see this is a painful subject," Emily said.

"It's not serious, we're just dating."

"What does that mean?" Arlene asked Emily.

"It means they're not boyfriend and girlfriend, or am I off base?"

She wasn't.

"He took her to Charlie Trotter's," Margaret objected.

"What's that?" Arlene asked.

"It's a four-star restaurant. You have to make reservations months in advance."

"Who is this lucky boy," Emily asked, "or shall he remain nameless?"

"Max."

"Maxwell?" Arlene asked.

"Maximilian, sorry."

"Max Power," Justin said, a joke Emily didn't get and that Sarah didn't appreciate.

His name was Max Howard. He helped run the main website for the Obama campaign. Margaret offered that he was older than Sarah, in his mid-twenties. He was a graduate of DePaul, though Margaret wasn't sure if he was actually a Catholic.

"Jesus, Mom."

"Well, these are the kinds of things you have to find out."

"Somebody please kill me," Sarah said.

"We're just joking," Margaret said.

"It's not funny."

"Oh, please. After the grief you two have given me about Ron."

"I think I'm ready for some salad," Emily said, eyeing the line. "Shall we?"

The buffet held no surprises, though Arlene cooed over the cream-of-chicken soup, a childhood favorite. Justin skipped the salads completely while Emily went back for seconds, feeling virtuous as she loaded her plate with leafy greens. By the time she was ready for her main course, he was on to the dessert table. She and Margaret chose the chicken Florentine, which they both found a little dry. Sarah barely ate, leaving half of her salmon. She wiped her nose with a bedraggled tissue, and though Emily wanted to know more about her life in Chicago, she held off. Margaret's man-friend she didn't consider polite dinner conversation, and so they picked at inconsequential topics—the economy, the war in Iraq, Guantánamo Bay. The waitress refilled their drinks and recapped the Steelers game for Arlene, a welcome intrusion, as no one seemed to have anything to say.

Justin and Sarah were both ready to go. Rather than prolong the agony, they decided to have coffee at home. The Carnegie could wait, and she could use the tiramisu. In the car, for the second time today, they thanked her. Driving at night tired her eyes, and when, with great concentration, she'd pulled safely into the garage, Justin knocked his door against the wall.

Inside, Margaret apologized for him. Emily shrugged as if it were nothing.

Sarah went straight up to bed, but came down minutes later to announce that Rufus had eaten her toothpaste, which explained why he was hiding under the dining room table. Somehow he'd snitched the tube off the bathroom counter. He'd also gotten into her wastebasket and shredded her used tissues all over the carpet.

"Honest to God," Emily said, as Margaret knelt beside her and helped clean up the mess.

"That can't be good for his stomach."

"I hope it hurts," Emily said, scrubbing at the bath mat with a wet washcloth.

"You don't mean that."

"I just wish I knew why he does these things."

"He's probably angry that you left him home alone."

Emily told her about him gnawing the chair leg and peeing on the carpet in front of her.

"How old is he?"

"That's why it upsets me. I'm afraid he's going to die soon, and I really don't want him to."

"I'm surprised he's lasted this long."

"I know," Emily said. "We've been very lucky with him. He's still a jerk."

"He's better than Duchess ever was."

"Remember what Dad used to call her?"

"The Worst Dog *Ever*," they said in tandem.

Downstairs, Arlene had dessert ready, and the conversation continued, spreading backward into the past, making stops at Panther Hollow and Chautauqua, her parents' house in Kersey and Calvary Camp. Dogs, vacations, boyfriends, neighbors. The Millers' grog parties. Sleepovers at the Pickerings' House of Fun. Emily was mildly surprised to hear Margaret recall those years with laughter. To Emily they'd been a running battle, one that even now she had to concede she'd lost, and yet here was Margaret beside her, reminiscing wistfully on Christmases past. Going downtown to see the windows at Horne's and Kaufmann's with the crowds, then meeting Henry for a leisurely dinner at Klein's. She still had the wooden blocks he'd crafted for her. She was saving them for her grandchildren, whenever that might be—making them all turn to Justin, speechless and suffering above his empty plate.

"Justin will take care of the dishes," Margaret said, and without a word, he did, then vanished.

Outside, the Coles' lights strobed over the yard.

"I wish we had our tree up," Emily said.

They'd all do it tomorrow, Margaret promised. She'd wake up early and make French toast. If it was cold enough, they could have a fire like old times.

Arlene needed to leave; she was falling asleep. When should she come by in the morning?

They saw her off, waving from the doorway. "Drive safe!"

Margaret wanted to read her book, and though Emily would have liked to stay up and talk, she was pleased with the way the night had ended.

"Maybe tomorrow we can sit down and go over a few things Gordon's been putting together for me."

"Did you want to do that now?"

"No, tomorrow's fine."

"All right. Sweet dreams."

"Sweet dreams, dear."

Margaret went up, leaving Emily to put out Rufus and close the down-stairs. As a young mother, she'd required a kiss from her children before sending them off to bed—Henry had gotten one too—but had stopped the practice when they were teenagers. Now she wished she could hold Margaret's face in her hands the way she used to, delivering a theatrical smack on her pursed lips—"Mmwa!"

She was wrapped in this daydream when she walked by Henry's office and saw Justin at his desk, tapping on his laptop. She'd thought he was upstairs. In profile he reminded her of Henry, the same strong jaw, and she imagined that somewhere there was a girl who would love him despite his awkwardness and terrible hair.

"Hello?" she said. With his earbuds in, he didn't hear her, and she had to flick the light switch.

"Hey, Gram."

"What are you doing?"

"Checking out the Hubble."

"What's that?"

"The Hubble telescope? They've got this site where you can see what they're looking at."

He leaned aside so she could see the screen. It was supposed to be a galaxy, but all she could make out was a white smudge in the night sky.

"Is that what you want to do—explore space?"

"If I could," he said. "Not many people get to."

"If you want to, you will." She laid a hand on his shoulder. "Now, don't stay up too late."

"Okay."

"Sweet dreams."

"Sweet dreams," he said.

She had to leave the front hall light on for him, and the one in the stairwell, and the night-light in their bathroom, which bugged her, accustomed as she was to turning everything off. The bathroom wastebasket was a mass of Sarah's tissues, easy pickings for Rufus in the morning, and with a sigh she lifted out the plastic Giant Eagle bag, knotting its handles together, took it downstairs and brought up a new one.

In her own bathroom, patting her face dry before applying her moisturizer, she heard a voice and froze, holding the towel to her chin. From the hot-air register in the corner came the sound of the TV in Margaret's room. In bed she could still hear it faintly, a pitched conversation, and covered it with her radio. Hadn't the day gone on long enough? It was her fault, she thought. She was too used to living alone. While she loved them all dearly, she'd forgotten how exhausting other people could be.

EARTHLY POSSESSIONS

One of the sorrows of her life was that her children were not good with money. While the economy rose and fell, their losses were constant. No matter how well they were doing, or how many hours they worked, they couldn't save.

Having come from a town where there was literally a wrong side of the tracks, Emily had friends in grade school who wore patched and faded hand-me-downs and used oaktag to plug the holes in their shoes. There was no shame in it. An honest propriety obtained. No matter how poor they were, mothers didn't allow their children to leave the house wearing ripped or dirty clothes (a point Margaret as a teenager refused to understand or honor, leading to much screaming).

It was not poverty or its semblance that Emily was afraid of as much as the loss of opportunity. Her father, who'd dreamed of being an architect, had had to leave school for a lack of money. He worked, comfortably enough, for forty-five years as a building inspector, approving the visions of other men. She never heard a bitter word from him, but after her mother died, while she was cleaning out his desk, among his mechanical pencils and rubber stamps she found tubes full of grand, intricate plans for a courthouse he'd designed. The date in the legend was 1931, the year she was born, a decade after he'd quit school, and she imagined him coming home nights and conjuring up this gaudy monument to the Second Empire—in Kersey, in the midst of the Depression—knowing it would never be built.

Emily didn't want her children to be rich, or even professionally successful. She wanted them to fulfill their responsibilities to others and to themselves, that was all. They both had so much promise (she would never believe she was mistaken in this), and yet they seemed so unhappy, so easily defeated. While she was openly skeptical of Kenneth ever making a living with his photography, she understood it was his love. No one was more upset when suddenly, as if time had expired, he decided to quit it altogether and throw himself into selling advertising for Lisa's father, a field anyone could see was a bad match for his gifts. He knew he was wasting his talent. It was clear when they spoke on the phone, his accounts of his workday full of self-deprecating jokes. She found herself encouraging him to pick up his camera, in what must have seemed an about-face from her earlier position. When pressed, he was defensive, which she read as resentment— of her as well as the job. Maybe things would change when the kids were through with school, but for now this was his solution.

Margaret had never discovered her true vocation. Like many of her generation, she'd dropped out of college, a mistake Emily blamed for her later troubles. Through her twenties, she hung around East Lansing, waiting tables and tending bar, sharing cramped apartments with friends of equally dubious means and a succession of men who disappeared before anyone could meet them. She was thirty when she met Jeff, and spent the next twenty years as a full-time if not always dedicated homemaker. Now, alone in their old house, she worked as a receptionist at a suburban hospital, where her status as a recovering alcoholic wasn't a problem. The divorce settlement had been equitable. She'd gotten the house, but now she was solely responsible for the mortgage. Between alimony, child support and her paycheck, often she couldn't cover her monthly expenses, and Emily had to help.

The main problem, as Emily had seen from the beginning, was that they were living beyond their means. She and Henry didn't start out in the house on Grafton Street. It had been a dream. They had saved and done without, though Henry's parents could have easily lent them the money. As the junior engineer in his department, Henry worked the shifts no one else wanted, banking as much overtime as he could. Westinghouse was booming, which meant sometimes for weeks she would eat her dinner and go to bed alone, but gradually, by sticking to a strict budget, they'd put together enough for a down payment and to qualify for a mortgage.

Only then, when they could actually afford a nice place, did they start shopping.

Invariably, when she told this story, one of the children would say, "Yes, but how much did a house cost back then?"—as if that somehow voided the moral. They didn't understand. The price wasn't the point.

Being bad with money, they disliked discussing it, as if they were being reprimanded for something not their fault. It must have seemed unfair. They had worked, they had tried, and yet the numbers were implacable. No answer they gave would change the balance, and so they weathered Henry's and then Emily's lectures in silence as payment for the check that would temporarily refill their accounts.

It was this hopeless resistance Emily had to overcome, the afternoon of Christmas Eve, as she ushered Margaret into Henry's office and closed the door. The tree was trimmed, the children fed, the lunch dishes done. On Henry's desk rested a thick manila envelope, one of three that Gordon Byrne had prepared for her. The second was for Kenneth. In fairness to him, she would send it off later this week, once the Christmas rush was over and there was less chance of it being lost by the post office. The third she kept for her records, and to have one handy in the house, if and when necessary.

Inside the packet, along with a copy of her will and her basic tax information, was an appendix listing her assets—fully itemized bank and brokerage statements, the contracts and current balances of her annuities, the contents of her safe-deposit box, the most recent appraisal of the house, the title to her new car, and, in her own tremulous hand, a dozen pages cataloging her jewelry, her silver and wedding china and crystal, the better furniture and Oriental rugs and artwork, even Henry's old woodworking machinery, now valuable antiques. As she'd compiled this daunting inventory, she recalled Matthew's warning not to lay up treasures on earth but in heaven. It hadn't escaped her that the possessions which meant the most to her—her books and music—were considered relatively worthless. As if to correct that misapprehension, she went back and, at the very top, above everything, added Henry's Bible, a true heirloom.

Margaret took the chair to the side of the desk, her back against the wall, hands clasped in her lap like a prisoner facing interrogation. Emily assumed Henry's spot. Originally the pantry, the office was a windowless box topped with a do-it-yourself drop ceiling, the frosted middle panel of which held two fluorescents that didn't quite illuminate the room. Emily clicked on the gooseneck desk lamp, training it on the blotter like a spotlight, flipped the envelope over and slid out the packet.

The last time they'd gone over her arrangements, they'd argued, but that was when Margaret was still drinking. As with any decision involving large sums of money, one's final instructions required an uncomfortable honesty. Trying to protect the children, Emily had made her reservations about Margaret formal and binding, naming Kenneth, who was younger, her sole executor, an act she would defend to this day and that she hoped Margaret, in her new life, could appreciate.

Her instinct now was to approach the subject head-on. This talk was necessary, if unpleasant, especially with all the changes in the estate tax. She didn't want to let things get emotional, and she'd long given up on disarming Margaret.

"Here is everything," she said without preface, patting the top sheet, "that you and Kenneth are going to need when I die. The biggest change is that I've made the two of you coexecutors, if that's all right."

She thought this would please her, but it was possible Margaret was still nursing that old hurt, because she showed no sign of relief or gratitude, just gave her the same grim face. Did Emily really think she could be exonerated so easily?

"After you both have a chance to go over it, you and he should talk about how you want to handle things. Justin and Sam are of age now, so the whole trust thing doesn't apply, but everything else is pretty much the same. It's relatively straightforward. The important thing is to make sure you pay half of the estate taxes within ninety days, that way the state gives you a discount."

"Okay."

"Right now the total is under the federal limit. That may change next year, depending on Congress, so check with your accountant, or with Gordon. He's going to be the one you'll be sitting down with when the time comes. The estate will be paying for him anyway, so make good use of him."

"His card's in there?"

"Right here. And this is a power of attorney I've had him draw up, so either of you can act for me in case I'm incapacitated. I've also asked that no extraordinary measures be taken. After what happened to Louise, I don't want there to be any question about that. I'm keeping that my decision, not anyone else's. I hope you understand."

"Of course."

On she went, pausing every so often to impress upon Margaret this or that fine point. Emily herself would have been asking questions and taking notes, but Margaret never interjected, merely nodded along, as if reserving judgment until she could parse the whole document. Emily summarized the sections and passed them across the blotter to her— Gordon's cover letter, the will itself, and then the separate, impressive addenda.

"If you want the car, you'll have to establish fair value and deduct that from your share."

Given the state of their minivan, this made sense, but Margaret let the offer pass untouched. Likewise, she didn't volunteer any preferences for the furniture or the dishes, as if that could all wait till another time.

"That's it, I guess," Emily said. "Unless you have any questions?"

"Not right now."

"Thank you, dear. I'm sorry we had to do this today, but it's something that had to be done."

"I know," Margaret said. "Thank you. It's just a little overwhelming."

"Consider it your reward for putting up with me all these years."

"Don't joke."

"Sorry." She hadn't meant to, it just popped out.

"You're the one who's put up with a lot," Margaret said. "I know I haven't been the easiest daughter in the world. I'm trying to do better."

"You are."

They both rose, and, as had become her habit since finding sobriety, Margaret hugged her, patting her back. "I love you, Mom."

"I love you too, dear," Emily said, but once Margaret was gone, she clicked off the lamp and sat for a moment alone, scattered and unsatisfied, trumped somehow. She thought she'd feel better after their talk, as if, in preparing to leave this world, she might purge the past and unburden herself. Instead she felt empty, and foolish for thinking either of those was possible, whether that was her fault or not. She thought of all the time they'd wasted, all the pointless battles they'd fought, and while she knew in her heart that she wanted more than anything for the two of them to be reconciled, finally, she couldn't shake the idea that they'd both waited till the last minute, and now it was too late.

THE GIFT

Christmas Day it rained and Sarah spent the afternoon in bed. Her cough worried Margaret. Tomorrow, early, they were headed back to Michigan, where it was snowing. The children were supposed to go skiing over New Year's with Jeff's family at their place in the U.P.

"He can't expect her to go if she's like this," Emily said.

"Of course he will," Margaret said, as if it wasn't a question.

Emily wanted to suggest they stay until she was better. Anything to prolong their visit. After that first interminable day, how quickly the time had passed. She could feel it flowing beneath them like an undertow.

With Margaret and Arlene helping, there was no room in the kitchen. "Too many cooks," Arlene joked, but the turkey was perfect. They ate dinner and let the dishes sit as they gathered around the fire, drinking coffee and admiring the tree, sharing their old stories. Rufus lounged at Emily's feet, his head resting on a new stuffed Eeyore as if it were a pillow. Before long Sarah excused herself, thanking everyone for her presents and blowing good-night kisses so she wouldn't infect them.

"It's okay if you want to go up," Margaret told Justin, engrossed in his new iPhone. "I'll take care of the dishes."

"Merry Christmas," he said, giving each of them a hug.

"I'm glad I saved my receipts," Arlene said when he was gone, because the sweater she'd given him was a medium and he was a large now. She'd also given Margaret a second copy of *Eat, Pray, Love*—the first coming from Kenneth and Lisa—but overall their gifts had been a success.

Margaret poked the fire and sat on the floor by Rufus, smoothing his coat with one hand. Emily had asked her not to get her anything too dear—her gift was just them being there—but the shot of Emily on the dock at Chautauqua with all the grandchildren that last summer was precious. Where on earth did she find it?

"You're not the only one with pictures."

"I can't believe it's been seven years."

"I can," Arlene said.

As the last log collapsed and the fire dwindled, they picked at the box of Bolan's chocolates Arlene gave her every year, though they were already stuffed with pumpkin pie and Christmas cookies, until, groaning and sticking out her tongue, Margaret fit the lid back on.

Over Emily's protests, all three of them cleaned the kitchen. The machine could fit only so much. The crystal and the pots and pans they had to do by hand. Margaret washed while Emily and Arlene dried. They worked together easily, hip-to-hip, a team, gabbing and laughing, then falling silent again, busy putting things away, and Emily was content. As gloomily as the day had begun, it had ended well. If this was their last Christmas, then this was the memory she wanted Margaret to keep.

By the time they finished, Arlene needed to get home. She was coming to the airport in the morning to see them off, but Margaret walked her to her car and hugged her goodbye.

"The cold feels good," Margaret said on the stoop, waving after her.

"Of course it's going to snow tomorrow," Emily said.

"As long as it holds off till the afternoon."

"I think it's supposed to." It was just a couple of inches, though for an instant she pictured a storm pushing in early, closing the roads, making them stay a few more days.

Inside, the grandfather clock bonged, reminding her that they had to get up in six hours.

"It really isn't such a bad little tree," Margaret said.

"It turned out nice, didn't it?'

"That's what Linus says in the show."

"I get it."

"It did turn out nice. Everything did."

"Did it?"

"It did. Thank you for having us."

"Of course," Emily said. "You know you're always welcome."

"I know."

"I wish Sarah felt better."

"I hope you don't get what she has."

"Maybe she could come to Chautauqua this summer? She could bring Max."

"I'll tell her you said that."

"I barely talked to her at all."

"I know," Margaret said. "I'm sure she feels bad about that."

She offered to help lock up, but Emily told her it was okay, by now she had it down to a science. They hugged good night at the bottom of the stairs—"*Feliz Navidad*," Margaret said—and Emily went through the rooms, turning off the lights. She left the tree for last, parting the screen of the fireplace and scattering the embers, then standing back and noting its speckled reflection in the front window, and her own silhouette against the stairs. Yesterday she'd been desperate. Today she felt love. Was it just Christmas? If the clock struck now, would the first spirit appear, take her hand and show her the folly of her ways? At her age, it was dangerous to think the past was all she had, her life already defined, when every day was another chance.

In bed she wondered if she believed that. In the morning she tried again, but her mind wasn't pliable enough, and there was no time.

They had to be out of the house by five-forty-five. She was used to waking early, but alone, at her own pace. She rushed through her shower so Margaret could hop in after her. She would have made them breakfast, but Margaret said they'd get something at the airport. They still had to pack.

Outside it was night. Under the streetlights, the asphalt was drying in patches. To Emily's dismay the *Post-Gazette* hadn't arrived yet. She fed Rufus and brewed a pot of coffee, made herself an English muffin and waited. She'd told Arlene five-thirty. When the clock struck the half hour, she mulled calling her, and then, before she finished her cup, the doorbell rang.

Arlene apologized for being late. "I'm surprised you're not in the car already."

"They're still getting their act together."

They saw nothing of them until exactly five-forty-five, when Justin bumped his suitcase down the stairs. Minutes later, Sarah clunked down with wet hair, followed by Margaret carrying a heavy duffel bag and shouldering an overstuffed backpack. She grabbed her jacket and scarf from the closet. No, no coffee, they had to get going. Emily held the front door for her, staving off Rufus with a hand.

"Have you got everything?" Arlene asked as they turned onto Highland.

"If not," Margaret said, "it's too late now."

Downtown they had the tunnel to themselves. The Parkway West was empty, only a few unlucky truckers working on Boxing Day. In back, sandwiched between Margaret and Justin, Sarah dozed with her mouth open. The sun wouldn't be up for another hour, and Emily kept to the right lane, driving the limit, yet she felt like she was speeding. She thought it was wrong that she should have to help them leave.

They climbed Green Tree hill, swung under the Norfolk and Western trestle and through Carnegie.

"How are we doing on time?" Arlene asked, as if she were going with them.

"I think we're okay," Emily said, though it would be close. To get the bags on the plane, they needed to be there forty-five minutes before departure.

They didn't have time to park the car. Emily pulled up to the curbside check-in and they all piled out into the cold. A skycap helped Justin unload the way-back, the hazards flashing over their faces while Margaret dealt with the ticket agent. There was a state trooper sitting behind them, so Emily could leave the wheel only briefly to say her goodbyes—sloppy and impromptu, not at all what she wanted—before they were through the doors and gone.

It was a shock, back in the car, to find that, once again, it was just herself and Arlene.

"I hope Sarah's okay," Emily said.

"She was pretty miserable."

"I did like her hair like that."

"I got used to it."

She didn't want to be alone, and they had to get off at Edgewood anyway, so she suggested breakfast at the Eat 'n Park, coupons be damned.

"I actually have one," Arlene said, patting her purse.

"Well," Emily said, "this *is* a Merry Christmas."

HOUSEKEEPING

Though their visit had been short, and relatively quiet, she felt the change in the house immediately. Upon coming home, she waved Arlene away and closed the door and was alone again, her peace and privacy restored. The tree still lent its festive presence to the living room, but without the heightened sense of expectancy that made Advent her favorite season. There was nothing to wait for—the holiday was over. She wouldn't see them till the summer, for one week, Sarah possibly not until Thanksgiving, if then.

"Yes, Mr. Poofus," she said, taking his face in her hands, "it's just us. You don't have to share me with anyone."

He followed her through the upstairs as she stripped off the sheets and pillowcases. Justin had dropped his wet towels on his unmade bed, provoking an "Honestly" that Rufus thought was directed at him. Margaret, sleeping in her old room, had pushed the keepsake pictures on her dresser to one side to make space. Along with a full glass of water that left a ghostly ring on her nightstand, Sarah had forgotten her phone charger, still plugged in and drawing electricity. The hall bath's shower caddy held someone's fancy shampoo and conditioner. From the hook on the back of the door hung a red plaid nightshirt. Emily gathered these fugitive pieces in a box she quarantined in Henry's office to mail at some later date, and kept going. She moved the booze and did a complete redistribution of the Kleenex. Once started, it was hard to stop, as if by keeping busy she might not miss them. Room by room, she cleaned and rearranged and straightened, and in a few hours changed everything back to exactly how it had been before, wiping away any trace of disorder, as if they'd never been there.

UNDER THE WEATHER

It started with a harmless cough, a dry tickle that progressed, overnight, to a scratchy throat. She began to sneeze—sometimes so uncontrollably she wet her pants, though that could happen at the best of times. Her head filled with mucus, plugging her ears, and she felt blunted and dull, as if she were moving underwater.

Being sick was news. She made use of it, broadcasting to all points as if something interesting had happened to her. On the phone with Margaret she called it Sarah's Christmas present, a joke she recycled for Kenneth, who worried it was strep. She appreciated his concern but discounted his diagnosis. Sarah didn't have strep, just a bad cold. No, as Arlene warned, at their age the thing Emily needed to be careful of was pneumonia.

"What are you taking for it?" they asked, and gave her the names of pills she'd never heard of and didn't trust.

She needed to rest, everyone agreed, but there was too much to do.

"Like what?" Margaret asked, and then suggested Arlene could return Emily's library books and pick up her mother's good tablecloth.

"I'm not bedridden," Emily said. "I just don't feel well."

"I'm sure she'd be happy to help."

"I promise, if I need help, she'll be the first person I call. How's that?"

"But you won't," Margaret said. "Because you're stubborn."

Later, Arlene called to offer her services.

"Why do I feel like I'm being ganged up on?" Emily asked, when of course she'd brought it on herself. Of the modern saints, she admired, above all, those martyrs who suffered in silence—Bonhoeffer, von Moltke—partly because she couldn't.

Ten in the morning and all she wanted to do was sleep. She wrote her thank-you notes, befogged, made herself some soup and toast for lunch, tipped back a noxious capful of DayQuil and put herself to bed. It was blustery out, the telephone wires swinging, and for a while she lay watching the changing light on the ceiling and listening to Rufus breathe, her swirling thoughts magnified by the silence. Her lungs were tight, her sinuses clogged, and, contemplating the closed door, she recalled how when she was sick as a child her mother would make soup and bring it up on a tray, tucking a napkin into the neck of her pajamas. Being cooped up in a room with two dozen first-graders, her mother was always coming down with something, and several times as a teenager Emily had the chance to return the favor, ceremonially bearing the tray from the kitchen up the stairs and down the hall. "Bless you, dear," her mother said helplessly, propped on her pillows, and Emily felt the satisfaction of repaying a debt, just as now, though she protested she would be fine, she felt she'd been left to fend for herself, and, overcome by weakness and the unfairness of it all, gave in to childish tears, then, spent, descended into a restless sleep, dreaming of summer in Kersey, and Henry and her in London, trying to flag a taxi and having no luck. They were stuck in the middle of a roundabout, traffic surging from all directions. Every time he stepped into the street she was afraid he'd be killed, and tried to pull him back to the curb, tugging at the sleeve of his old trenchcoat.

When she woke, the room was dark, the covers smothering her. She was sweaty and flushed, feverish, a development the thermometer confirmed. The Bufferin hurt going down.

She put on her robe and slippers and fed Rufus, but had no appetite herself. She sat at the breakfast table, rumpled and fusty, picking at some leftover turkey and mashed potatoes, dreading every swallow. It was too late to call Dr. Sayid's office. Instead she called Arlene, who agreed her plan made sense.

In the morning she was hoarse. Tiffany at Dr. Sayid's office took pity on her and fit her in. Arlene drove, reprising her old role of chauffeur, for which Emily was grateful. The Taurus stank freshly of cigarettes, but she was too far gone for it to bug her.

She'd been seeing Dr. Sayid since Dr. Runco retired, leaving him his patients. From the first she liked him better, which came as a great surprise. He was younger, yet formal in his manner, crisply enunciating each syllable in a charming Bombay accent. A fellow crossword fiend, he'd done his residency at Johns Hopkins, and, unfairly perhaps, she considered him sharper than Dr. Runco, a graduate of her own alma mater, Pitt. As her father would say, he was on the ball. He was also more direct with her, treating her as an equal, which, not being squeamish, Emily appreciated. He could deliver the worst news with no preliminaries whatsoever and expect her not only to accept it but to immediately discuss treatment options. At this point in her life, as she told anyone who would listen, that kind of practicality was exactly what she needed.

Today, after a half hour in the crowded waiting room, she saw Mary, the nurse practitioner, who briskly took her history, checked her vital signs and updated her chart. Mary swabbed the back of her throat, making Emily gag, asked her to change into a flimsy gown and left her alone again.

Waiting and illness were both a kind of limbo. Combined, they produced a hypnotic daze, and sitting there on the paper-covered examining table in the spare little room decorated with anatomical drawings, aware of her faulty posture, Emily experienced a blank timelessness, as if the rest of the world and not she had come unmoored.

She saw Henry in the dream, hailing a black cab—Death, she suspected, or was that too simple? She grabbed at his coat, trying to hold him back. She'd never had a dream like that about Louise, only the one in the museum, the two of them browsing the endless glass cases of stuffed birds, all silently, a scene out of Louise's favorite, Bergman. She would have loved to hear what Louise made of it.

When the doctor walked in she tried to smile for him, as if she were putting up a brave front. He apologized for taking so long. He didn't seem surprised to see her, and rolled his stool over. Under his lab coat he had on a striped tie topped with a perfect Windsor knot. "All right, let me take a look at you." He clicked his penlight and peered into her mouth. "Wider, thank you. Oh my, yes. I can see why we're having trouble swallowing. You've got some redness on both sides."

"You think it's strep?"

"There's a strain that's been circulating." He felt her glands, turning her head right and then left. "We'll have to see what the culture tells us, but I'd be very surprised if it isn't."

He stood and warmed the disc of his stethoscope between his palms before having her lean forward and breathe deeply. As he moved it from place to place on her back—"Again," he said—she marveled at how unaccustomed she'd become to another's touch.

In the midst of this, there was a knock on the door. The doctor pulled her gown closed before calling, "Hello, yes?"

It was Mary, with a printout for him. The test had vindicated Kenneth—it was strep.

The doctor was also worried about her weight. She needed to be gaining, not losing. "Tell me what you had to eat yesterday."

She was too miserable to defend herself, and told him the truth, essentially. How could she explain? The fridge was stuffed with leftovers, she just wasn't hungry.

He shook his head as if it were unacceptable. "You have to do better—for yourself and for me as your doctor. You can make my job easier or you can make it harder, it's up to you."

He prescribed antibiotics, and a nasal spray for her sinuses. He also wanted her to supplement her diet with Ensure, and had Mary give her a sample can which Emily was embarrassed to carry through the waiting room.

"I've got some at home if you want it," Arlene said in the car. "It's really not so bad."

"It's old people chow."

"We're old people."

"What I resent is the implication that I can't take care of myself."

"You're a terrible sick person," Arlene said, "you know that?"

"I know. I'm sorry. You're a good one."

She scoffed. "I overcompensate, that's all."

"Me too," Emily said, "I just go the other way."

"Probably healthier for you."

"I doubt it." And that, being the truth, they let stand as the last word.

They swung by the Rite Aid on Highland and dropped off her prescriptions. In the far corner, customers were lined up against the wall and sitting in the blood pressure chairs. The pharmacist said it might be a while, so Arlene drove her home and settled her in bed. When Emily resurfaced, hours later, on her nightstand sat a small white bag with her pills, the stapled receipt holding it closed. Emily had to put on her glasses to see how expensive it was and then wished she hadn't.

TAKE WITH FOOD, the label warned.

Arlene was way ahead of her, bringing up a steaming bowl of turkey noodle soup on the same varnished rattan tray the children used to serve Henry breakfast in bed on Father's Day. As she settled it over Emily's legs, she leaned in, treating Emily to a close-up of her scar. The new skin was the color of bubble gum. On the surface of the soup floated dozens of tiny yellow circles of fat like breeding amoebas. The turkey chunks were stringy, the carrots pale orange coins.

"Did you make this?" Her voice was a whisper.

"I got it from the Crockery while I was out. I know how you like them. All I did was stick it in the microwave. If it's too hot, I can add an ice cube."

"No," Emily said. "Thank you."

"Eat," Arlene said, trying a Yiddish accent, "it's good and good for you."

She was right—the broth was rich and salty—but each mouthful stung going down. It was an effort, and Emily found herself apologizing.

"It's okay," Arlene said. "Just eat what you can. Maybe we'll have some ice cream later, how does that sound?"

She was enjoying playing nursemaid too much, and yet what a relief it was to cast off the last shreds of her dignity and surrender to her. Emily had no strength left, and let her open the cider-colored vial and tip out her pill, a formidable tan football. Arlene passed her a glass of water and took it from her when she was done, then decoded the instructions of the nasal spray so all Emily had to do was squeeze the thing twice and sniff in before handing it over and going back to sleep.

Later, waking in the dark, she told Arlene it was okay, she didn't have to stay the night. Arlene laughed. She hadn't. It was morning. She'd slept at home and let herself in with a key. She was making oatmeal for her, if she was hungry.

"Thank you," Emily said.

She thought they'd caught the infection early enough and that with each dose of Levaquin, once she established a base, she'd get progressively better. She was right about one thing—this was just the beginning.

She'd forgotten what it was like to be sick. The days were shapeless, her room a burrow. Arlene made it too easy, pulling the blinds and closing the drapes, taking Rufus downstairs with her. When the phone rang, Arlene answered. When the mail came, Arlene brought it up with Emily's lunch. It was the darkest part of the year, when the arrival of the spring seed catalogs was all that sustained her, and now she didn't have the energy to read them. The pills gave her diarrhea, taking away what little appetite she had. Her mouth was foul, the roof tiled with dried mucus. On her nightstand gathered unruly blossoms of used tissues and stale glasses of water. Henry ran after the cab, and she ran after him, his trenchcoat flapping behind him like a cape. Sometimes when she woke, the radio was playing softly, and sometimes she only thought it was, imaginary viols sighing fantasias composed by her own ears. She missed church for the first time in ages, along with the crossword, and then, Tuesday, woke blearily to a new year. She noted, more with ironic astonishment than self-pity, that time had literally passed her by.

"You've got your sense of humor back," Arlene said, checking the thermometer. "That's a good sign."

"I suppose it is," Emily said, though she wasn't trying to be funny.

She was tired of lying in bed, and pestered Arlene to let her go downstairs in her robe and slippers and sit at the breakfast table with the paper while she made their lunch—grilled cheese and tomato soup. The stovetop was spotted with grease, and Betty was supposed to come tomorrow. Out of habit, Emily wetted a sponge.

"Sit," Arlene said, as if she were talking to one of her students. "Do you need to go back to bed?"

"I'm feeling much better," Emily said, but her voice was a husk.

"I'm glad. Now drink your juice."

"Did you water the tree?"

"I watered it when I watered the plants this morning."

It was hard for Emily to imagine anything going on in the house without her knowledge, and as grateful as she was, it was also, subtly, an affront. There was so little she could call her own.

Under the table, as if starved for attention, Rufus rested his head on her knee. After they ate, he preceded her upstairs, curling around the far side of her bed where the box spring blocked the gray light from the windows. He flopped down, rolled over, and in minutes was dreaming, his scraping snores providing accompaniment to a Debussy étude.

She knew it was perverse, she knew she needed to rest to get better, yet she resented that, with so many things that needed to be done, nothing was expected of her. She leafed through her seed catalogs, dog-earing pages, and sniped at the *Times* crossword. As she was rereading her mother's tooled leatherette copy of Hardy's *Life's Little Ironies*, a sour, too-familiar stench reached her—Rufus had let one loose.

"P.U.," she said, and then, when he didn't wake up, called out loudly.

He knew what it meant, but didn't budge.

"Go."

He looked up at her moonily.

"*Go*," she said, and he did, settling by her dresser, huffing once. "You know I love you, but you stink."

Her intention was not to nap but to get back on a normal schedule, especially with Betty coming tomorrow, but *Life's Little Ironies* was not Hardy's best, she was full from lunch, and the bed was warm. When she'd read the same sentence three times with no success, she closed the book and, holding it to her chest like an amulet, closed her eyes.

When she opened them it was dark out—tricked again. The streetlight was on, and she could smell onions frying in butter. Rufus was gone, a blow, since she'd hoped to feed him his dinner.

The Bolognese Arlene had made upset her stomach, but Emily didn't mention it, or that she thought it an odd choice. Never having had to cook for a family, Arlene had a limited repertoire, and Emily counted herself lucky that it wasn't her game-day chili. Under Arlene's watchful eye, she ate with gusto and then offered to help with the dishes, only to be rebuffed.

Arlene wouldn't let her wipe down the counters either.

"There must be something I can do." But her voice undercut what she was saying.

"You can go sit down and rest, that's what you can do."

In protest, she let Rufus out. They were getting low on treats, so she added it to the list Arlene had started.

"What are you putting on there?" Arlene asked, as if she were trespassing.

"Only the most important thing in the house."

Later they had ice cream, which Emily didn't want, after the pasta. She appreciated that Arlene wasn't pushing the Ensure, but once she left, Emily had to use the john. She was noisy, and reached over Rufus, who was flat on the bath mat, to flick on the fan.

"I'd say I'm sorry, but turnabout is fair play."

Before bed she set her alarm, something she hadn't done in years. In the morning, achy and muddleheaded, she showered and dressed as if it were a regular day. She brought in the paper and made herself toast and tea, stirring a spoonful of honey into her cup. She did her dishes and took her next-to-last pill, and by the time Arlene arrived, she was plucking ornaments from the tree and fitting them into their boxes.

"What are you doing?" Arlene asked, aghast.

"What does it look like I'm doing? I'm taking down the tree."

"It can't wait till the weekend?"

"It's easier when Betty's here."

"Oh my God," Arlene said. "Margaret was right. You'd rather kill yourself than let someone help you."

The irony of this insult was self-evident, Emily thought, given Margaret's history, but she didn't take the bait. "That's not true. I appreciate everything you've done for me. Honestly, I don't know what I would have done without you. But I can't stay in bed forever, that's not going to help me feel better."

"Thank you, but . . . Just don't overdo it. I'm supposed to be looking after you."

"And you did a fine job of it," Emily said, presenting her upright self, with a model's flourish of a hand, as evidence.

"You still sound awful."

"I only have one pill left."

Arlene remained skeptical. Betty knew the situation, and all day the two of them watched Emily, as if testing her. She pretended to ignore their scrutiny, using her rare moments alone to rest and regroup. Together they wrestled the tree out to the curb, along with the garbage, and stored the ornaments safely in the basement.

At the end of the day Arlene asked Betty for a ruling, casting her as an impartial observer, but, having worked for them so many years, and preferring to continue, Betty wisely refused to choose a side.

"I don't think you're a hundred percent yet," she said, "but you're getting there."

Emily paid her and they saw her off, leaving them to play out an awkward scene in the front hall. Arlene, trying to do her duty, wanted to stay and make dinner. Emily, exhausted from putting up a front, wanted her to leave so she could collapse in peace. She thoughtfully considered her offer, as if she might accept it—because she *was* grateful, and Arlene had been a dear—but she hadn't fought all day not to win her independence, and gently she said, "Thank you, but I think I can manage."

"Okay," Arlene said, with reservations—or, did Emily imagine it, with relief? "You've got to eat, though."

"I will."

"I'll call you tomorrow to see how you're doing."

"You don't have to."

"I know I don't have to."

Emily reached into the closet and handed her her jacket, helping her find the armhole. "Let me call Margaret."

"I'm many things, but a tattletale isn't one of them."

"I didn't say you were."

"She'll call me right after she hangs up with you anyway."

"Checking up on me."

"She worries about you—for good reason."

"That's a switch."

"I think we're at the time of life when we all worry about everyone."

The idea lingered after Arlene was gone, like a phone ringing in a quiet house. Though they all lived alone, and preferred to, they were all worried about one another, equally. Why had it taken them so long to arrive at this point? Shouldn't it have always been that way?

She coated her throat with honey and practiced speaking in a normal voice before calling Margaret, who sounded surprised to hear from her. She was glad she was feeling better.

"Arlene was a huge help," Emily said. "Thank you for siccing her on me."

"It was entirely her idea."

"Entirely."

"Almost entirely."

"Well, thank you."

"You're welcome. Now you just have to keep eating healthier."

"I am, I am," Emily said.

For dinner she made a plate of leftovers, but wasn't hungry, and ended up scraping most of it down the disposal. She felt bad, after all her promises. Selfish and deceitful, her mother would say—the worst thing a person could be, the complete opposite of Jesus Christ, the impossible model to which Emily spent her childhood being compared and yet for whom, as with her mother, she felt an unending love. She also missed the tree with its merry lights, and the crèche, and the boughs on the mantel, as if all of their work today now counted against her. Hadn't she gotten what she wanted? Her wounds, if she had any, were self-inflicted, and rather than nourish the misguided feeling that she was the victim of some injustice, she put Rufus out and went up to bed obscenely early, thinking she would read. The Hardy was no better than before, and despite the live broadcast of the Philadelphia Orchestra, she dropped off with the light on, missing the end of Schubert's Unfinished Symphony.

In the morning, for the first time in a week, she felt rested. She slathered butter and raspberry jam over her toast, and drizzled honey into her teacup. After breakfast she took her last pill, pitching the vial in the kitchen trash as if declaring victory.

Upstairs, as she brushed her teeth, pacing by the windows overlooking the street, she half expected Arlene to pull up in her Taurus. After a cleansing night's sleep, Emily was disappointed that Arlene had accepted her dismissal without a fight. The house was spotless, but she needed to run out to the bank and the post office and the grocery store—and the library, if she had time. Instead, to her amazement and frustration, she puttered around the downstairs, waiting for Arlene to call, as if only she could release her.

INGRATITUDE

Every year the same maddening pas de deux occurred, with only the most minor variations. The week after Christmas, Emily wrote her thank-you notes and posted them, expecting—if not directly then at least shortly—an equal number in return.

The habit, ingrained in her by her mother, was more than a genteel nicety, reflecting, as it did, the bonds of love and respect upon which all relationships depended. As a child Emily had spent whole afternoons drafting hers, writing to the Brandy Camp and Elbon and Dagus Mines branches of the Waites and Bentons, bending low over her desk with the tip of her tongue clamped between her teeth, taking pains to reproduce her award-winning penmanship. Those were the war years, and her family didn't have a lot, so any present was special. *Thank you so much for the bracelet. It is beautiful. I will wear it with my blue dress.* Just hearing how pleased her Aunt June had been to receive her card was a gift in itself.

As a mother, Emily had enforced and supervised the process, providing reminders, addresses and stamps. When they opened their presents, it was Kenneth's job to log what each of them had received, from whom, and before they bagged the wrapping paper and carried their booty upstairs, she let them know what was expected of them.

Henry, being a partner in the larger entity of Mr. and Mrs. Henry Maxwell, already represented by Emily, was not charged with this task, just as he was not asked to buy Christmas presents for anyone except her. His responsibilities were technical (making fires, putting up and taking down the tree, train and lights) and financial (paying for everything), while hers were domestic and social, including—though this was self-imposed, a leftover from her mother's day—not adding to his.

Kenneth, ever dutiful, finished his thank-yous before Margaret started hers, though his were slapdash, as if he'd rushed through them just to be done. Due to larger curriculum changes, in the early seventies the Pittsburgh schools dropped writing, and his cursive never improved. A five-year-old's scrawls could be charming, but not a fifth-grader's, and as he grew older, Emily vetted his efforts like a teacher correcting homework, more often than not sending him back to his desk so that it became a struggle, and unpleasant, to the extent that the mere mention of thank-you notes met with a groan—a mistake, since it awakened her sense of outrage, which only escalated the situation. Occasionally he was confined to his room until she deemed his work suitable.

Margaret simply didn't care. Thank-you notes belonged to the same category of useless formalities her square parents followed blindly, like sitting down to meals at prescribed times or going to church on Sunday. People should give gifts because it made them happy. There should be no obligation involved, no guilt. Writing a thank-you note for a gift you didn't like was hypocritical. Her ditzy hippie logic exhausted Emily, and though she and Henry were united on this front, they had bigger battles to fight with Margaret, meaning that around this time of year Emily would get a call from her mother (she couldn't stay on long—it was too expensive), letting her know that she'd received Kenneth's nice note.

Now the wave Emily sent out traveled farther, as if the scope of her life had widened, when, at her lowest, she felt it narrowing down to this house, this room, this moment. Though she would dearly love to, she would never see Ella's apartment in Cambridge, or meet her friend Suzanne. The same for Sarah and her beau in Chicago, and Justin and Sam off at college. Their lives were beyond her reach, just as hers had been when, at Pitt, every month she received a check for five dollars from Aunt June, along with a letter detailing the antics of Chester, her Siamese, and updating her on the progress of the new superhighway going through DuBois. Emily had faithfully answered those missives from home, but with platitudes—happy chatter of classes and dances rather than what she was really doing. And why? Just laziness, and some overweening idea of privacy, as if Aunt June might show up at the door of her sorority in her moth-eaten mink with Chester in hand and demand to stay the night.

A thank-you note was so little to ask—the minimum, really. Maybe it was a sign of her age, but lately she awaited them with greater anticipation than she could muster for any gift.

The first, as she could have predicted, came from Arlene, in her elegant hand, on monogrammed stationery. Arlene herself brought it up with the rest of the mail to Emily's bed during her convalescence. Politeness required Emily to say she could have saved herself a stamp, when both of them knew such a shortcut would have been improper. Arlene, for all her faults, had impeccable manners, as had Henry. During their initial dinner at the club, way back in '51, Emily's mother had been impressed by how gracious the Maxwells were as a family, their sense of etiquette far more important than their money, though her father, cowed and out of his element, said in the car that having both wasn't a bad package deal.

The second, which arrived when Emily was feeling better, was from Lisa, also on monogrammed stationery (a gift from Arlene), and neatly done, though devoid of emotion. As if to make up for it, Kenneth's, which followed a day later, closed, *Much love from all of us*, and listed not only himself and Lisa and the children, but Muttly and Fenway, their two goldens, complete with cartoon paw prints.

Margaret's followed not long after, a full-fledged letter, no surprise, since her new ideals prized, above all, communication and gratitude. She thanked Emily for having them, for the plane tickets, for her gifts, and finally for their good talk, which she obviously remembered differently—again, not a shock, as everything that happened to her now happened for a reason, and therefore had to be received positively, as a gift from God, including, presumably, Emily's death.

She thought that Ella's would be next, or possibly Sarah's, her prejudice against the boys having been borne out more times than not, but for days the mail was skimpy and impersonal. Their mailbox was old, a wrought-iron shell bolted to the brick and so heavily coated with black Rust-Oleum that the open rosette which let her glimpse an envelope within had skinned over. Just before lunchtime she heard the lid clank shut, only to go out, defying the cold, and discover it was empty, the mailman a figment of her desire.

A week passed, then the weekend. Monday was the fourteenth. She was painfully aware of the date because her estimated taxes had to be post-marked by midnight tomorrow. It had been three weeks. She was carefully writing out her checks to the U.S. Treasury when the mailman delivered Justin's note.

It was exactly what she expected: three lines in slanting block print cataloging the clothes he hadn't asked for and wishing her a happy new year, finished at the bottom with a squiggly signature. The stamp was stuck on crookedly, the envelope postmarked Silver Hills, meaning he'd dispatched with the onerous chore the last thing before heading off to school. That was fine—that was all she wanted, a simple acknowledgment. She might even give him brownie points for beating out his sister.

The next day nothing came, and waiting in line in the post office, she glanced at the display racks of overpriced Valentine's merchandise and imagined how the children would feel if, as an experiment, she didn't send them a card. Rude as the idea was, it might teach them a lesson, though more likely they wouldn't care, and she would only be depriving herself. As Margaret's two poles illustrated, you couldn't force someone to be grateful.

Martin Luther King Day she knew there was no mail, then forgot and only remembered again later, when it was overdue, throwing her into a bad mood. She understood Sam, but Ella? Sarah? Could theirs have pos-sibly arrived when she was sick and gotten lost?

In four days it would be a month—more than enough time, by any measure. Arlene thought so too, since she was facing the same quandary. Betty agreed, nodding in sympathy.

Could Emily hold her tongue that long? Because prompting her chil-dren was not Arlene's job. Like them, the task belonged to Emily. She remembered her mother, and her own problems with Margaret, the in-tractable past, and wished that, just once, she didn't have to call. But, like every year, she did.

FORGETFULNESS

In the middle of the afternoon, as she detoured through the dining room on her way to the kitchen for something pressing, she discovered Rufus sitting at attention on the back stoop in the cold, peering forlornly through the French doors.

"Did someone forget you? Is that what happened? I'm sorry, Boo-Boo. I don't know where my mind is today. Next time say something."

Then, later, when the toilet paper in the downstairs bath ran out, she threw the gold, spring-loaded spindle in the trash and held on to the empty cardboard tube.

"Seriously," she said, regarding the irrefutable proof in her hand, as if someone had played a trick on her that wasn't funny.

MYSTERY!

Unlike Arlene and the children, Emily wasn't big on TV. She'd witnessed its awkward first steps and sixty years later remained unimpressed. Each technical advance did little to conceal the fact that it was an unserious medium, a lazy way to fill the hours—as some wag put it, chewing gum for the mind. From time to time, of a Saturday afternoon, Henry planted himself in front of the Pirates game for a couple of innings, but more often he had Bob Prince on the radio down in the basement, providing background for whatever project he was lost in. They might watch Huntley and Brinkley together before dinner, the disjointed opening of the scherzo from Beethoven's Ninth introducing the equally chaotic news of the day, but they didn't have favorite shows the way the children did, and by the time cable colonized Highland Park, the children were gone, and Emily saw no reason why they should pay for something they received for free.

The one exception to this summary judgment was PBS, whose *Masterpiece Theatre* miniseries were consistently worthwhile. Week after week, year after year, she and Louise would get together with a glass of Chablis or two to watch the BBC's eight-part adaptation of *Middlemarch* or *The Mayor of Casterbridge* or *Northanger Abbey* and fall heart and soul into the familiar world of Victorian England, where the rambling manor houses were ivy-covered and candlelit, and corseted desire beat beneath layer upon layer of lush costumes.

As a girl she'd been a devotee, as her mother was, of Hardy and the Brontë sisters, yearning, in tumbledown Kersey, for a noble, soul-shattering passion. Now as she watched, gray and middle-aged, she recalled those still hours, lying belly-down, propped on her elbows behind the sofa, hidden in the warm gap by the radiator, lazily kicking her feet in the air, crossing and uncrossing her ankles, the book flat on the carpet. Even then the movies had infected her. At thirteen she imagined entering the same swagged ballrooms and salons, and watching Laurence Olivier's brougham depart from behind the same mullioned windows as Vivien Leigh or Merle Oberon.

How powerful the romance of the past was, and how sad, all the lost possibilities, despite how well things had turned out. A country mouse and an outsider herself, she had been these tentative heroines, had stepped innocent and unschooled into high society and made her way despite a paralyzing self-doubt. To see that part of her life reflected in them now, after the fact, was bittersweet—the dream, having been achieved, was over. If there was a role for her and Louise in these period pieces, it was no longer the yearning ingénue but the faithful retainer, Miss Haversham or Mrs. Fotheringill, played by a craggy character actress or fading grandame, whose sudden illness would force the rival sisters to stop quarreling and band together, and yet Emily could not bring herself to accept anything less than top billing, still susceptible (there's no fool like an old fool, her mother loved to say), after all these years, to the formula of longing.

Another, less high-minded British import they lapped up was *Mystery!*, with its Edward Gorey credits and clever, near-spoofs of Agatha Christie and Dorothy L. Sayers, both of whom held places of honor on Emily's bedroom shelves. While violence of any kind repulsed her, she relished a good murder. She and Louise were puzzle lovers, and made a game of staying a step ahead of Miss Marple and Lord Peter Wimsey, sorting through red herrings and teasing out intrigues among the suspects. The world of the twenties was as elegant as that of its Edwardian predecessor, with shooting parties and touring cars and gleaming rail coaches nothing like the cigar- and mildew-smelling one she and Henry endured from York to London. It was a fantasy, a place where wit and a simple moral logic prevailed, and every Monday, while the rest of Pittsburgh was glued to their football, she and Louise gave themselves to it eagerly.

Later, *Mystery!*'s offerings would grow more modern, encompassing not only the war years, an epoch for which Emily still had untapped feelings, but also contemporary England, for which she had none. In an unnecessary concession to realism, instead of rolling meadows and misty heaths, these new series featured the gritty streets of working-class cities like Manchester or Liverpool, stark tower blocks and run-down council flats and scummy takeaways. The stories were less mysteries than police procedurals, office-bound and charmless, nearly American. Their heroines were middle-aged inspectors with complicated relationships, and the crimes themselves revolved around larger issues like drugs or terrorism or immigration. As much as Emily admired Helen Mirren, she missed the sly comedy and blithe repartee, and when, several years ago, PBS announced a new season of Poirot, she and Louise awaited the initial episode with high hopes. The actor who played the detective was the same, the set design equally sumptuous, yet as they watched, Emily felt a helpless nostalgia for the earlier version, as if, across the intervening decade, something had been irretrievably lost.

Now, with Louise gone and *Masterpiece Theatre* stretching well beyond her bedtime, the only shows Emily watched regularly were the morning and evening news, mostly for the weather, though lately the presidential race had piqued her interest. She understood that she was different, that she was voluntarily missing a large part of the culture. Arlene had her soaps, and every night after supper played *Jeopardy!* and *Wheel of Fortune*, and Emily had seen how the TV sucked the children in, but for her it posed no temptation. She attached no personal virtue to this abstinence. As with smoking, she counted herself lucky not to have fallen into the habit.

Several Christmases ago, Kenneth had given her a DVD player to go with her VCR. He'd had all their old home movies on Super 8 and VHS transferred to six slim discs, a wonderful present, and yet, besides that visit, she'd never removed them from their handsome folder. This year, because it was the kind of thing Kenneth remembered, he'd given her—along with all the other useless treasure—the complete Lord Peter collection, a boxed set with every episode of her favorite seasons from the seventies.

Just the idea of sitting down with a glass of wine and savoring them again was enough to warm her. Impossible as it was, she wished she could go back and see them with Louise for the first time. She imagined starting from the beginning, rationing herself an episode a week to make it last. Occasionally, of a Monday evening, she thought of opening them and popping one in. It had been thirty years. Surely there would be much to discover. She intended to—she honestly meant to—because it *was* incredibly thoughtful of him to remember, and she *did* love the old programs, but there was always something else to take care of, and by that time, most nights, she was too tired to do anything but read a few lines before drifting off, and for whatever reason, as January turned to February, she left them sitting in the TV cabinet with the home movies, where they remained, a pleasant memory, pristine in their shrink-wrap.

PF

The groundhog was wrong. Spring was at least six weeks away, Easter even longer. It was the dark time of year Emily dreaded, the promise of better weather a taunt as one dispiriting system after another swept across the Great Lakes. Snow, sleet, rain, fog. The sun came out every few days, and the slush melted, only to refreeze overnight, triggering pileups on the Parkway and making their hill impossible. Not even the Subaru could handle black ice, and instead of risking life and limb, she stayed in, the list on the refrigerator growing a second column.

The snow crusted over so that when Rufus tried to reach his usual spots in the backyard, his legs broke through and he sank up to his tags. She was afraid he would hurt himself, and called Marcia to ask if Jim would come over after work with his snowblower and clear a path. Marcia did it herself, in sweatpants and olive barn boots. Buster refused to go out in this mess, she said, as if he were wise rather than spoiled, but Emily was grateful, offering her hot chocolate, and the two had a nice visit.

Emily thanked her, maybe too abjectly, saying she never could have done it herself.

"Please," Marcia said, "anytime. If there's anything else we can do, don't hesitate."

"Maybe, if it's not too much trouble, could you bring in some wood for the fireplace?"

From childhood Emily was used to storms closing roads and knocking out power, and guarded against the eventuality as if 51 Grafton were a pioneer homestead. Besides a store of candles in the sideboard, each room had its flashlight. When the forecast was bad, she took them out of their drawers and tested their batteries, then set them around the house in convenient locations, as if preparing for an attack. She kept Henry's old transistor radio handy, in case later on the authorities might be broadcasting lifesaving information. She still had a rotary phone that plugged into a wall jack so she could call without electricity, unlike Arlene, whose fancy cordless wouldn't work in an emergency. Upstairs in the linen closet she had extra flannel sheets and blankets, and a down comforter. In the basement, consigned to a masking-tape-labeled trash can, were her old long johns and ski sweaters, her last line of defense. Thus girded, she awaited the blizzard.

The greatest indication that it was coming was how excited the weathermen suddenly became. Days before it was scheduled to hit, they grew expansive, smiling like salesmen, as if, for once, they had a sure thing. As it neared, moving across the plains in a rainbowed cubist wave, they turned serious, listing precautions she'd already taken, and still they hedged, their predictions vague, ranging from two inches to two feet, depending on the storm's track and their different computer models. They wouldn't risk their reputations by actually forecasting the weather, leaving Emily to imagine the worst.

When she was in the third grade, a bad storm closed down Kersey for a week, followed by a cold snap, stranding an older woman from outside of town who belonged to their church. She ran out of coal for her furnace and soon went through her woodpile. In the end she resorted to breaking up chairs for her fireplace. That was where they found her, according to the schoolyard gossip—wrapped in blankets by the hearth, sitting upright, white as a plaster saint.

Nothing like that would happen. Her fears now were more practical—pipes freezing and bursting in the walls, water pouring through the living room ceiling—though she could not stop her mind from showing her the most lurid possibilities. One recurring scene wasn't that far-fetched: falling in the backyard as she refilled the big tree feeder and then lying there in the snow, croaking for help. She dismissed it, yet each time she ventured out with the sunflower seeds she bundled herself up as if she were crossing the Antarctic and then gingerly fit her boots into her old footprints.

Like the weathermen, she eagerly tracked the front as it swept up the

Ohio River Valley. Margaret said it had passed well to the south of them, and still dropped five inches.

"Looks like we're going to take the brunt of it," Emily said with a strange pride, as if this privilege had been reserved for Pittsburgh, the city drawn together by the threat.

It would arrive that night, the heaviest accumulation taking place between midnight and four in the morning, which was somehow unfair. She couldn't protect the house if she was asleep. She wanted to stay up and see the snow fall, watch it silently bury the world while she sat warm and dry inside, the furnace purring away in the basement. Instead, she arranged some logs on the grate and shoved balled newspapers under them before heading to bed, in case she woke up later and the house was cold. She thought she would have trouble sleeping, but dropped right off.

In the morning the street was a sea of white, the Millers' hedges bent under the load, the tree limbs and telephone wires coated. The sun was out, though it was still snowing wispily. The room was chilly, but no more so than any other day. Her radio worked, and the light in the bathroom. They'd been spared, all her preparations for naught. She felt slightly silly—Chicken Little—until she noticed that the display of the microwave read PF, for power failure. The interruption must have been brief, because the clock on the stove had the right time. It was probably just a flicker, nothing sustained, and yet, though it would have made absolutely no difference, she was disappointed that she'd missed it.

"You won't believe it, I slept right through it," she told Kenneth, incredulous, as if telling a joke on herself, then, once she was off, wondered why. Was she hoping to show him how accustomed she was to living alone, or trying to make him feel guilty? Maybe both. She was still gnawing on the question as she went through the house, opening and closing drawers, putting away the flashlights until the next time.

BEE MINE

It was a Wednesday, so Betty was there when the oversized red envelope arrived—proof, Emily said, that at least somebody loved her. She'd sent valentines to all four of the grandchildren, yet none of them had reciprocated.

They still hadn't. The writing was Kenneth's.

The card was a pop-up: Winnie-the-Pooh in a striped bee costume, suspended by balloons high above the Hundred Acre Wood, floating skyward as he licked honey from one dripping paw. No salutation or message, just *Love, Kenneth & Lisa*. Emily thought it was wrong that after all these years she still felt a twinge of distaste at the sight of her name.

"That's sweet," Betty said.

"I really wasn't expecting anything," Emily said, because it *was* a surprise, and she wondered if it had anything to do with the whole fiasco of the thank-you notes. She set it on the mantel, where she passed it often, but rather than a source of joy, it quickly became a reminder of her own shortcomings, prompting pointless self-recriminations until she moved it to a less-trafficked spot, on the sideboard in the dining room.

Sunday, when she picked up Arlene for church, she noticed a similar card on her mantel. This one showed Piglet balanced precariously on Pooh's shoulders, trying to poke a hanging beehive with a stick. Instead of Kenneth's block letters, it was signed in Lisa's girlish script—no accident, Emily thought. When she got home, she removed her card from the sideboard, folded it closed and slipped it into her secretary, and then, feeling entirely justified, lifted it out of the drawer again, stalked to the far end of the kitchen and shoved it in the trash.

A BAD HABIT

Rufus used to love the snow. She remembered mornings not so long ago when, like a child, he couldn't wait to get outside and romp around the untouched yard, dashing back and forth, rolling so his snout was powdered and he stank wetly when she let him in. Now he hesitated at the open door, glancing up at her dolefully—couldn't they skip this part and go straight to breakfast?—and then barely stepped off the porch to do his business. He no longer lifted his leg, as if that were too much trouble, just thrust his hips forward with his tail raised flaglike behind, looking around as he drained his bladder.

All he wanted to do was eat and sleep, and even at these favorites he'd noticeably slowed. When Margaret had brought Doctor Spot to Chautauqua, they had to keep an eye on Rufus or he'd poach his bowl after gulping down his own. Lately he'd taken to carefully chewing each morsel, as if his teeth hurt. He still badgered her for it, especially in the afternoon, with the days so dark, but sometimes he didn't finish his dinner, and she wondered if she should switch to canned food, though she feared that might provoke his farting problem.

The sleeping worried her—the depth and extent of it. While Emily had trouble sleeping through the night, he could circle three times and curl up anywhere and be snoring away in seconds, lost to the world. He disappeared for hours, sacked out in the children's windowless bathroom, then padded downstairs and found her working in Henry's office, resting his head on her thigh to be petted. He seemed listless and glum, and while she still teased him for being old or fat ("El Tubbo"), it was no longer a joke, and she did so gently.

He had trouble standing after lying down for a while. He pushed himself upright with his front legs easily enough, but raising his back end took an effort, and looked painful. It wasn't the dysplasia common to the breed, but the same arthritis that plagued her when she sat and read too long. His hips were just stiff. The vet recommended fish oil pills so powerful-smelling that Rufus refused them unless they were buried in his food. He'd been taking them for months and she wasn't sure they were helping, or if anything would. She sympathized. It might have just been her imagination, and she didn't like to think this way, but he seemed as resigned as she was.

For years he'd been the first one up, coming to her side of the bed and staring at her in hopes of getting his breakfast a few minutes early, a habit that annoyed Henry. Now he waited till she was out of the shower to leave his nest of blankets. He was still greedy, pushing past as she opened the bedroom door, clattering down the stairs and then standing there at the bottom looking up, wagging his tail. Mr. Impatient, she called him. Mr. Demanding.

Like Duchess before him, he'd gotten into the bad habit of anticipating her every move, but, unlike Duchess, he was uncertain, and so, though he preceded her into the kitchen, he had to glance back to make sure she was still right behind him. In doing so, he slowed, weaving, and to avoid tripping over him, Emily had to veer left or right. Sometimes he turned that way as well, nearly taking her out at the knees, making her stumble and stop short, or the two of them would become entangled, Emily straddling his back or falling across him, saving herself against the counter and then yelling at him to get the hell out of her way.

"Why do you do that?" she asked. "Sometimes I swear you're trying to kill me."

It wasn't his fault. The kitchen was small. He couldn't help being underfoot, especially when he was excited, and while she feared falling—how could she not, when it was all people talked about?—she was only seriously afraid of falling on the stairs. They were steep and treadless, polished hardwood. She could see herself tumbling down, somersaulting in a ball, her neck and spine vulnerable, landing awkwardly, her bones broken, and then not being found for days.

Living alone, she naturally imagined herself dying alone. She pictured Rufus lying by her side, waiting for her to wake up and feed him, saw him sniffing her face and baying. She felt bad for whoever discovered her. The odds were with Marcia, or possibly Arlene. They both had keys. What would they do with him while they were taking care of her? Rufus and Buster didn't get along, and Arlene wasn't a dog person. Emily could see Margaret taking him. Kenneth's would actually be better for him, with their big backyard, but Lisa would never agree to it. Conveniently, she had allergies.

The issue was moot—or at least Emily planned on outliving him. A pricklier question was whether he would be her last dog or not. She felt disloyal weighing it, yet the idea of being totally alone was even more discomfiting. She'd preemptively ruled out a puppy. She didn't have the energy to start all over again. Maybe an older rescue dog, they were supposed to be harder to place. A golden or a setter. She'd always liked water dogs.

For now she babied Rufus, plumping his bed and giving him kisses and softening his kibble with chicken broth. The cold lingered, so there was still snow on the ground, and in the afternoons she laid a fire and he came down, drawn by the smell, and slept by it while she read in Henry's chair. From time to time, as the stereo played and the pendulum of the grandfather clock flashed through its prescribed arc, she glanced up from the page to find an idyll—snow falling outside, flames leaping within, the faithful hound dozing on the hearth. Lying there on his side, he looked peaceful, his profile regal, the scion of a kingly line. She never felt tenderer toward him than when he was asleep.

He was her dog, just as Duchess was Henry's. Henry had never liked him, said he was too sneaky, and accused Emily of letting him take advantage of her. She defended him, though it was true. He could be sweet, keeping her company, and then a minute later wander into the kitchen and stick his nose in the garbage. He would eat anything—lettuce, tennis balls, wallets. Once he'd devoured an entire belt of Henry's, leaving just the buckle on the floor. For a week they found scraps of leather in his poo. There was no denying it, of all their dogs he was by far the worst, and yet that incorrigibility lent him a roguish charm. He wasn't dumb, like Duchess. He knew what he was doing, he just didn't care. His defiance, like his appetite, was a force of nature, and to see him so diminished was hard.

The day after Washington's birthday was a Saturday, and gray, almost no light penetrating the blinds, and while Emily was tempted to sleep late, she also had a long list of errands, the most important of which was buying the makings for a crumb cake she'd promised to bring for coffee hour tomorrow. As she showered, she made her grocery list, and was repeating it in her head when she opened her bedroom door. She wasn't thinking of Rufus, right behind her, newly awake and ravenous. Her sole focus was *baking powder, vanilla, light brown sugar, pie pan*. She only had to make it to the pad on the refrigerator, but she'd been forgetful lately, and didn't trust herself. She was on a mission, and strode into the hall before he could cut in front of her.

She glimpsed him peripherally as she turned at the head of the stairs. He was scurrying, trying to cut tight inside her, ducking through the gap between the newel post and her right leg. She could see he was going too fast and braced herself as he took the corner and his rear end went out from under him.

"Wait!" she commanded, too late. She was firmly planted, and he bounced off her leg, twisting, missing the first step completely, and sledded down sideways, out of control.

She froze, clutching the railing, and though it was useless, reached out her other hand, witchlike, as if she could magically stop him as he clunked and bumped from step to step, legs flailing, nails scrabbling for traction, finally rolling over on his shoulder and landing with a crash that shook the whole house.

She hurried down, gripping the railing, afraid he'd broken something.

He was limping, and seemed dazed, not looking at her, and she wondered if he had a concussion.

"You're okay," she said, kneeling to hold him so she could check his ribs and legs. All she felt were his lumps. "I know, that was scary. What do I always tell you: you need to be careful on the stairs. How does that feel? Okay, let's see your other paw."

She didn't find anything obvious. He still limped, favoring his rear left leg. She watched him with a clinical eye until she realized he was heading for the kitchen. He wanted his breakfast.

"You are something," she said. "I don't know what, but something."

She was equally amazed that in the midst of the emergency her list hadn't evaporated. She wrote it down while he ate. Baking powder, vanilla, light brown sugar, pie pan.

Of course, the vet wasn't open yet. If it was an emergency, she could leave a message—pointless, though she did anyway, explaining the situation. To her astonishment, they called back right at eight. If she was worried about him, by all means she should bring him in. "At his age," Michael the nurse said, "you want to be careful," because they knew Rufus there, and they knew her.

She had to help him into the Subaru. He could get his front paws up onto the rear deck, but she had to bend down and cradle his butt and lift him in—a move that she realized, even as she was doing it, was probably unwise.

Emergency or no, she still had to wait twenty minutes, enduring the stale hits and insulting commercials of some mysteriously chosen soft-rock station. Rufus strained at the leash, trying to reach all the different smells, while Emily recalled taking Margaret to the emergency room when she sprained her wrist ice-skating in Panther Hollow. She and Kenneth had collided and fallen awkwardly, and to this day Margaret claimed, partly though not completely joking, that Kenneth tripped her. Third grade, so she would have been ten. 1963. Not merely Henry and her parents, but Jack Kennedy was alive. The Vietnam War hadn't officially begun. Was it possible? Like any memory, it was a trick, tempting her to feel what was now entirely imaginary. She would not be comforted, though she could clearly see Margaret's thumb poking from her cast, crowded with the magic-markered names of her classmates.

"You're all set," Michael said, opening the Dutch door to the back.

"Hang on," Emily said, because Rufus was already pulling her out of her chair. "He thinks he's going to get a treat."

"Only if he's a good boy."

Dr. Magnuson was her favorite, she was grateful he was in today (Dr. Sharbaugh, his partner, could be distracted and curt, uninterested in Emily's history). Like Dr. Sayid, he was younger, and possessed a quiet decisiveness that calmed her. He was also very large, taller than Henry, a burly pink Swede with steel-rimmed glasses and lank, near-white hair. His lab coat only made him more imposing, yet he was soft-spoken and open, an attentive listener. His hands were thick mitts, and as he gently probed Rufus's back and hips and belly, he reminded her of a kindly giant in a children's story.

"He may have strained a ligament, but I'm not finding anything that would make me think it's more than that."

"Thank you so much," she said, holding a hand to her breastbone. "The way he fell, I thought for certain he'd broken something."

"You'll want to watch his output for a day or two, just in case. If you see any blood, either in his stool or his urine, I want you to bring him in right away."

"I will."

"I'd say he's very lucky."

"Did you hear that?" Emily said, nose to nose with Rufus. "You need to be careful. You can't go pushing in front of people whenever you feel like it."

The cost of the visit, as she would tell Arlene with pop-eyed astonishment, was highway robbery, but honestly, what choice did she have? She did not completely mean this. While logging the amount into her checkbook annoyed her, the doctor reassuring her that it was nothing serious was well worth it. She'd expected much worse.

At the edge of the parking lot, Rufus gave her an opportunity to check his pee. The stream was clear, melting a yellow hole in the snow. At home, she watched him pick a spot in the backyard and squat, then tugged on her boots and her jacket and crunched her way to the pile—nothing unusual, just poo.

"I think you're fine," she told him, as if he were faking, but that night after dinner she went out with a flashlight to make sure.

The next morning his limp was gone. She made him sit before opening the bedroom door.

"You wait," she said, holding up one finger as she slowly backed toward the stairs. "Wait. Good boy." She knelt down. "Okay, now you may proceed."

Her plan was to make him sit and wait there as well, but he'd waited enough, and scooted by her on the outside, clattering down the stairs and then spinning around at the bottom, looking up, his tail wagging, to see what was taking her so long.

"Excuse me," she said. "Let's try that again."

They began every day with this battle. At first she used treats to get his attention, which worked but which also made him drool all over the floor, and when she weaned him off them, he lost interest. He went two days, three, being good, then completely ignored her, turning at the bottom and racing for the kitchen as if he could get his own breakfast.

She didn't think he was too old to learn, he just didn't want to listen. It was a matter of being consistent. If anyone could do that, she could.

She stood at the top of the stairs, waiting for him to reappear.

He finally did, looking up at her expectantly.

"Let's go," she coaxed.

She clapped her hands.

"Come on."

He blinked at her vacantly, a blatant challenge.

She sighed. It was like having a child. His stubbornness spurred her own, but there was no place for her anger, which was doubly frustrating. He had to learn his lesson, for his own good.

"If that's how you want it," she said, "I can stand here all day."

EXPRESSIONS OF SYMPATHY

Lorraine Havermeyer was dead. Arlene didn't have all the details. She'd just gotten a call from Peggy Stevenson, who'd talked to Sukie Beach, who was friends with Roberta Joyner, who lived in the Webster Hall apartments. Apparently it was sudden, because she'd been at brunch on Sunday and seemed her usual bubbly self.

"That's awful," Emily said.

"I wonder how Edie's doing."

"I know."

"She had to be upwards of ninety."

"Somewhere around there," Emily said. "Still, you never thought of her that way."

"She always had a lot of energy."

"More than I ever had. Oh my. Lorraine."

"I thought you'd want to know."

"Thank you."

It was Thursday, early morning, and piercingly sunny, which added to the shock of it. Betty had come the day before, and the news made a mockery of her clean house. She couldn't picture Edie without Lorraine. Emily had considered them indestructible, a Greek chorus somehow immune to the follies and fates they reported. Like the death of anyone in their circle, it brought Emily closer to her own, as if they'd all moved up in line.

"They haven't set a date but I'd imagine it's Saturday."

"They're still at Ascension?"

"So you know parking will be a headache. Remember Millie Bennett's? What a debacle that was."

Emily had been thinking the exact same thing and was relieved that

Arlene would say it out loud. Death made her feel petty and self-involved, her current life unworthy of deeper inspection.

"We should send flowers," Emily said. "What did we do for Gloria's? That was nice."

"That was the lily wreath. I wasn't wild about the stand."

"What if we do the lilies in a vase?"

"It would be cheaper *and* nicer. Want me to order it?"

"Please," Emily said. "Just let me know what I owe you."

"Any preference, in terms of a vase?"

"I trust your judgment. Something simple."

"Gotcha," Arlene said.

Normally a call this time of day was an intrusion. Now, stunned and rudderless, Emily didn't want to get off, but finally let her go.

Poor Edie. Emily knew from losing Louise the desert emptiness she was facing, and was uncomfortably aware that if not for Arlene she herself would be totally alone. Was that why she'd wanted to keep talking, to say she appreciated her company, despite all their squabbles, or was death making her sentimental? She hadn't been that close to Lorraine.

The *Post-Gazette* ran her obituary the next day, topped with a soft-focus shot from another era: a dimpled, dark-haired girl in her twenties wearing a peaked garrison cap. As a child during the war, Emily had envied the WACS and WAVES who scaled rope ladders and elbow-crawled under barbed wire and danced the Lindy with their fellow GIs shipboard. From her seat in the rear balcony of the Penn Royal, she sailed to exotic ports and stumbled into foggy intrigues like Ann Sheridan. With her photographic memory and love of cryptograms, she thought she would make a good spy, and planned on signing up when she was old enough, but of course that, like so many of her vicarious lives, never happened, and to discover, too late, that Lorraine had actually been what she'd idly dreamed of becoming was humbling. How could she have been ignorant of this?

She parsed the long column and learned that Lorraine was only eighty-eight and had been born in Albany. During the war she'd been stationed at the naval yard in Hampton Roads, Virginia. After her honorable discharge, she was an auditor and later worked in employee benefits at Dravo, where she met her husband Edgar, retiring in 1982 after thirty-five years of service. She enjoyed quilting, cross-stitch and other needlework, and donated many pieces to UPMC-Oakland's neonatal ward. She was predeceased not only by Edgar, but by her five sisters.

Emily had often heard of Edgar, and seen pictures of Lorraine's children, grandchildren and great-grandchildren, but had no inkling of this other side of her—the quilting, for instance—and wondered if she'd known Lorraine at all. Emily herself had never fully divulged her history to anyone besides Henry and maybe Louise, but she'd never considered her past interesting. Like Kersey, it was something to shrug off. She went to elementary school, she went to high school, she went to college. She imagined friends from the club poring over her obituary. What about her life was surprising?

"I think I knew that about her," Arlene said. "She handed out uniforms or something. I can't believe they used that picture. When I die, promise me you'll get one that looks like me. Kenneth must have some."

"Agreed."

"I heard from Peggy that she went in her sleep."

"That's the way to go." Henry hadn't, nor Louise, and she felt unaccountably jealous, as if this final mercy had been withheld. Louise had been dead—hard to believe—for nearly a year now. Emily could just call back her voice, and how she perched sideways on the edge of her couch, ladylike, skirt smoothed, knees together, to stab an olive with a toothpick or pour them each another glass of wine. She should really visit her and Doug, but she hadn't been to see Henry or her parents in ages. When the weather turned, she'd take a day and make the drive to Kersey. It might be the last time.

Looking out the front window, she thought, as always, of visiting Kay Miller, though Kay would have no clue who she was. Emily knew the place, it was maybe ten minutes over the bridge. She really should. There was no excuse not to.

She sulked the day away, dumping her cold cup of tea in the sink, sighing as she logged the usual troop of jays and nuthatches and titmice in her bird journal. She didn't recall this black gloom descending when Millie

Bennett or Gloria Albright died. She suspected the weather contributed to it, and her worries about Rufus. Louise had been waiting for spring. "If I can just hold on till then," she said, "I know I'll feel better. The days being longer makes such a difference."

Emily herself felt the same way now. The flower show was only three weeks away but seemed far off. She'd been cooped up in the house too long, at the mercy of her own claustrophobic thoughts. Kenneth was coming for Easter—Lisa too, but they would steer clear of each other—and then it would be spring and she'd be busy in the garden. In the summer she lived in the backyard, weeding and sunning with Henry's transistor radio playing QED, enjoying leisurely meals on the porch, a glass of chilled Chablis with dinner. Late July, when the humidity grew oppressive, she'd close up the house, trusting Jim and Marcia to water her garden, and head for Chautauqua, where for a week the whole family would be reunited. More than anything, that was what she looked forward to, that week of renewal, at the end of which she would be desperate to get back to her solitude. It was all a cycle, this was just the hardest part. Logically, if she could make it through the dregs of last winter, the long, awful vigil by Louise's bedside, she could make it through this. After Henry, she could make it through anything.

In the morning, getting dressed, she discovered a dry-cleaning tag pinned to the cuff of her beaded jacket. The last time she'd worn it had been at Gloria's funeral. She wondered if anyone would notice, and thought, of all people, Lorraine would.

The service was scheduled for ten, meaning they needed to be there by nine-thirty at the very latest if they wanted a parking spot. Emily called ahead and Arlene was waiting for her at the bottom of her stairs. She'd had her hair done, the rich, artificial henna making her face seem pale.

"Morning," Emily said.

"Morning."

For a while they rode in silence, like strangers carpooling to work. They crossed the Fern Hollow bridge and snowy Homewood Cemetery slid by on the right, the headstones and mausoleums dotting the gentle hills. Arlene flipped down the vanity mirror and freshened her lipstick, then snapped shut her clasp purse.

"I expect it will be catered."

"I'd imagine so," Emily said.

"Remember Gene Hubbard's?"

"I doubt it will be that lavish."

"Whoever did his, that's the kind of reception I want."

"The cannoli."

"The cannoli, the crab puffs, the little cheese-and-spinach thingies."

"Empanadas."

"And no sandwiches. I don't want people to have to make their own sandwiches."

"It's not a picnic," Emily said, egging her on.

"That's right. And it's not a pick-up dinner party. No eating off of your knees. Give people a table so they can eat properly."

Once, Emily would have thought this conversation the height of crassness, but as a regular guest at these all-too-frequent gatherings, she harbored the same complaints, and the same hope that her own reception would be a success. She'd begun planning her service directly after Henry's, choosing the music and the readings, tinkering every so often with improvements, updating her ideas and filing them in a folder she kept with her most important papers. To impress upon the children that she was serious, she occasionally brought up the topic, but, as with her will, Kenneth and Margaret were uncomfortable discussing it. They probably thought her morbid or obsessed. Emily couldn't explain: making her wishes plain, once and for all, was comforting. She trusted they would honor them. In case there was any confusion, each time she made changes she sent Gordon a copy for safekeeping. The Bach toccata, the Buxtehude prelude, the Libera Me from Duruflé's Requiem. Just thinking of the sequence of pieces warmed her like a pleasant memory. The great shame was that she wouldn't be there to hear it.

They came down Forbes, through Carnegie-Mellon, the wide plazas and crisscrossed walks of the campus deserted after last night's frat parties. In Oakland, the restaurants were closed. Crammed in nose-to-tail, students' old Volvos and Camrys filled every available parking spot.

Church of the Ascension was a squat armory of black stone tucked behind the more imposing St. Paul's on Fifth Avenue, and only a few blocks from Webster Hall, convenient for members of their set who'd relocated from Squirrel Hill and Edgewood and Fox Chapel. Emily was familiar with the lot from a decade of dropping the children off to catch the bus to Calvary Camp. Land was too dear here, so close to the university. In the front there was barely enough room to angle the two charter buses so their noses infringed upon the sidewalk; the narrow alley that ran around the side was a fire lane; in back there were just three stunted rows—the one along the wall handicapped, the middle reserved for clergy and vestry, leaving parishioners to vie for the spaces against the fence or roam the streets. Even in the summer, with Pitt on vacation, Henry had to put his flashers on and double-park on crowded Ellsworth as the counselors pitched in to lug Kenneth and Margaret's footlockers and sleeping bags to the open cargo hold.

Today the church was offering valet parking. Near the stairs a pair of attendants in matching jackets and watch caps stood by a line of orange traffic cones.

"That's smart," Arlene said.

As glad as she was not to have to find a spot, Emily had never let anyone drive the Subaru, and relinquished her keys with some misgiving. She was also not sure if she had any ones to tip him with afterward, and on principle resented the pressure. This was exactly the kind of thing she hoped to spare her guests. No one would have to pay to see her off.

The stairs were oversalted and treacherous, grains like shattered safety glass crunching underfoot. Arlene clung to the railing as if it were a lifeline, Emily steadying her elbow. An usher saw her struggling and opened the heavy door for them.

As Emily stepped into the dim narthex, the bass drone of the organ and stuffy, tallow-scented air enveloped her, inducing a cleansing reverence. She liked the idea of shedding the world, and her worst self, if only temporarily. They were early, the pews nearly empty. On all sides, the vault amplified the low murmur of voices, a cough, the scuff of shoes on marble. She accepted a program from an usher, and together she and Arlene processed down the aisle, surveying the scattered mourners as they searched for a good seat. Myra Frost and Barbara Chase turned to them as they passed, and Emily dipped her head in greeting. Peggy Stevenson was there with Bev Howard, and two rows beyond them but still a respectful distance from the front, Rand and Graceann Beers, tan from their time-share in Delray Beach, their teeth unnaturally white.

"I'm surprised none of the family's here yet," Arlene said once they'd gotten situated.

"I'm sorry. I thought we'd have more trouble parking."

"I'm not complaining. Do you see our lilies anywhere?"

"They're just to the left there."

"I swear I'm going blind."

"On the steps." Emily pointed. "I like the vase."

"I asked for the plainest one they had."

"They did a nice job. You'll have to let me know what I owe you."

The crowd straggled in, stooped and doddering, propped up by the young like the walking wounded. Most they hadn't seen since Christmas, some since Thanksgiving, and their presence was a relief—like that of Claude and Liz Penman, though she was still in a chair and appeared to have lost weight. As at any club function, a few would be conspicuously missing, their health speculated upon endlessly.

While Arlene craned around, Emily appraised the program as if they were at a concert. She expected the selections to be interesting, given that Lorraine and Edie were what Doug Pickering called culture vultures, but she was startled to find, right at the top, her Buxtehude Prelude in G minor.

Had she mentioned it to Lorraine? Because Donald Wilkins hadn't played it in ages. The rest of the program was fairly standard, some florid Charpentier and the always safe Clarke, a couple of Bach warhorses. Besides the Buxtehude, it might have been thrown together on short notice by any musical director.

This is mine, she wanted to protest to Arlene—she had the papers to prove it—and only held back out of shame. Was she really that selfish?

No, because when the organist played it, with Lorraine's family and

Edie gathered in the two front pews, surrounded by a heartening show of old friends, Emily felt the same sense of peace that came over her at home. He rushed the limpid middle section, but on the whole she was pleased.

Father Waters delivered the homily, on the use God had for each of them. Like Father Lewis at Calvary, George Waters was on the civilized side of the Anglican debate, which, from countless coffee hours, Emily understood as a power struggle rather than a referendum on gays, though, as usual, the right-wing types aimed their arguments at the most vulnerable minority, a tactic which seemed decidedly un-Christian to her. In the diocesan newsletter, Father Waters had written an open rebuke to the new bishop of Pittsburgh, who was threatening—as leverage, if nothing else— to seize the assets of several prominent congregations, among them Calvary, prompting talk of lawsuits. She was predisposed to listen to Father Waters, yet as he spoke of Lorraine's many roles as daughter, wife, mother, grandmother and friend (nodding to Edie), though Emily knew she was wrong, instead of contemplating her own usefulness, her mind circled back to the impossible coincidence, trying to conjure an explanation. It bothered her that it bothered her. Did she think herself better than Lorraine, somehow more deserving or worthy of Buxtehude's genius? She could just hear her mother dressing her down for thinking she was special. *I don't know where you got that idea, because that is not how I raised you.*

The Charpentier, blaring, brought her back to the present. To stanch her thoughts, she concentrated on Father Waters leading the prayers, asking God to protect and sustain his servant Lorraine in eternal life, a promise Emily needed to believe in and wished earnestly for Lorraine, and, by doing so, regained herself.

During the pensive, somber Bach, she decided it wasn't Lorraine or Louise or the Buxtehude that had her so overwrought, but the tenuousness of everything. It had been a rough winter, with Arlene going into the hospital, and Sarah giving her her cold. It was no exaggeration to say the next funeral she attended could be her own. She expected the worst now, not out of self-pity (though heaven knew she wasn't immune to it) but because at her age, realistically, that was what awaited her. Most of the time she distracted herself from that base knowledge by crafting her elaborate plans.

Here, faced with the smallest chink in them, she panicked. Her death would not be special, and why should it? Her mother was right. They were all equal in the eyes of God.

The reception was in the refectory—a buffet ranked with chafing dishes and round tables set along the walls—but before the guests could sample a bite they had to run the gauntlet of the receiving line. Lorraine's family was well represented, a husky, rosy-cheeked clan of Scandinavians. Neither she nor Arlene knew any of them. The hall was high-ceilinged, and with so many people talking, Emily couldn't hear well. She followed Arlene, moving from person to person, offering her hand and leaning in to introduce herself and convey, over and over, the same condolences. "She was a dear, dear friend, always interested in everything."

At the very end, the family had thoughtfully included Edie, who, rather than sobbing and stricken, was smiling, her face fixed in a beatific rictus, as if she were being congratulated. Beside the clan of pale giants, she seemed small and dark and fragile. For the first time Emily could recall, she embraced Arlene.

"I had no idea Lorraine had so many children," Arlene said.

"They've been so wonderful," Edie said. "Father Waters did such a nice job. And thank you both so much for the flowers."

Edie opened her arms and Emily held her a moment, then let go, the smell of her powder lingering. She wanted to say she was sorry, that she knew it was a terrible loss, but Edie was beaming adamantly, and she deferred to her better judgment.

"It was lovely," Emily said, nodding to reinforce her point. "The music was beautiful."

THE DAMAGE

It wasn't until several days later, unlocking the car after picking up her dry cleaning, that she saw the scratches on the door. Twin zigzagging gashes, as if someone had taken a barbecue fork to her paint job.

She stopped, arrested, her keys still in the lock, and made the same incredulous, disgusted face she made when she found a mouse stuck to a glue trap in the basement. She rubbed at the gouges with a gloved thumb, as if they might come away with the gray winter buildup of dried salt, but the clean smudge only made them more noticeable. They were deep, revealing a lighter color underneath—primer or bare metal. Possibly a body shop could buff them out, that would be the cheapest route. She wasn't sure what her insurance covered, or what this might do to her premiums. In any case, it would be expensive and time-consuming.

Up until then she'd been having a productive afternoon. She didn't let the discovery deflect her, continuing on to the post office and the library, yet even as she crossed off these errands, a feeling of pointlessness overtook her, all of her care and diligence squandered by a momentary lapse. Because her intuition had been correct. There was a good reason she hadn't wanted to give up her keys, and now she scolded herself for not listening to her inner voice.

There was no way to prove it had happened at the funeral, and even if she could, who would take responsibility? Not the valets. No doubt the company protected itself with a clause on their claim checks saying she was entrusting the car to them at her own risk. And imagine—she'd tipped them.

"It was bound to happen sooner or later," Kenneth said, a notion she rejected yet could not logically refute. Bostonians, he and Lisa were accustomed to dings; it was part of driving in the city. They'd never think of fixing something as small as a scratch, but of course their battlewagon had two hundred thousand on it, where her car was brand-new. As always when she sought his advice, he brought forth his store of experience, making his case, and then, reflecting further, retreated to a perfect disinterest, as if the decision and its consequences were hers alone, which they were. What she wanted was for him to tell her what to do—as Henry would have, cars being his province—but Kenneth was unwilling to prescribe his opinions, and she hung up even more frustrated than before.

Margaret sympathized. The minivan's transmission was slipping again. The estimate was more than the damn thing was worth, but she didn't have the money to replace it, so for now Ron was letting her drive his BMW, an arrangement she wasn't entirely comfortable with, given the uncertain state of their relationship, the particulars of which she didn't feel like getting into. As interested as Emily was in Margaret's love life, she recognized that Margaret had once again trumped her problems with her own, indirectly belittling them, and rather than try to refocus the conversation, she changed the subject.

Betty recommended a product she'd seen on TV. You squeezed a blob of this compound on the scratch, then let it sit for fifteen minutes. What happened was that the chemical broke down the paint so when you rubbed it around, you were covering the scratch with the original color. All you needed was a rag. Toni had used it on her Beretta and it looked like new. Betty still had the tube somewhere downstairs. "Before you use it," she said, "you definitely want to test it on a part of the car you don't see, like the edge of a door or something."

Normally Betty was the voice of reason, but in this case one look at her rickety little Nissan disqualified her. Emily thanked her for her offer as if she might take her up on it later, but for now she was still making up her mind.

After transferring and putting her on hold twice, her insurance company said she was covered for the repair, but, naturally, only after she'd fulfilled her deductible, which was five hundred dollars. As to whether filing a claim would affect her premiums, the representative (Alicia, whose name Emily had jotted down to have some record of the conversation) couldn't say. That would depend on a number of factors. Would she like to speak with an adjuster?

Once again she faced the classic dilemma: the onetime lump sum vs. the endless monthly payment. At her age, every financial decision she made had to take into account her life expectancy, as if she were betting against herself. The idea that someone besides her children should profit from her death, or her lack of clairvoyance in the matter, was insulting, yet so often that's what it came down to.

"No, thank you," she said, and, once off, marveled again at how the industry worked. Essentially they insured themselves against paying any claims. The only recourse, she thought, would be to go and burn down their headquarters, forcing them to submit a claim to *their* insurer. But then, of course, they'd both simply raise their rates—like the oil companies, passing their expenses but not their record profits along to the consumer.

The next day, unable to bear the unresolved issue any longer, she made an appointment at the dealership. The next Monday she drove out to McKnight Road in a spitting rain and waited two hours in a stifling room with a rotating cast of fellow Subaru owners while a TV blared idiotic talk shows.

The bill was just under five hundred dollars, so she'd made the right choice by not filing. This was no consolation. Neither, strangely, was the pristine finish of her driver's-side door. When the car was new she often caught herself admiring her reflection in the deep azure clearcoat. Now each time she gazed upon its glossy surface, instead of the pleasure of perfection, she saw only the flaw of her lost four hundred and seventy-eight dollars, and vowed she would never be so careless again.

SPRING AHEAD

Saturday night, after putting Rufus out one last time, she added an hour to the wall clock in the kitchen. She'd had a glass of wine by the fire, and poked hopefully at the controls of the stove and then the microwave, the blue digits racing past the correct time before she could stop them, and had to go around again.

The newscasters didn't have to remind her. She'd been waiting all day. It was the only thing on her calendar.

God, she thought, *if that isn't a sad commentary.*

She used the square-shanked key to do the grandfather clock, inserting it into the face painted with the heavens and twisting gently, letting the chimes play to the end before continuing, afraid she might damage the mechanism.

"Go on up," she told Rufus, who was watching her from across the room. "I'll be there in a minute."

He went, leaving her to fine-tune the universe. Technically they were supposed to change their clocks at two in the morning, as if—Margaret had complained as if it were a personal affront—no one would notice. Unlike Margaret, Emily didn't feel cheated out of an hour. She saw daylight savings as a fresh start, like punching a reset button. At this stage of the winter she'd do anything to hurry the season along. With every twist of the key, she was that much closer to Easter, and Kenneth's visit.

Upstairs she fixed the banjo clock in the den, the old white-numbered clock radios in the children's rooms, and finally the trusty one on her nightstand. She undid Henry's Hamilton from around her wrist, pulled the stem out and rolled its ridged edge between her thumb and forefinger, then set the watch on her dresser.

She read for a while, some middling library mystery, her body not yet honoring the change. Downstairs, prematurely, the grandfather clock struck eleven. She couldn't recall the last time she'd been up this late, and tried not to let the chimes intimidate her. Tomorrow would be here soon enough, her mother used to say, encouraging her to put away the Little Golden Book she was reading and sleep. Then, as now, she reluctantly marked her place and turned out the light.

Lying there with the false hour glowing over her shoulder, she reflected on the arbitrary, changeable nature of time, and how, at her age, she was almost free of it. The idea pleased her, as if she'd discovered something elemental. Springing ahead was an official admission that no clock could ever measure the rotation of the earth, or the earth around the sun, birth and death, the turning seasons, the thrust of new shoots. Though she couldn't quite say why it was a comfort, floating in this unmapped, in-between state, she appreciated time being imaginary and malleable, as if, knowing its secret, she might loosen its hold on her. But in the morning, when she woke, it was still dark out, and she was a full hour behind. She had to hurry to get ready for church and then was late picking up Arlene.

THE FLOWER SHOW

They came every year, like pilgrims. Women of a certain age, her mother called them, a polite way of saying old bags. For months they'd been saving the date, the invitation to members stuck to the fridge, pinned to the kitchen bulletin board. This was the real beginning of spring, the gathering of the tribe. Survivors, believers, they flocked from across the city, made the trek in to gritty Oakland from the tony suburbs, curling around the Gothic rocket ship of the Cathedral of Learning, back past the library and Flagstaff Hill to the edge of Schenley Park. There might be snow on the golf course, the trees bare, but inside the peaked glass palace of Phipps Conservatory, the world was in bloom.

Along the walkway leading to the new welcome center, before they even reached the front doors, Emily and Arlene had to stop and marvel at the beds of frilly, butter-colored daffodils open well ahead of schedule, as if they belonged to a different climate.

"You think the ground is heated?" Arlene asked, snooping about for a wire.

"I imagine they're transplants. This mulch is new."

The lobby of the welcome center was all light and curved white walls, a dozen conversations mingling, filling the atrium. From the domed ceiling hung a massive chandelier the color of marigolds, made from hundreds of tubes of blown glass like the balloons clowns twisted into animals for children. It was supposed to be modern and whimsical but was merely labored and ugly—at that scale, aggressively so.

"Oh my," Emily said.

"I think I like it," Arlene said.

"You're not serious."

"I am."

They checked their coats but kept their pocketbooks. Rather than ask Arlene to attempt the sweeping, ramplike staircase, they took the elevator up the one flight with several brightly dressed garden club types, one of whom steered a gray-wheeled walker.

The door rolled open on lush jungle—towering palms and rubber trees, stands of bamboo, a profusion of orchids, but also overflowing baskets of hydrangeas, and along the low red-brick walls, orderly borders of white tulips. The air was moist and warm, the dripping humidity at once foreign and familiar, exhilarating. To Emily, the smell of wet, turned earth was a promise. In a few weeks she'd be on her hands and knees in the backyard, happily occupied, the long winter forgotten.

That was how time passed—waiting through everything else to do the thing you wanted. How little fell into that category now: Easter, her garden, Chautauqua. She thought there should be more to live for.

They escaped the busy crossroads of the Palm Court with its benches and piped-in Mozart and wound their way back through the rocky grottos. Underfoot, the concrete was wet in patches, as if a hidden stream had slipped its banks. A Girl Scout troop passed them coming the other way, snaking by single file. "It smelled like butterscotch," one said, making Emily smile.

Like the aviary or Buhl Planetarium, the conservatory was a magical destination for young and old. Over the years she'd faithfully taken the children and grandchildren, and it was impossible to walk the meandering paths without seeing Margaret or Sam dashing ahead of them, then turning around to hurry them along to the next wonder. Kenneth loved to hide beneath the stone bridge in the Fern Room and menace them like a troll, his hands curled into claws. Half forest, half maze, the place was straight out of a fairy tale, though, like a fairy tale, once the children reached their teens, it no longer enchanted them. Now, as with so many things, with Louise gone, the only person she had to share it with was Arlene.

The day was overcast. With just the natural light filtering through the panes, Arlene couldn't decipher the helpful labels on stakes. Emily craned in to read: *Swiss-Cheese Plant (Monstera Deliciosa).*

"Is it supposed to smell like Swiss cheese? It doesn't look like it."

They sniffed. They shrugged. It was a mystery.

In the Serpentine Room, among the fragrant hyacinths and delphiniums, they came upon another ridiculous glass sculpture, this one a cotton-candy starburst, utterly incongruous.

"Don't tell me there's one in every room."

A large placard gave the artist's name. She had to try it twice—Chihuly.

"I think he's supposed to be famous," Arlene said.

"Can't he be famous somewhere else?"

They strolled on.

"Look at those," Emily said.

"Aren't they funny."

"Are they jack-in-the-pulpits, maybe?"

"I don't know what they are."

"Do you like snapdragons?"

"I do like snapdragons."

In the Fern Room, syrupy strings embellished a familiar melody Emily couldn't quite place. "What is this awful music?"

"Sounds like 'Moon River.'"

"Why on earth would they play that here?"

The humidity grew oppressive as they penetrated deeper into the rain forest. In the Orchid Room a drop of water splashed off her shoulder. The windows were steamed, weeping green streaks of algae. Fans blew, making the heavy fronds nod.

"Watch out for this," Arlene said, pushing aside a strand of Spanish moss.

"Thank you."

Arlene stopped by the goldfish pond—a homely touch in all the hot-house exotica, Emily had always thought, though the children were fascinated with it, begging Henry to install one in the backyard, a bill she successfully tabled, knowing that, like the Millers', it would quickly lose its novelty and become a breeding ground for mosquitoes. The fish hung suspended, undisturbed by their presence, lazily flicking their tails, bending the gridlike reflection of the ironwork ceiling.

Emily didn't find them at all interesting, and instead watched Arlene cough long and hard into her fist, then lift her chin and clear her throat. Her scar was just a faint pink seam cutting through her deeply creased forehead. She hadn't stopped smoking, as the doctor ordered. Besides being wobbly on her feet, and her eyesight going, even when she was at rest she wheezed emphysemically, like now, breathing with her mouth open, lipstick on her front teeth. She was three years older than Henry, and he'd been gone almost seven years. Emily knew how quickly a person's health could turn, and wondered if the Eat 'n Park episode was isolated or the beginning of an inexorable slide.

Should she tell her she was worried about her?

She could hear Henry say yes, definitely, but now was not the time. She would have ample opportunity in the car, though this stirred memories of trying to reach Margaret as they drove home in their old station wagon from ballet class or riding lessons. Somehow Emily was never gentle, never politic enough. Thin-skinned herself, she had a talent for saying precisely the right thing to escalate the situation. "Do you think I should be happy you were suspended and not expelled?" Arlene might be offended, or hurt, or merely irritated. Knowing how hard quitting would be, she'd asked Emily not to think badly of her if she couldn't, and Emily had agreed. That wasn't what this was about. If she kept smoking, she wouldn't be around for Emily to think badly of her. Was that what she wanted? The last thing Emily wanted to do was harangue her. That's how it would sound. She'd have to bide her time and find the right moment to drop a calm observation free of judgment. *You don't sound well,* she might say, instead of *You sound awful.* Or, *That woman with the walker seems to get around nicely,* instead of *You're going to fall and break something and then you'll be in real trouble.*

NO WHEELCHAIRS, read a sign by the opening of the Stove Room, STEEP RAMP AHEAD. Trailing, Emily dawdled, as if giving Arlene the option. The path dropped down around a curve, a mossy rock wall rising on one side, water welling from the bottom. Arlene never hesitated, using the handrail to steady herself.

"Watch," she warned Emily, "this is a little slick."

Below the curve, they passed through a tunnel, the air surprisingly cool and dank. The ramp on the far side wasn't much more than a gentle rise. Emily suspected the trustees were just covering themselves.

The highlight of the room was the chocolate tree, the name of which excited the children but in itself was less impressive than the banana trees with their tempting green bunches.

"They always look upside down to me," Arlene said.

"I used to know the reason they do that."

They'd had enough of ferns, and retraced their steps through the Serpentine Room and the Palm Court to the South Conservatory, where all pretense of imitating nature gave way to a symmetrical display of pastel tulips and stepped reflecting pools framing another dreadful blown-glass confection. They liked the Sunken Garden and its trickling fountains better, though a wailing toddler strongly disagreed. Emily felt a bit tired herself, but kept on, knowing there wasn't much farther to go.

Mercifully there was no music in the Desert Room—Kenneth's favorite, with its baked air and austere rocks and potted cacti: bunny ears and squat barrels and man-sized saguaros. Beside a massive aloe with bladelike leaves stood a denuded, sawed-off trunk about four feet high with a sign: I'M NOT DEAD, I'M DORMANT. It was supposed to be a joke, though Emily failed to see the humor. She immediately rejected the idea that it might apply to her.

"What does it say?" Arlene asked, and shouldered in close as Emily read: "African tree grape. As winter approaches and the amount of natural light decreases, African tree grapes lose their leaves and become dormant, just like maples and oaks. Watch for new leaves to appear in the spring."

"That makes sense."

"I guess it's not spring yet," Emily said.

As they pressed on, surrounded by teeming green life, the bare stump nagged at her. Like the gussied-up garden club ladies, they'd come to celebrate beauty and renewal, to worship perfection and pick nits, but now the falseness of the entire enterprise struck her. Where were the blighted and dried-up plants, the withered and sere? Hidden away, discarded. Why did it bother her? Was it just the sign, and her too-hasty denial? She knew she was being morbidly sensitive, taking it personally, and yet the more she pondered her reaction, the more she resented the African tree grape, as if whoever included it did so just to puzzle her.

The Victoria Room was entirely black and white, Doric columns and plaster casts of classical statuary rising from an inky pool. Emily supposed the design was meant to point up the decadence of those turn-of-the-century botanists who finally succeeded in breeding black orchids and roses, but why were visitors (in this case two noisy boys) encouraged to monkey with a console on the railing that controlled the fountains?

The East and Broderie Rooms were taken up by similar dioramas, fussy fantastical stage sets meant to astonish, one all blue, the other all white, including live butterflies.

"It's too much," Emily said.

"I like the butterflies."

"That's about it, though."

They'd completed the main circuit, and their feet hurt. They'd seen enough for one day, they agreed. They'd come back when it was warmer out and tour the Japanese and aquatic gardens.

"It was nice," Arlene said, looking about the Palm Court as they waited for the elevator.

"It always is," Emily said.

There was nothing they wanted in the gift shop, and the café was too loud and expensive. On the way out, Arlene couldn't pass the wishing well without digging in her pocketbook. She did this everywhere they went, and had for years, it was a compulsion with her. At their age, Emily wondered, what was there left to wish for?

Arlene turned to her. "Do you have a penny?"

Emily sighed and fished one from her change purse.

"Thank you." She dropped it in and smiled as if she knew she was being childish.

Outside, they returned to the gray world of Pittsburgh, which now seemed even deader and more dormant than before. Dark-bottomed clouds sat right down on the treetops. The air was bracing and smelled of mud and last fall's leaves. It would rain later—no, it was already starting, drops dotting the sidewalk, dappling the car windows.

They'd arrived early enough to find a space in the long atoll that bracketed Edward Bigelow's statue. Emily unlocked the doors with her remote, the lights winking acknowledgment, and they hustled across, ducking inside just as the downpour struck, drumming the roof, plinking white off the hood. Emily got the wipers going, and the defroster.

"I think we were very lucky," Arlene said, wheezing.

Emily was tempted to bring up her smoking, but thought it would be small of her right then, and agreed. It was so rare that they could say that. And to think she'd begrudged Arlene a penny. At the mercy of the fates, they needed all the luck they could get.

"You know," Emily said, "I get half of your wish if it comes true."

"Is that how it works?"

"In a capital market, yes."

"You already do anyway."

"How's that?"

"I wished that we'll both be back next spring."

Why was she so surprised? Because she hadn't been thinking of Arlene in nearly the same way? Or because she didn't think the odds of that happening were very good?

"That's a nice wish," Emily said. "I hope it does come true."

THE PROBLEM WITH GOOD FRIDAY

For weeks she'd been trying to pin down Kenneth on the specifics of their visit. Were Ella and Sam still coming? What time did they expect to arrive? Please, she needed to know as soon as they booked their flights so she could plan accordingly. Betty was coming special, and she had food shopping to do. Her real worry was that while he waffled and stalled, Ella might make other plans with her friend Suzanne. He refused to commit to anything, saying it depended on whether Lisa could get Friday off. As crazy as it sounded, the Cambridge Public Schools didn't consider it a holiday.

She knew he wasn't telling her the truth. Like Henry, he didn't want to disappoint her, and often withheld upsetting news until it was too late for her to intervene. The promise of their visit had sustained her for so long that any deviation from the ideal felt like a slight. Maybe in her frustration she was being uncharitable, but behind his evasiveness she sensed the hand of Lisa. It would be just like her to drag her feet and then cancel at the last minute.

Last Christmas when they visited, Lisa had affected a fraudulent helpfulness, cheerily pitching in with the children to clear the table and do the dishes rather than sit and talk over coffee. She joined the family around the fire, playing Scrabble and Parcheesi, but said little to Emily, and nothing of substance. They'd never gotten along. It wasn't as if there'd been a honeymoon and then a falling out. Over the years their mutual dislike had calcified, their relationship fixed and incomplete. Emily didn't expect that to change now. While she was aware it was a great failure of character, she wasn't magnanimous enough to forgive her. In fact, she held it against Lisa that by surviving Emily she might think she'd prevailed.

The shame of it was that Henry's mother had been so kind. Lillian had taught Emily so much that she would always be grateful to her. Coming from Kersey, alone in a forbidding city, Emily had been eager to learn. As a new mother-in-law, she'd wanted to do the same for Lisa, but from the beginning Lisa acted as if she knew better—as if, in her insistence on passing along those time-tested lessons, Emily was ignorant and out of touch. Any motherly advice she might give, Lisa would counter by citing her gaggle of friends, all of whom relied on child care while they worked full-time. Emily thought it only common sense to protest this scheme of things, voting in favor of her staying home until Ella was at least three or four, a suggestion that more than once met with disdainful silence.

Emily tried to appeal to her counterpart, on generational grounds, but, having resorted to nannies herself, Mrs. Sanner sided with Lisa. Born on the North Shore, Ginny Sanner belonged to a loftier set than Emily had ever aspired to, the world of Miss Porter's and sailing lessons on the Vineyard. There was nothing Emily could teach her daughter, nothing practical, that is, unless one included the outmoded principles—prized only in places like Kersey—of frugality and basic etiquette.

Emily liked to think she didn't need anything from Lisa, yet Lisa held the ultimate power over her—the ability to deprive Emily of time with Kenneth and the grandchildren. Even Margaret at her worst understood that family trumped their personal battles. Lisa felt no such compunction. Thanksgiving was typical. She invited Emily to the Cape, belatedly, knowing she wouldn't have time to make arrangements, sentencing her and Arlene to the buffet at the club.

It wasn't the first perfunctory invitation, transparent to all involved. Their every exchange—channeled unfairly through the intermediary of Kenneth—involved calculation and subterfuge, and Emily feared this was just another instance. Lisa wasn't a teacher but a guidance counselor. How hard would it be to take the day off?

The problem, Kenneth said, was that she'd used the last of her vacation days for their twenty-fifth anniversary trip to Florida, and her principal wouldn't let her take a sick day to make a three-day weekend.

"What if she was actually sick?" Emily asked.

"It's too obvious."

"But the three of you are still planning on coming?"

"We're still planning on coming."

That hard-won admission should have been a victory—Ella coming by herself would have been enough—yet Emily still felt cheated, as if once again Lisa had publicly insulted her.

Why did she let it bother her? Honestly, she didn't want to see Lisa, had nothing whatsoever to say to her. The visit would go smoother without her. It was just pride.

"I swear," Betty said over their plate of Milanos, "you two are a pair."

"I beg your pardon, but I am nothing like her."

"I bet she says the same thing."

"What is that supposed to mean?"

"Nothing, Emily. Just that it's nothing new between you two. I wouldn't have the energy for it. It's like me and Jesse. It's not that we're getting any mellower in our old age, we're just too tired to fight all the time."

"It's not all the time."

"Just whenever you're together."

"Not true," Emily protested, as if it were a joke, but later, making the bed in Kenneth's room, she realized it was technically untrue for another, uglier reason. She and Lisa didn't even need to be in the same place to argue. A face-to-face confrontation was rare, and by design they barely spoke on the phone. No, at this stage all Emily had to do was think of her.

CURIOUS

Of the grandchildren, Ella had always been her favorite. Slim and bookish, she reminded Emily of her younger self, a judgment that changed only slightly when, her freshman year at Wellesley, Ella declared that she was—and had always been—a lesbian. Kenneth had broken the news to Emily, joking that he and Lisa weren't exactly shocked, as if Emily, who was, should have picked up on the clues.

Emily wasn't sure what those would be. Compared to Sarah, who'd inherited Margaret's and her own straight nose and high cheekbones, Ella was plain, a bit moon-faced and weak-chinned like Lisa, but still appealing. Dimpled and long-limbed, she had a nice smile and a lean figure perfect for evening wear. Her hair was bobbed but not severe. She wasn't a tomboy, like the few Emily had known in her youth, but a shy, smart girl. Emily had never been distressed at Ella's lack of boyfriends, attributing it not to any lack of attractiveness or desire but to her seriousness and discriminating taste. In retrospect, Emily wasn't sure if she'd been fooled or if she'd fooled herself.

Ella Bella met a fella, she used to tease her, and she supposed she just assumed that would happen. In her vicarious pride she'd anticipated those same milestones she herself had felt lucky to reach: marriage, children, grandchildren. Not that Ella couldn't have all of these things—times had changed, there were infinite variations of family—and yet Emily, while righteously vowing to be supportive, had to admit some sadness at the revelation, as if life had suddenly gotten harder for Ella, and Emily could do nothing to protect her from it.

At first, Emily half entertained the idea that this adamant and showy stand was just a phase, like Margaret's many attempts to scandalize them, or her own overeager rejection of Kersey. In her sorority, it was common for sisters to share a bond as strong as—if not stronger than—any fleeting romantic attachment to men, who orbited the house like distant, mysterious planets, making brief, seismic contact and then receding without explanation. Women would always be more understanding, their feelings toward each other deeper, more complicated, for better or worse. It might be that Ella, never outgoing, had mistaken the quieter, more reliable affections of friendship for love. Emily wondered what tenderness had moved and then convinced her, and when, though as time passed, this line of questioning grew more and more moot, so much so that Emily realized it might be perceived as objectionable (by Lisa, if no one else), and set it aside.

Ella and Suzanne had been together nearly a year. They shared a one-bedroom in Somerville with a Scottie named Jack Sparrow. Suzanne was getting her PhD in environmental engineering at Tufts. Emily had seen pictures of her—a gaunt blonde with a ponytail and a marathoner's body, always sporting a windbreaker and athletic sunglasses for some outdoor activity—but had yet to meet her in person.

While Emily was supremely interested in the domestic arrangements of all her grandchildren—as she was concerned with their well-being and happiness—she drew the line at their intimate lives. She might picture Sarah and her beau Max enjoying a glass of wine at a candlelit restaurant or kissing on a balcony overlooking Lake Michigan, but her imagination, possessed of a delicate censor, didn't follow them any further. She wasn't interested in the couplings of the boys and their various girlfriends, the mechanics of which she expected were similar, the commonplace ecstasies of the young. Though she wished it did, the same decorousness didn't extend to Ella and Suzanne.

Despite herself, at the most inopportune moments (speaking to Arlene about them, or on the phone with Kenneth) she was seized by visions of them in bed—not vaguely pornographic, let alone *in flagrante*, just the two of them lying there side by side, occasionally reading, sharing the covers and pillows like any other couple. This pointless voyeurism disturbed her, signaling, as it did, her ongoing confusion and curiosity about Ella's orientation. Whenever Emily's mind strayed toward the bedroom door, she tried to remember what a pleasant, helpful child Ella had been, a proud holder of yarn and folder of towels, and what joy Emily had taken in her company, the two of them kindred spirits. Back then, unfairly, she often fantasized about how much easier her life would have been if Ella had been her daughter. Did she still feel that way?

Just the fact that she had to ask made her worry. She considered herself tolerant and cosmopolitan, as if by leaving Kersey she could escape its small-mindedness. In her childhood the Italians and Swedes lived on the wrong side of the tracks, and were thought not just poor but filthy, breeding freely like animals. Well into the 1980s, her Grandmother Benton used the term "darkies," and parroted the racial clichés of her youth. Her own mother, a dedicated teacher and proud suffragette, had a habit of reading names from the paper and asking, "Is that Jewish?" Henry and the children were properly horrified. Emily, knowing the climate that bred such ignorance, was both more forgiving and more resigned. Isolated and intractable, they were victims of the times. As sad as it was, nothing would change their views except death. She was afraid that in this case she might be the same, that somehow, unconsciously, against her will, she harbored a deep-seated prejudice against a person she adored, and, terrified that Ella might find out and their relationship might change forever, Emily tended to overcompensate, as she did now, smothering Ella in a hug the moment she stepped through the door and holding on too long. Rufus capered around them, barking as if Emily were being attacked.

Even in her bulky old peacoat Ella was willowy, her wrists bony—just as Emily had been at her age.

"Look at you," Emily said. "You're wasting away to nothing."

"I am not."

"*Down!* I'm kidding, you look good. You look happy."

"Hey, Grammy," Sam said, and lightly embraced her by the shoulders, as if she might break.

"Hi, Mom," Kenneth said, and set his bag down to kiss her cheek. There were more in the car, and the boys went to get them.

"So," Emily said, hanging up Ella's coat, "how is Suzanne?"

"Good."

"I wish she could have come."

"Her dad's having an operation, and she really wanted to be there for her mom."

"I'm so sorry."

"It's okay, it's minor."

"How old is he?"

"Older than Dad."

"At that age nothing's minor," Emily said. "Please let her know we're thinking of her."

"I will."

"How's Captain Jack?"

"Good."

"Good."

She beamed, overwhelmed by Ella's presence. Emily had so much to tell her, yet her mind, so full just moments ago, was suddenly blank. As her imagination veered down the hall in the apartment she'd never see, in panic she reached out and took Ella in her arms again. "My Ella Bella."

"Grammy, are you okay?"

"I'm just so glad you could come. It feels like I haven't seen you in ages. Come, sit," she said, patting the couch. "Tell me everything that's going on with you."

THE GROWN-UP TABLE

Perhaps it was nostalgia, or just the stubbornness of memory, but she could never separate the grown-up versions of the children from the children they'd been. Margaret had been turning heads for nearly forty years—sometimes with dire results—yet she would always be the chubby, sullen third-grader who hid candy in her room. Justin, the budding astrophysicist, would forever be the oversensitive boy who burst into tears because he put the wrong soap in the dishwasher. Not proud of her own earlier self, Emily understood that imposing these old roles on them was unfair, and did her best to follow their new pursuits and celebrate their latest triumphs.

In Sam's case, this was difficult. He was the youngest of the grandchildren, and the most troubled. As a preteen he'd been banned from their local mall for shoplifting, and with a friend was responsible for setting fire to a neighbor's toolshed. After he was suspended for breaking into the school store, Lisa had him tested, fishing, Arlene suspected, for a diagnosis of ADD, a condition she regarded, from a lifetime of teaching, as arbitrary and convenient, and which the doctors confirmed, prescribing drugs that supposedly would help him focus. Even with medication and a special diet, he'd been held back his sophomore year and was failing several classes before Kenneth and Lisa transferred him to the Milton Academy (at the Sanners' expense), where he did well enough to get into Clark University, a nontraditional college, as if a lack of structure might help him. He lasted only half a semester there, moving back home and enrolling at Bay State College, which neither Emily nor Arlene had ever heard of.

Now, at the dinner table, when Emily chose her opening and casually asked, "And how is school?" she was prepared to be encouraging.

"Actually I'm taking a break right now."

"Oh," Emily said, trying to temper her surprise. She'd had two glasses of wine and this was news to her. "Are you working, then?"

"I am."

"Doing what, if I may ask?"

"Working at Bob's."

"Forgive my ignorance. Who is Bob?"

"The store," Ella said.

"They're a chain," Kenneth said. "They sell clothes."

"What do you do there?"

Sam had taken a bite of cheesy potatoes, as if his part in the conversation were over. He nodded and swallowed. "Pretty much everything. Stock the shelves, do checkout, whatever they need."

"His official title is sales associate,'" Kenneth said.

"How do you like it?" Arlene asked.

Sam shrugged. "It's okay."

"It's just temporary," Kenneth said.

"Of course," Emily said. "I assume you're going back to school in the fall?"

"I haven't figured out what I'm doing yet."

His answer, like his others, stumped her. He seemed unconcerned, or uninterested, as if he'd had enough of the subject, and though Emily sensed that pressing him further would serve no purpose, she couldn't let such an alarming statement go unchallenged.

"I know your Aunt Margaret wishes she'd stayed in school."

"It's true," Arlene seconded.

"We've already discussed it," Kenneth said.

"It may not seem like it because you're young, but you only have so many opportunities in life. You don't want to wake up twenty years from now and find you've missed the boat."

Sam had stopped eating and waited for her to finish with his hands in his lap, as if he were being punished. "I'll try and remember that."

"I'm not saying this to pick on you. I'd say the same thing to Ella."

"Right."

"I would."

"Except you wouldn't have to, because she's Ella."

"I'm staying out of this," Ella said, holding both hands up.

"I'm just one person voicing her opinion," Emily said. "I'm sorry I brought it up."

"It's fine," Kenneth said, as if he were the final arbiter.

"If it's no trouble," Arlene said, "I would love a tiny piece of ham."

For the rest of dinner they stayed away from the topic, as if it were closed. It wasn't until Arlene was gone and the children were upstairs watching TV that Kenneth sat down with Emily in the living room and told her the real story. Sam had actually been taking a full course load and holding his own until he'd come down with the flu the week before midterms. His teachers let him reschedule the tests. He studied extra, he claimed, but failed all four badly, and decided to withdraw while they could still get a partial refund.

"That's why he was so upset."

"It would have been nice to know that," Emily said. "I don't know why I bother calling you. You never tell me anything."

"Mom." He shook his head as if she were being unfair. "We didn't think broadcasting it would help the situation."

"That's fine. I'm not going to offer my opinion when it's obviously not wanted."

She let this sit.

"It just happened a couple weeks ago," Kenneth said. "We were hoping he'd stick it out, but he was already on academic probation and didn't see a way he could bring them all up to B's. The hope is that he can take a couple of them over the summer so he can really concentrate on them and bring his average up."

"Is he going to want to go over the summer?"

"That's what we're discussing. He's pretty discouraged."

"Naturally," Emily said, thinking it wasn't an isolated case of bad luck, just an extension of his usual troubles. "Having Ella for an older sister can't make it any easier."

"You really touched a nerve with that one."

"Should I apologize, or would that just make things worse?"

"That's entirely your call."

"I should say something to him."

Kenneth agreed, but left her to figure out what that might be. The whole sibling issue was a minefield. She couldn't blame Sam for being jealous of Ella. Emily could honestly say she hadn't known of his situation and that, like it or not, she would always worry about him. It was neither an apology nor a reprimand, which she thought fitting, since they'd both been at fault, but when she called him out of the den for a quick word and delivered her brief speech in the hall, it was received with the same indifference he'd shown at the table, and though they embraced as if they'd made up, she felt no closer to him.

She fretted over it in bed. Her concerns weren't personal. Hurt feelings were the least of it. His quitting worried her, and his prospects, as she cast ahead to the future. Unlike Ella or Sarah, he had no particular skill, no unique talent or personality beyond his mother's sullenness and a penchant for getting into trouble. She could see him working at this Bob's and living at home indefinitely, never finishing his degree, like Margaret. She imagined Kenneth was disappointed in him, and that was sad. But he was young, it was possible he might change. Or not. That would be awful. While part of her protested that she was being melodramatic, she saw the larger issue as practical, and far-reaching. If he kept on this way, what would become of him?

POWER OF ATTORNEY

She'd instructed Kenneth to bring his copy of the will so they could go over it together. They didn't have to be at the airport until five-thirty, and after they came back from church and changed out of their good clothes and made sandwiches from last night's ham, she led him into Henry's office and shut the door behind them.

"Have a seat."

He did without a word, setting his backpack on the floor between his feet.

Even if his silence was meant to be respectful, she wished he weren't so solemn. Why did people treat death like an embarrassing family secret? She was braced for a replay of her meeting with Margaret, but also eager to be done with it once and for all, thankful that this was the last time she'd have to explain herself.

She slid open the file drawer and lifted out the thick manila envelope with both hands. Since Christmas she'd revisited the will and its appendices many times, with an eye toward what Kenneth would need to know, since he'd most likely shoulder the bulk of the executor's duties, and the pages were fringed with pink Post-it notes.

"That's very funny," he said.

"What?"

He reached into his backpack and withdrew his copy, setting it on the desk beside hers. It was layered just as thickly with yellow Post-its.

"That is funny."

What was funnier was that their queries were perfectly matched.

While she spoke, he took copious notes on a legal pad, flipping the pages, stopping her every so often to ask for clarification. In contrast to Margaret, he'd always been a good student, a spelling bee finalist, conscientious to a fault about homework, excited by the possibility of extra credit. She attributed his eagerness to please to Henry, but she'd been the one with straight A's, the one whose report cards were celebrated and saved. If Margaret was cursed with her temper, Kenneth had inherited her diligence.

As they went over each point in detail, she was gratified that he'd taken the time to understand her, and relieved. Why had she been worried? She should have known she could count on him.

A week later, floundering, as was her habit in the wake of their leaving, she took Rufus out for his constitutional one bright, chilly morning only to discover, on the slate square of sidewalk directly in front of their steps, like a hex or a warning, a pair of black spray-painted arrows pointing downhill, bracketing the number 392.

She peered around at the empty lawns and driveways and porches, as if whoever was responsible were watching. Rufus looked up at her, wondering why they'd stopped.

She would have suspected gang graffiti, which had been a problem in the alley behind Sheridan, except it was small and artlessly done. Its sloppiness looked official, the harbinger of some public works project, a new sewer line or fiber-optic cable that might intrude on her summer. Besides marring her front walk, the inscrutable numerals promised a chaos she was powerless to stop, and sent her off up Grafton, frowning at her bad luck.

As they wended along, Rufus pausing to nose the budding hedges for a proper spot, she searched the sidewalk for similar hieroglyphics, and the street, hoping to divine the path of the coming disruption, but found none. Instead of their usual route, she didn't turn left at Sheridan but continued uphill to Heberton, crossed and came down the far side of Grafton past the Millers', interrogating the pavement, which itself seemed, except for a few minor fissures, in decent enough shape.

Last fall the gas company had dug up the corner of Farragut at the foot of the hill, right by Henry's old bus stop. The patches were still visible, grafts of lighter-colored asphalt. Farragut had been red brick when they'd moved in, and remained so well into the eighties—lumpy and frost-heaved, the bricks cracked and chipped, slippery in wet weather, but beautiful too, especially in the fall, the overhanging limbs forming a tunnel—when the city resurfaced it a smooth uniform gray. Emily wondered who had made that decision, what bloodless committee. Certainly no one who'd ever lived there.

They went all the way down to the stop sign at Highland and came back up their side, past Louise's. Rufus lagged behind, his head drooping. He panted as if he'd run for miles, and she slowed to let him catch his breath. There was nothing by either manhole, or the storm drain in front of the Conroys'. She was baffled by the absence of any other markings, as if, once she established a pattern, she'd be able to solve the mystery.

As she was mulling this, Marcia Cole emerged from her house, wearing a warm-up suit, her hair tucked under a Penguins cap. She'd taken up running to lose weight, and though so far she showed no visible results, every morning Emily saw her chug past, red-faced and sweaty. Marcia hefted one leg, propped a sneakered heel on the porch rail and began stretching as if she were training for the Olympics. Buster, who'd followed her out, sat imperiously at the top of their stairs, swishing his tail. Emily tightened her grip on the leash, but Rufus failed to see either of them until Emily hailed Marcia—"Morning"—at which point Buster scooted across the lawn and up the driveway, headed for the garage.

"Do you know anything about this 'three-ninety-two'?" Emily pointed, though it was impossible for Marcia to see anything from there.

Together they walked over to the square in question and studied it as if it were a clue.

"That's weird," Marcia said.

"It must have just happened. I've been around all week and haven't seen or heard a thing. Have you?"

Marcia stooped and tested the paint with a finger. "It's been here a little while at least."

"Since yesterday, do you think?"

"Probably. I guess. I don't know. You say you haven't seen any others?"

"We just did the entire block."

"Hunh." Marcia raised one knee high and hugged it against her chest, then the other. She went back and forth a few times, an impressive display of flexibility. "You might try calling the city and asking if anyone there knows what's going on."

"I was planning on it."

"I've got to run—literally—but let me know what they say."

"I will," Emily said, and watched her jog off, her bottom wobbling, and thought she wouldn't have the courage to do that in public.

Inside, she refilled Rufus's water dish and gave him a treat, then fetched the phone book and sat at the breakfast table with an orange and a cup of tea and the directory open to the blue pages, going down the rows of numbers with a finger, pressing 1 for English and then waiting on hold, watching Buster crisscross the backyard with impunity. She gave her name and address and described the markings repeatedly, only to be told, again and again, that they had no information on any upcoming project involving Grafton Street. Worse, the people she spoke to weren't interested, as if she were wasting their time—when the converse was true. She kept a list of all the departments she contacted, and though she spent a good chunk of her morning on it, in the end no one could tell her who the number belonged to.

If no one cared, she thought vindictively, then no one would object if she went out now with a wire brush and an acid bath and scrubbed it off, or took Henry's power sander to it. What was stopping her? It was her property. But while she protested that she was within her rights as a homeowner, she also feared the repercussions of such a rash act, which could easily be mistaken for vandalism. She could just see the mark from her front window. Like the scratch on her car, it quickly became irresistible, a goad, an insult. From then on, ten, twenty times a day, she would crane over the radiator and part the curtains to make sure it was still there, as if, on its own, it might magically disappear.

THE CRUELEST MONTH

She knew these dismal gray days too well, the dregs of another Pittsburgh winter, the sky like soot above the rooftops. Spring was so close—the wait was excruciating. All she wanted to do was go outside and scratch around in her flower beds, take a peek under the blanket of mulch to see what had come up—her reward for all her hard work in the fall—but the weather wasn't cooperating. It snowed on her crocuses, burying them completely, Buster's tracks a dotted line across the yard. She fought back with tea and oranges, melba toast dabbed with unsalted butter. The radio was calling for freezing rain, a wintry mix that could tie up the school buses. The breakfast nook was drafty, and she retreated to the living room, reading *Middlemarch* with an afghan over her lap, the lulling trumpets of Gabrieli on the stereo, the shifting polyphony putting her to sleep.

She woke to the grandfather clock marking ten-thirty. Sleet tapped at the windows. Rufus sat staring at her, asking to be let out.

"You can't be serious," she said, and then, at the back door, "Quick-quick."

Watching him pick his way over the crust, she thought if she could just hold on a few weeks longer, she'd be all right. The sun would resuscitate her, burn away this feeling of uselessness. She'd throw open the windows and walk Rufus around the reservoir, wipe down the chaise longue and bask in the yard.

The phone broke through her reverie. It was almost with relief that she moved to answer it. She hoped it might be Kenneth, though they'd just talked on Sunday. More likely it was Arlene, or Betty, asking if there was anything she could bring on Wednesday.

"Hello?" Emily said, but the woman on the other end was already talking:

"—and thank you for your time. The committee to elect John McCain would like to remind you that the presidential primary will take place on Tuesday, April twenty-second—"

"This is not the way to win my vote," Emily said, as if someone listening in might register her displeasure.

Outside, Rufus was barking. As Emily hung up to tend to him, the doorbell rang.

"What now?" she said, because suddenly the place was a madhouse.

It was Marcia in her Penguins cap, down jacket and sweatpants. Instead of her usual sneakers, she wore snow boots, the Velcro tabs flapping loose. Emily was pretty sure she was no longer working. For days her little hybrid didn't move.

"I just heard," Marcia said. "I'm so sorry."

Emily had no idea what she was talking about, but nodded, maintaining a concerned neutrality. "Thank you, but what exactly is it that you heard?"

"About Mrs. Miller."

"Yes?"

"I'm so sorry. I know you were close."

Kay gone, and Emily had never visited her. Could it really be true?

Yes. Jim had been keeping an eye on the place while it was for sale. The family had called to let him know.

In back, Rufus continued his racket, but now he seemed far away. Marcia stood on the stoop as if waiting for an invitation.

"Thank you," Emily said.

"If there's anything we can do."

"Thank you, that's very kind."

That was all Marcia wanted to tell her. Once she was gone, Emily thought it was unfair, leaving her alone with the news. As she made her way to the back of the house, where Rufus was still going on ferociously, she reflected that Louise had died in the spring, also her father. To make it through the darkest days only to succumb—she suspected there was a lesson in it, one that, in her position, didn't bear closer examination.

She gave Rufus his treat, dropping it without looking. It hit the floor and split, one piece shooting under the lip of the dishwasher so that she had to toe it out for him.

"You stink," she said, because he was wet.

Kay. Tiny, birdy Kay with her bangs and bangles and cancerous pink cans of Tab. She was the first of their circle to wear a bikini to the Edgewood Club. With her tomboy's body she could get away with it, unlike Emily, who felt she was putting herself on display. Kay was a fiend for tennis, and worked on her tan all summer long, holding one mahogany arm beside Emily's. Every day they were at the club. They took turns driving, loading the kids into those massive old station wagons, wearing nothing but their suits and T-shirts, their hair reeking of chlorine.

When were Jamie and Terry going to let her know, or did they think there was no one left on Grafton Street?

They wouldn't be far wrong. Of the old crew, she was the last, and once again she wondered where the years had gone, and why she was still alive.

The rest of the day she waited for their call. When it finally came, from Jamie, late that afternoon, she was grateful not to be forgotten.

"Your mother was always so chipper," Emily said, and though it was true, she felt false, having put off seeing her for so long—forever, now.

Arlene had known Kay, years ago. In the seventies they'd been members of the same ski club, taking trips to Banff and Vail and once even Austria. Emily wanted her to be more upset.

"I guess what I'm saying is, it wasn't unexpected."

"It felt unexpected to me," Emily said.

"How long had she been there?"

"That's not the point."

"I understand what you're saying," Arlene said, but obviously she didn't.

Neither of the children was surprised. They were both sorry, and asked Emily to please pass their condolences on to Jamie and Terry. Kenneth remembered Kay dressing up as Pinocchio for Halloween. Margaret recalled sleeping over, all of them staying up late to watch Chiller Theater, and then in the morning Kay making them chocolate chip pancakes. Even more than Louise, she'd been the fun mom of their set, instigator of water fights, architect of miniature golf birthday parties, their yard the neighborhood playground. In the past Emily might have been jealous of the children's easy affection for Kay; now she was pleased, as if these memories were a gift she could give her.

The memorial service was held at Eccles Funeral Home, across the river in Aspinwall, the same place Kay had had Dick's. It was fine, if lightly attended—another hazard of outliving your friends. Rather than disfigure the guest book with her shaky handwriting, Emily had Arlene sign for both of them. The family had placed framed pictures of Kay at various ages around the room, a tactic Emily found manipulative, the embarrassing hairdos and saddle shoes wrenching her back through the decades to her own lost childhood. Her mother and father, the war, the Penn Royal—how was that world gone now, and everyone in it? Kay's grandchildren were bored, dressed up in their church clothes, clustered at the end of the front row. Emily and Arlene's lilies shared the dais with two identically gaudy arrangements. The room was windowless, the air warm and stagnant, and as Jamie read a long, gently comic remembrance of her mother's love of weddings, Emily thought she'd been to so many of these that she'd become a critic.

She was here because she'd loved Kay, because for so many years their lives and families had been intertwined, yet as she sat waiting for Jamie to finish, her mind catching on the undeniable reason for the gathering, Emily thought she was mourning the passing of that happier time as much as she was Kay. Was it just selfishness, or at this point was every loss personal? Though she knew it wasn't true, looking back from this bare, ugly room, life seemed meager and short, unfairly so. At the end, had Kay felt cheated too?

Afterward, the family invited everyone to join them for an informal reception at Atria, an overpriced fish place farther upriver. Emily had no real interest in going, but felt obligated, and glanced over at Arlene as if she might rescue her.

No, they would do what was proper.

They stayed just long enough to have a glass of wine and touch base with Jamie and Terry. Out of habit they called her Mrs. M., a name she hadn't answered to in years. It was plain they had no idea who Arlene was. Jamie, who'd always been smart and confident, had married an orthodontist and lived in the suburbs of Denver with their five children. Terry, who'd had a boyhood crush on Margaret, was balding and twice divorced and working for a plastics company in McKees Rocks. Emily couldn't help but compare them to her own children, as if she and Kay were still in competition.

"I'm afraid we have to say goodbye or we'll turn into pumpkins," Emily said, leaning in and kissing Jamie's cheek. "It was lovely to see you. If you're ever in the old neighborhood, please drop by. I'm not planning on going anywhere for a while."

Outside, it felt like they were escaping. The car was damp, and Arlene turned on her seat warmer. Rush hour had begun, the traffic on Freeport Road crawling by the dingy strip malls. Somewhere in the sprawl behind them was the nursing home Emily had never visited, the carpeted halls and beeping machines. Dusk was falling, the sky in the west smudged red beyond downtown, warning lights blinking on the locks as they crossed the Highland Park Bridge. Just over the dark hillside that rose before them, the zookeepers were feeding the animals, hosing out the cages.

"Thank you," Emily said. "I'm glad we went to the reception."

"You didn't want to at first."

"I think I've had enough of these things."

"It's true," Arlene said. "They tend to blend together after a while."

"I've never been a great fan of Eccles."

"Oh, I know. It's depressing."

"I don't see why they have to have the casket there. Is that supposed to serve as proof? I don't need any more proof."

"They were glad to see you."

"I was glad to see them. It's been a long time."

This nostalgia was dishonest. As she had since she'd heard the news, she wanted to confess that she'd been a bad friend, and a coward, letting her memories of Louise stop her from visiting Kay when she was all alone in that place, and that she would never forgive herself. She recalled the confession of sins, the boundlessness of it: *for things done and left undone.* Yes, exactly. She wasn't sure she could wait till Sunday. Tonight, perhaps, as she lay in bed, she could offer this latest failing—surely not her last—to God, for who else would absolve her?

At the end of the bridge, she had to choose which way to go—straight, for Regent Square and Arlene's, or right, for home. It had been a long day, and she was relieved when Arlene didn't ask what her dinner plans were.

They swung down onto Washington Boulevard, past the old driver's test course and state police barracks, where Henry had taken the children to get their licenses. The make-believe streets had been converted into a fancy bike track, with painted lanes and high-banked curves like a raceway.

"I'll never get used to it," Emily said.

"You wonder whose idea it was."

"Not mine, that's for sure."

Dropping her off, Emily suggested that if the weather didn't improve, they might try the Van Gogh exhibit at the Scaife. Not this weekend—they didn't want to fight the hordes—but maybe Monday? Just to get out of the house.

"I've been wanting to see that."

"We could have lunch there and make a day of it."

"That sounds lovely," Arlene said, and so it was settled.

Driving home through the wet streets of East Liberty, Emily cast ahead. Sunday they had church, Monday the Scaife, Tuesday breakfast at the Eat 'n Park, Wednesday Betty came. And still that left tomorrow and Saturday to get through on her own.

She should have asked Arlene to have dinner with her. She wasn't sure why she hadn't. Just tired. She caught herself biting the inside of her cheek—a habit her mother detested—and made herself stop.

Along Grafton, the streetlights were flickering on, a dull silver. As she slowed for her driveway, the Millers' house loomed darkly behind its hedges, inescapable, the gables sharp against the sky. The idea that it was haunted now was silly. She frowned at herself, shaking off the thought, and made the turn, concentrating on keeping the car centered so she wouldn't scrape the fence.

She'd left a light on for Rufus, but still he was upset, huffing at her back as she fixed his dinner. He sneezed as if he were scolding her.

"Shush," she said. "Stop acting like a brat."

The words were barely out of her mouth when she realized she was talking about herself. Kay was dead, and here she was sulking like a child. It was her own fault. What did she think would happen? At their age, once you went into a place like that, you didn't come out. She was just lucky Henry never had to go to one.

She needed to eat something, but she wasn't at all hungry, and poured herself a glass of wine. She took it into the living room, put on some Bach and sat in Henry's chair with her shoes off, sipping and admiring the designs in the Oriental rug. She hadn't had much of a lunch, and a pleasant fatigue settled on her, suspending all thought. She sat back and closed her eyes and imagined falling asleep here. Who would care?

As she was picturing herself waking up in the middle of the night in her good clothes, the phone rang. The machine was on—in her funk she'd forgotten to turn it off. After a brief wait for the message to play, a cheery voice spoke from the kitchen: "Hello. This is Lynn Swann with the Republican Party of Western PA. We'd like to remind you that Election Day is Tuesday—"

"I know when it is," Emily said.

She sat back and closed her eyes again, but the mood was ruined. It wasn't even six-thirty and all she wanted to do was crawl into bed. She thought of Kay and remembered Louise near the end, telling her she just wanted it to stop. Was that okay? They were alone in her room, one of her rare lucid days when the pain medication was working. She was afraid the boys wouldn't understand. Of course it was, Emily said. She still believed that. It wasn't giving up when there was nothing left anyway. The problem was, by that time you couldn't do anything about it. She imagined Kay never had that choice, and wondered if she would. She'd made her wishes known to the children. What more could she do?

Her mouth was sour, and she could feel the beginnings of a headache, a dull pulsing like a heartbeat behind one eye. She pushed herself out of the chair and padded to the kitchen. She rinsed her glass and stuck it in the top of the dishwasher, poured herself a tall glass of water and then, without hope or desire, began searching through the cupboards for something to eat.

ALMOND BLOSSOMS

Even on a weekday the Van Gogh was a zoo. The galleries were teeming with schoolchildren and harried docents attempting to shout above the din. Loosed from their buses, the children chased one another as if in gym class, squealing and slipping on the polished marble floors. The museum offered an audio tour of the exhibit, so even the solitary strollers gathered in packs, silently paying homage before the more famous paintings. To Emily they looked like the subjects of some mind-control experiment, pressing buttons on a small black box wired to their heads.

As she and Arlene waited for the crowd around *Sunflowers* to disperse, they browsed a wall of canvases inspired by the Japanese—Hiroshige in particular, a favorite of hers. Under a dark sky, hunched figures hurried over a bridge in the pouring rain. Emily shivered in sympathy. The weather outside wasn't much better, a fact accentuated by the high plate-glass windows that gave on to the sporadic traffic and shiny black asphalt of Forbes Avenue below. She'd checked her coat downstairs, and now she felt a chill settling in.

"Look how wild the river is," Arlene said. "That's what I love about him, everything's in turmoil, everything's in motion. Look at those brushstrokes."

She might have been criticizing her own work, the polite, dingy still lifes that absorbed light instead of freeing it. Emily, who'd never painted anything more ambitious than her kitchen, knew she was being too hard on her, and softened, watching her lean closer and squint at the boatman caught in the current. Barring a miracle, this would be the last time either of them would see these big Van Goghs. She so wanted to enjoy them, to drink them in, and yet, as much as she admired Arlene's enthusiasm, there was something that prevented Emily from fully sharing it, distracted by the children and the drab streets outside. It seemed a less than ideal way to experience art, and for a brief and selfish instant she understood why the black market thrived. To be alone with a masterpiece was to possess it wholly. No guide's or bystander's commentary intervened, no curator's notes printed in foot-high letters on the wall, just you and the painting, and in that quiet space, intimacy, connection and, perhaps, communion. She wanted to be moved, to be thrilled, and how was that possible in a room full of third-graders?

Moments after she'd given up hope, as she and Arlene maundered along the Japanese wall, they stopped before a simple canvas, a branch of an almond tree in bloom. It was minor, Emily didn't recognize it. The flowers themselves did nothing for her, but the blue Van Gogh had chosen for the air captivated her—rich and bright, near aqua with a milky whiteness to it, a loudness which would have been laughable on the trim of a house and was nearly an affront here, yet from her first glance Emily couldn't look away. For months she'd been dreaming of spring. Here it was in all its gaudy freshness, made present through the plainest of emblems—a flower, a branch, the sun-warmed air. While Arlene moved on, Emily lingered, concentrating, as if by paying enough attention she might imprint the vision on her mind.

Part of it, she thought later, when they were almost done, was the surprise, the shock of that wild blue. *Sunflowers* and *Crows over a Wheatfield* left her indifferent as a cat, yet that first glimpse held the force of discovery, and an unforgettable one. It wasn't simply the unexpected that moved her. The grimness of these past few weeks had left her susceptible. How strange that his choice of color, made so long ago, was waiting to dispel her gloom at just that moment. And to think she'd felt it despite the chaos all around her. She couldn't imagine a greater testament to the power of art, and wasn't that why they were there, to have their faith in it renewed?

On the way back to the elevators, she made a point of stopping for a last look, and was pleased to find the blossoms held her now, as if she'd overlooked them.

"I think this is my favorite."

"It's nice for a study," Arlene said. "I'm more partial to *La Berceuse*."

"That's completely different."

"True. There are so many great pieces here it's overwhelming. I'm glad you suggested it."

"I am too," Emily said.

The café was jammed and expensive, but the onion soup warmed her. She asked Arlene if she minded if they took a peek at the gift shop, just for a minute. She wanted a print of the picture to take home, though, when she thought of her walls, there wasn't space for anything new. Maybe the upstairs hall, or in Kenneth's room looking out on the backyard. They didn't have one anyway, only *Starry Night* and a couple of other icons. She turned the postcard racks until she found it, but they couldn't reproduce the blue. It looked flat and lifeless, unworthy of the original, and she left empty-handed, knowing, in time, with nothing to remind her, she would lose that feeling of wonder.

DRIVE-BY

The next week the weather finally turned, releasing her. The snow thawed, soaking the yard, dotted with Rufus' handiwork, some from as far back as November. She scooped it one disintegrating pile at a time, surprised at not just the amount but the variety—chalk-white, brick-red, dark olive. He ate the same food every day. The different colors, she reasoned, must have come from his treats.

The front wasn't nearly as bad, but still had to be picked up. As they melted, the dirty mounds left by the plows yielded their treasure. She was out by the curb in her work duds, bent over with a plastic Giant Eagle bag in one hand, gathering the cracked coffee cup lids and flattened straws and soggy cigarette butts, when someone flying down the hill honked at her.

In a single motion, more out of reflex than neighborliness, she glanced up from her task and raised an open hand as the car flashed by, a big white SUV she didn't recognize. It had deeply tinted windows, which Emily associated with drug dealers and East Liberty, preening teenagers who blasted their stereos so loud the sound shook the air. She was certain she didn't know anyone who owned a car like that. It paused at the stop sign and turned left onto Highland, revving as it accelerated away.

Was it a joke? Were they making fun of the old lady, trying to frighten her? She was sure she presented a spectacle, a geriatric parody of Millet's *The Gleaners* in her headscarf and Henry's ratty old plaid shirt and her dirty buckskin gloves. She peered up and down Grafton to see if anyone else was watching. When a VW bug turned onto the block from Sheridan, she bent her head as if immersed in her work but kept an eye on it as it passed—harmlessly—and then felt foolish, used, though she couldn't precisely say why.

She dismissed the entire business with a shake of her head, aware that she was being thin-skinned, and moved on to her next job, cleaning out the fridge to make room for the groceries she would buy this afternoon. With the last of the sharp cheddar, she made herself a grilled cheese for lunch, and killed off a jar of pickles that was past its expiration date, and still, sitting there chewing, thinking she should refill the feeders, she couldn't stop seeing herself bent double, defenseless, the SUV flashing by, and her hand shooting up too eagerly.

"I know it's hard to believe," her mother once said, apropos of a playground scrape at school, "but not everyone in the world is your friend." Emily thought she'd learned her lesson. Hadn't she tried to teach her children to be more cautious, or did one's sense of trust come from somewhere deeper? For most of her life she just expected things would work out, that people would be kind. Now she recognized her good fortune for what it was. She'd been lucky in so much, it had left her woefully unprepared for old age.

She was contemplating this when, behind her, from the front of the house, the lid of the mailbox squeaked open and then clanked shut, an always promising combination of notes. She stalled, rinsing and racking her dishes, then crossed the living room to the bay window and leaned over the radiator, holding her breath as she peeked through the curtains. The mailman was well past the Coles' and headed off down the block. She checked the street for cars before opening the front door, grabbed the mail, gently closed the lid and slipped back inside before anyone could see her.

THE VIRTUAL TOUR

They came early one morning, like gypsies, in a noisy caravan—an aged stake truck and a humongous new pickup towing a trailer loaded with mowers. There was no name painted on the doors, which suggested to Emily that the motley army of young men gathered on the sidewalk in front of the Millers' was being paid under the table. They all had tall coffees they balanced on a bumper or a tailgate, and she wondered how many of the cups would find their way into her bushes.

They deployed without orders, as if they'd done this before. A pair strapped on leaf blowers, clamped earphones over their baseball caps and racketed away. A second pair gassed up the mowers and followed behind them, standing like charioteers to guide their machines across the lawn. The grass was still wet, but apparently that didn't matter. A third pair attacked the hedges, sweeping the chattering blades of their trimmers in long arcs, planing the faces, squaring the corners.

While Emily was pleased that someone was finally taking care of the place, their sudden entrance and the noise they gave off felt like an assault, landscaping as mechanized warfare. She'd been working away peacefully, enjoying the sun and the call-and-response of birdsong. Even Rufus had seen fit to join her, snoring on the warm slab of the back porch.

She refused to let them ruin her morning, and retreated to her garden, plucking up weeds, moving her stool a couple of feet at a time, doing her best to ignore the roaring, and then, as she was eating lunch, it stopped. She thought they might be taking a break as well, but no, they were rolling the mowers onto the trailer and tying them down, and by one o'clock they were gone.

The Millers' yard, she had to admit, looked much better. The hedges, naturally impressive, were perfect. They'd pruned back the rhododendrons by the porch, edged the beds and mulched them with red cedar chips, creating a pleasing contrast. Later, walking Rufus, she saw that they'd aerated and fertilized the lawn, and wondered how much it all cost.

The painters came next, in a white van with ladders on top and a rainbow on the side. They occupied the house for a few days, only to give way to a plumber, then an electrician. One afternoon, two deliverymen with a fancy hand truck wrestled several monstrous boxes up the front stairs; twenty minutes later they rolled out Kay's old stove and refrigerator and hauled them away.

The reason for all this became clear when a man in a station wagon uprooted the RE/MAX sign and planted one from Howard Hanna. The children had switched realtors, hoping to move the house.

The sign listed the agent's website. Emily felt strange punching in the Millers' address when it was right across the street. PRICE REDUCED! the header said. The pictures showed the neat yard and bare, newly painted rooms, alien without their furniture. The stove and fridge were buffed stainless steel. There was no trace of Kay and Dick—the slumber parties and Sunday brunches, the hot toddies by the fire after sledding. They'd even replaced the chandelier in the dining room. They were asking $385,000, $20,000 less than before.

At once the number excited and dismayed her. Since it had been for sale, she'd imagined what her own house might be worth—pointless, since she'd sacrificed the Chautauqua cottage for the sole purpose of staying where she was. Why was the idea of money so enticing? There was nothing she wanted. And still, the drop in price bothered her, as if the difference were coming out of her pocket. At some point Margaret and Kenneth would have to sell her place, and she wanted them to do well. There was solace in knowing the grandchildren would profit from their dearest investment. That was all Jamie and Terry were trying to do. It was unfair to hold it against them.

"I don't think they'll get anything close to that," she told Arlene. "Not with the way the market is."

"The kitchen's beautiful. I'd kill for that island."

"It's still a three-bedroom."

"You should see what they're getting for three bedrooms over here—little ones. It's crazy."

"I don't get it," Emily said. "But I don't get why those condos on Beechwood are going for half a million, if they're actually selling. Meanwhile, the city can't afford to pay the firemen."

"And yet they're going ahead with the Bore to the Shore."

"Another boondoggle."

"I'm just glad I have a place," Arlene said. "If I wanted to buy something on my block now? I couldn't afford it."

"And this is a buyer's market."

She mentioned the website to Margaret, as if she might immediately log on and corroborate Emily's thoughts, but Margaret was upset. Sarah had lost her job and was talking about moving back home. Out of reflex, Emily said if there was anything she could do, she'd be glad to. As always, Margaret brushed her off, as if she could handle her own problems.

Less comfortable talking about himself, Kenneth was more apt to humor her. He thought the price was right for a house that size, in that neighborhood. In suburban Boston, with that lot, it could run upward of a million.

"This isn't Boston," Emily said. "You know what I find surprising? They only have one-hundred-amp service. You'd think they would have upgraded at some point. The furnace and hot water heater look like they've seen better days. It's hard to tell from the pictures."

"Mom, are you thinking of making an offer?"

"Don't be a smart-ass."

He apologized, lightly, which made her feel as if she'd been touchy, and she decided they were done with the subject. Why did she think anyone would care?

The week before the primary, the website said there would be an open house that Sunday. The agent came by and hung another sign. At all hours of the day now, cars stopped and people hopped out to take pictures. The most brazen walked right onto the front porch and snapped away at the living room window. Emily tried to see the place through their eyes, as if she could imagine a new future there. A professional couple with young children. They'd covet the pocket doors and built-in bookcases while appreciating the half bath off the kitchen and the finished basement. She'd always thought it was charming, and had no doubt it would sell, maybe not at the asking price but eventually, and that was good. As much as she missed Kay, and those days, it had sat empty for too long.

Betty said she was sure it was a nice house, but it was way out of her range. "I guess some people have that kind of money. I don't."

"You know how much we paid for this place?" Emily said. "Sixteen thousand. And we thought that was a king's ransom."

"I bet it was at the time."

"It was! I remember the day we paid it off. Henry wrote the check and we opened a bottle of champagne."

"That must have felt good."

"Oh, no kidding," Emily said. Then why, after she and Betty cleaned up and got back to work, did it make her feel worse?

That world was gone, as sure as the Kersey of her girlhood, though she could recall her neighbors' faces—and their children's—as clearly as her mother's. The sale of the Millers' would make official her status as its sole survivor. She supposed the alternative was worse, though occasionally, stricken with self-pity after a lonely dinner and a glass of wine, she wavered. This was her world. As her mother forever counseled, she would just have to make the best of it.

Saturday, when Jim Cole came over to help take down the storm windows and put up the screens, she solicited his opinion. He'd kept an eye on the place over the winter, and confirmed that the furnace was older—but it was a Lennox, a reliable brand, and heated the place well enough, even on those cold, cold days they'd had in January, though to be fair, with the house empty then, the thermostat was only calling for sixty degrees. He didn't remember anything special about the hot water heater and thought it was probably all right. He took her word about the electrical service, and wouldn't speculate on the wiring. Anyone who was serious would have an engineer do a complete inspection, but he didn't notice anything too alarming, just the usual wear and tear for a place that age. Like the professor he was, he tended to qualify his answers, hedging until he seemed to have no opinion of his own. When she pressed him on the state of the foundation, he suggested she go over tomorrow and see for herself.

"Oh, I couldn't."

"Why not?"

"I wouldn't feel right. I know it's silly, but . . ."

He didn't contradict her. She was sure he thought she was fishing for permission, that, despite her protests, she wouldn't be able to resist. Though he'd been her neighbor for more than ten years, and was unfailingly kind, Jim Cole didn't know her very well. If it were their house for sale, she'd feel no compunction about snooping through their rooms. At the same time, she couldn't explain to him that her curiosity was strictly financial, because he wouldn't believe her, and so she handed him the next clean screen and let the matter drop.

It was this insult as much as her own resolve, the next day, that kept her from crossing Grafton and joining the parade of couples whose cars lined both sides of the street. She took it as a good sign that several came out and tramped around the house, taking pictures. They talked animatedly as they walked to their cars, and she wished she had a copy of the brochure they all came away with. She watched her prospective neighbors closely, paying special attention to the way they were dressed and how they held themselves, as if she were judging a pageant. Being a patient of Dr. Sayid, she wasn't surprised that several of the families were Indian. None, she noticed, was black. Her favorite was a couple that appeared to have come straight from church with two blond toddlers who scampered across the yard as if they lived there.

The open house ended at four, though the agent didn't leave till almost five. By then Emily had turned her chair around so it faced the living room again. Her desire to be inside Dick and Kay's place one last time hadn't lessened—had, in fact, only grown. All day she'd been dying to go over and introduce herself as a neighbor and old friend of the Millers', and while it meant nothing to anyone else, she was proud she'd held out, and congratulated herself, now that the opportunity had passed, for respecting their privacy.

THE LESSER OF TWO EVILS

Normally their presidential primary meant nothing, coming so late. Now, because Hillary Clinton refused to quit, Pennsylvania had suddenly become the focus of the campaign, the breaks in the evening news a battle of ads. Friday, Barack Obama, who Emily considered an opportunist and a lightweight on foreign policy, held a rally downtown which snarled traffic for hours. Monday Hillary was flying in for a last-minute whistle-stop.

As a lifelong Republican, Emily felt left out and vaguely jealous. She was not a fan of John McCain, and, really, there was no other choice. As she admitted to anyone who would listen, for the first time in her adult life she was thinking of not voting at all.

"If you *had* to vote for Obama or Hillary," Kenneth asked, "who would you vote for?"

"I wouldn't."

"If you had to. At gunpoint."

"I didn't know it was that kind of election."

"Every election is that kind of election."

"I would not vote for Mrs. Clinton at gunpoint. How's that?"

"I'm a little surprised."

"She already had her chance, and if you recall—how should I put this—let's just say it was messy."

"Compared to the last eight years?"

Knowing she regretted it, he would never let her forget that she'd voted for George W. Bush not once but twice. Not that it made a bit of difference in the greater scheme of things. She'd also voted twice for the original George Bush, and for Ronald Reagan, and Eisenhower, and three times for Richard Nixon. She'd voted for Goldwater and Gerald Ford and Bob Dole, knowing, in each case, that it was probably a hopeless cause.

She'd come to her beliefs honestly. Like most everyone in Elk County, her parents were Republicans, and were relieved to discover that Henry's family was active in the Pittsburgh arm of the party—the city, like so many at the time, being notorious for its Democratic machine. Coming from people who'd worked hard for everything they had, she prized, above all, self-reliance. Over the years she'd heard her notions of frugality and responsibility echoed by the GOP and only the GOP, and she'd been faithful. No one could accuse her of being a frontrunner. While Vietnam had obviously been a mistake, and Mr. Nixon a bad apple, the principles she subscribed to were inviolable. She still believed that, but the ongoing debacle of the last eight years had convinced her, and many of her club friends, that Mr. Bush and his cronies had betrayed the tenets of conservatism, and that the party had let them, sentencing moderates like herself who once made up the base to a kind of exile. An advocate for solidarity, Emily was more puzzled than angry at being cut adrift. What was the object of snubbing the old guard?

Kenneth, who grew up watching the Watergate hearings after school, welcomed her newfound disillusion. Their discussions were less heated now, as if they shared some common ground. Like her, he couldn't see Hillary winning. Neither did he see her minions shifting to McCain. California and New York were entrenched, as were Texas and the West. The election would come down to whether Obama could carry Florida and Ohio—the same states, Emily noted, where the more experienced Gore and Kerry had failed. As disgusted as she was with Mr. Bush, she liked reminding Kenneth that the country was necessarily conservative, concerned with family and faith and paying the bills. As always, they sparred to a draw, but now they ended their bull sessions with the skeptical hope that things had to get better, since they couldn't get any worse.

Margaret was of the opinion that Dick Cheney was a war criminal and anyone who voted for McCain was an idiot—views which she would have been surprised to find were not so far from Emily's, yet she broadcast them with such blithe self-righteousness that Emily couldn't take her seriously.

Obama should win, Margaret said, but probably wouldn't because large parts of the country were racist. As a teenager she'd had a penchant for dramatic overstatement, making the dinner table her stage, hoping to provoke Henry, and then, when he wisely didn't take the bait, accusing them of being sheep. Four decades later, she hadn't changed. She was just as emotional and absolute, just as dismissive and shrill. Worse, she seemed incapable of drawing lessons from her own experience, as if her personal politics weren't in some way to blame for her current situation. Knowing how sensitive she was, when Margaret went off about the Republicans running up the deficit, Emily refrained from pointing out that a Republican was paying her mortgage.

Early on, Arlene had made it plain she was voting for Hillary, and, as a woman, was thrilled to have the opportunity. Emily, who saw the Clintons' marriage as the very worst kind of compromise, regarded Hillary as the opposite of a role model. She understood Arlene's excitement in finally having a viable woman candidate. Too bad she happened to be Lady Macbeth.

Judging by the lawn signs up and down the street, her neighbors were solidly for Obama. CHANGE WE CAN BELIEVE IN, read the bumper sticker on Marcia Cole's hybrid. Emily thought Marcia was too old to buy such a grandiose slogan, but Marcia did a lot of things Emily considered her too old for. Maybe it was generational, the aging children of the sixties inflicting their revenge with the ultimate affirmative action. He'd been a senator for less than two years, and all Emily heard out of his mouth were platitudes. What maddened her was how the media compared him to Jack Kennedy, as if that were a good thing.

She would have been happier voting for John McCain if he wasn't so gung ho about the war. And if he hadn't been one of the Keating Five. And if he hadn't run out on his first wife after her accident.

It wasn't that she would have preferred Mitt Romney, who seemed too slick to her, or Mike Huckabee, who, like Hillary, didn't have the common sense or decency to give up. She would have preferred Bob Dole to any of them, or the original George Bush, who could still serve another term. Was it too much to ask for someone she could believe in?

She repeated her threat to not vote all the way up until Election Day. Far from a convert, more out of duty than anything else, she drove to Fulton Elementary School (now the Fulton Academy), where a chain of fluorescent-vested cops waved cars through the busy lot. She'd waited till midmorning to avoid the crowd, yet inside the echoing gym, dozens of people stood in line—most of them black, all of them Democrats. The Republican table was empty. She showed her license to Hazel Sayers from church, pulled the handle that closed the privacy curtains and with a grimace voted for John McCain. As she left the gym, a volunteer handed her a familiar sticker that said I VOTED TODAY. Emily pressed it to her bosom and wore it out into the world with pride.

THE MYSTERY OF MARCIA COLE

With spring came not just its buds and blooms but its mating rituals—all of them, it seemed to Emily, nocturnal. The peepers were peeping, Buster and his friends prowling the back alley, keeping her up with their serenades and lovers' quarrels. She had to close her bedroom windows to block out the carnal opera.

These were the hours she missed Henry keenly, the bulk and warmth of him against her reassuring. They spooned, his arm hooked around her ribs like a fallen branch, his knees tucked behind hers, then, without a word, they both rolled to face the other way, and she held him, kissed his back. In the morning he prodded her, wanting, and while she kept luxurious memories of those trysts, what she missed most was the smell of his skin.

One noisy night when she couldn't sleep, she threw off her covers and padded to the bathroom to take some Bufferin and refill her water glass. The moon was bright, laying shadows over the plush bath mat by the sink, and as she looked out onto the yard, she noticed someone standing on the Coles' back deck.

The figure by the sliding door was pale and still. At first Emily thought it was a trick, her fears conjuring a burglar from the darkness. Then the figure moved, lifting its face to the sky, and she could see it was Marcia, and that she was naked, her skin reflecting the moonlight.

It seemed to Emily that she was basking in it. There was something ceremonial and dreamlike about the scene, and Emily didn't dare move. Maybe Marcia was sleepwalking, or maybe she'd taken a sauna. She had to be freezing. Emily expected Jim to step out with a robe and lead her back inside, but after a few minutes Marcia turned and closed the door behind her.

Emily waited for her to reappear, then topped off her water glass and climbed into bed again. Rufus huffed once and subsided. It was two-thirty by her clock radio, and now she was wide awake. She was sure it was the lateness of the hour, and the strangeness of what she'd just seen, but along with her many speculations she tried to recall the last time she'd been outside like that, naked to the world, and couldn't. She remembered beaches and ponds, and, long ago, Henry's canoe at Chautauqua. The temptation was to go down right now and stand on the back porch in the altogether to prove she could do it, but it wasn't the same, and she immediately vetoed the idea as preposterous. No one wanted to see that ruin, least of all herself, and so she lay there waiting for the release of sleep, listening to Rufus wheeze and trying to think of anything besides Marcia shining in the dark like another moon.

BETTER OR WORSE?

Arlene had had a little accident. Just a fender bender, nothing serious. The first Emily heard of it was from Betty, who called to see if she could bring anything on Wednesday. Arlene had backed into someone in the parking lot at the Petco in Monroeville and broken a taillight.

"When did this happen?" Emily asked.

"Yesterday, I guess."

"Why am I just hearing about it now?"

"I just heard about it myself. I'm sure she's embarrassed."

"What happened to the other car?"

"Nothing. It was a truck. Supposedly her insurance will cover it."

"It's still going to be expensive. Plus the time and aggravation. That's not something you can drive with. I should check and see if she needs help."

"I'm sure she does."

"Thank you for letting me know," Emily said. "I can't say I'm surprised, the way she drives. She can't see."

"She can't."

"It worries me."

"It worries me too," Betty said, and the fact that she agreed pleased Emily, as if confirming a long-held belief.

"I'll talk to her."

"Good luck," Betty said, and let her go.

Emily made no pretense, as Betty had, of calling for some other reason.

"What's this I hear about you having an accident?"

"I knew I shouldn't have said anything," Arlene said.

"When were you going to tell me?"

"I didn't think it was that big a deal."

"A car accident's not a big deal?"

"I was going two miles an hour in a parking lot and bumped someone. That hardly qualifies as a 'car accident.'"

"Arlene, you can't *see*."

"I can't see at night. That's why I don't drive at night."

"For which we are all grateful."

"My eyes are perfectly fine during the day."

"When's the last time you had your eyes checked?"

"November, and they were fine."

"They were not 'fine,' and that was last year. You need to have them checked."

"I have my six-month appointment with Dr. Laughlin next week."

"I can drive you if you want."

"Thank you, that won't be necessary."

"It's not just me—Betty's just as concerned as I am."

"If I remember correctly, Betty was very concerned when you started driving again. I was too, but I didn't tell you you couldn't. I'm sorry. It's good of her to be concerned, and of you. I appreciate it, Emily, I do. But— and please tell me if I'm wrong here—this is the first accident I've been in this century, and it wasn't all my fault. I don't know what Betty told you, but the other driver was backing out just like I was, he just had a bigger bumper. Otherwise we wouldn't even be discussing this."

"I didn't hear that part," Emily said.

"It wasn't like I pulled out without looking. I looked both ways, several times. We just happened to pull out at the same time. It was a one-in-a-million chance."

"Maybe less than that."

"It had nothing to do with my eyesight."

"Which you're going to have checked."

"Because I'm aware that my eyes aren't as good as they could be, and I need to take care of them. Like anyone my age."

Having endured countless moments of terror as her passenger, Emily wasn't persuaded, but pressing the argument would do no good, and while she hadn't quite made her point, she'd at least registered her opinion.

"You're sure you don't want a ride?"

"I'm sure."

"I'd be happy to."

"I know you would."

It would serve Arlene right, Emily thought, if she had an accident on the way there—on the bridge, where there was nowhere to pull off—then dismissed the idea as spiteful. These little skirmishes brought out the worst in her. The infuriating thing was that she really had meant well—as she explained to Betty later.

She didn't expect to ever hear the results of Arlene's checkup, or only a bowdlerized version, but the following Wednesday, right after lunch, Arlene showed up on her doorstep sporting a trendily rectangular pair of glasses. She modeled them for Betty, turning her head one way and then the other. They were right, her eyes had gotten worse. The new prescription made a world of difference, especially driving, and she'd wanted to come over, first thing, and thank them for putting up with her. It was an apology, and yet Emily didn't feel vindicated. If anything she felt chastened, as if her argument had been false all along. While she laughed at Betty popping her eyes at how strong the lenses were, she couldn't understand why Arlene's good news should make her feel bad.

WHITE ELEPHANTS

Every May, as part of her big spring cleaning, Emily donated her cast-offs to the church rummage sale. Over the years she'd systematically emptied the basement and the garage, taking a victorious general's pleasure in the newly recouped space. The tables at Calvary had been blessed with an abundance of junk she no longer had any use for and couldn't fob off on the children: old dishes and Christmas lights and board games and steamer trunks and cameras and lamps and so many folding chairs. There were sentimental exceptions, of course—her golf clubs, Henry's jigsaw, Margaret's typewriter—though as she grew older, she found it easier to part with the tokens of their past. She was done storing things in the hope that someone would love them as much as she did.

She spent a morning in the corner behind the furnace, culling the most obvious pieces. This year's crop included a rusty cooler they'd used for picnics and backyard parties, a box fan that didn't fit Kenneth's window and two ugly beige card tables she'd bought for her long-defunct bridge club. It was a shame, the card tables were in perfect shape, but no, they had to go.

As tough as it was giving away merchandise she'd paid good money for, presents were even harder. She'd keep the bread maker for another year, though she had no intention of using it, and the Crock-Pot, and the red-enameled skillet like her mother's that Margaret had found at the flea market. No one would know if she donated them, and yet, out of simple etiquette, Emily felt obligated. It was doubly frustrating, leaving these unwanted objects to gather dust when she was getting rid of things that actually meant something to her.

Hardest of all were those remnants of Henry's she should have thrown out years ago, like the matching luggage they'd bought for their trip to England—four hardshell American Tourister suitcases the dark purple of raw liver, each with its own gold monogram and combination lock. Tall and narrow, they hailed from the era before wheels, and had a tendency to topple over at the merest touch. Emily couldn't remember the last time they'd used them, probably a Christmas visit to Boston when the grandchildren were little. She had a vague memory of filling one with presents. In any case, at least ten years. Since Henry died she hadn't used hers, as if breaking the set would be bad luck.

She tipped one to the light to read the initials—Henry's—and saw him in his trenchcoat, hatless, on some Midlands rail platform, the wind rearranging his thin hair. Rather than bother with a car, they'd taken trains, vetting the schedules like astrologers, working their way from London up through the Lake Country and the empty moors to Edinburgh. It was supposed to be romantic, the dining cars and long vistas, but each time they boarded, Henry had to navigate the treacherous metal steps and busy aisles with the two larger suitcases while Emily struggled behind with the smaller ones. When they reached their cramped compartment (in the movies they were much more spacious), he had to heft each bag onto an overhead rack, prompting muttering about how he was certainly getting his exercise this trip and then testy exchanges over how many clothes they really needed to bring and why they'd chosen to come in the fall. By their second week the ritual had become so unpleasant that neither of them commented on it, just lugged the bags on and off as if this were their sentence. And then, when they'd unpacked at the next inn and found their way around the quaint town, they softened. They hadn't come all this way to argue. Henry was accommodating; she was sorry. A nice rare lamb chop and a bottle of claret did wonders for their morale, a sinful dessert with clotted cream and then a tawny port, perhaps a nightcap of Drambuie for Bonny Prince Charlie, and arm in arm they weaved their way back through the ancient streets to their nest of a room and fell into bed, all the rigors of travel forgotten, all the joys theirs for the taking.

With an old dishcloth she wiped the handle free of cobwebs, then lifted the suitcase to test its weight—surprisingly light. She'd performed the same experiment last year, and the year before, the strength of her memories weakening her resolve, when, really, there was no compelling reason to hang on to them. Her days as a world traveler were over. That was fine. She wasn't the Elderhostel type, traipsing around the Holy Land with a visor and a canteen. If only they weren't monogrammed. She wished there were a way to remove their initials. She was tempted to mask them with electrical tape, a kind of blindfold, as if it would be easier to send them off anonymously.

These second thoughts stopped her, made her straighten up, take a breath and reconsider the whole set, the four of them huddled in the dankness like a family. They were more than forty years old, she'd never use them again and the children had their own bags. So why did she feel like an executioner?

"I'm sorry," she said, wiping down the sides. "Maybe your new owners will take you somewhere nice."

The decision sapped her as if she'd run a mile. She didn't bother with the far corner, just carried up what she had, one piece at a time. Rufus, who was afraid of the basement stairs, waited for her at the top, and then, as she came back from filling the Subaru, at the back door.

"Yes," she said, "thank you for helping. No, Boobus, you don't really want to come. I promise, it's going to be no fun. Go lie down. I'll be back in an hour." She kissed the top of his head and sent him off, listening for the clatter of his nails on the stairs. "Go on up," she said, and he did.

One of the pleasures of donating to the rummage sale was seeing what other people had dredged up before the public had a crack at it—an empty privilege, really, since she was done accumulating things. Part of it was simple curiosity, part a confirmation. Confronting the sheer bounty of junk made her grateful she'd already gotten rid of hers. Spread about the refectory like the treasure of an archaeological dig was the detritus of a civilization dedicated, it seemed, to leisure: lawn chairs and fondue sets and exercise bikes, children's skis and wooden tennis racquets still in their wing-nut-studded presses, Herb Alpert records and forgotten bestsellers, outmoded tape players and TVs and VCRs. So much of life, one might assume from this display, was a waste of time, but among the folding tables she recognized meaningful episodes from her own—the humidifier she set on a chair beside Margaret's and Kenneth's beds when they had bronchitis, or at least a reasonable facsimile; a Coleman stove like the one Henry brewed their morning coffee over on their camping trips before they had children; dry-cleaned sleeping bags, chipped punch bowls, space-age sunlamps. It was somehow comforting to encounter the same juice pitcher from the seventies decorated with a giant orange slice, as if, like one of Plato's ideal forms, it could never vanish completely. Despite herself, she pinched the little price tag on its string and then had to resist the bargain by walking away.

There were several coolers to choose from, including a newer-looking one with drink holders sunk into the lid, and several sets of expensive luggage. She eyed them as if they were competitors. The volunteers from the Altar Guild hadn't put hers out yet, and rather than wait and see what they were asking for them, she said her goodbyes and headed home, telling herself it didn't matter.

She told herself the same thing the next Sunday when they didn't sell and the youth group chucked them into a dumpster with all the other garbage to be hauled away and buried in some landfill. She'd given them freely, glad to have them out of the house. What happened to them after that was beyond her control, though, imagining their bags crushed beneath the ever-deepening layers, she understood it was all her fault, and now when she ventured down to the basement for a cardboard box or a screwdriver from Henry's workbench, instead of stopping and admiring the open space she'd created, she was reminded of how much she'd lost, and scurried back upstairs.

INNOCENT VICTIMS

Emily agreed, the *Post-Gazette* did seem to feature more upsetting stories lately, as if the city were declining by the day. The article that prompted this latest discussion, as they were warming up with their coffees at the Eat 'n Park, involved a fifteen-year-old girl from Brushton who bested her rival by opening fire on her Sweet Sixteen party. Three girls were dead, three more in critical condition at Children's Hospital. Arlene knew one of the families, if the father was the same Shawn Booker she was thinking of. She'd had him, oh, it had to have been thirty years ago. A nice boy, tall, always polite. It made her sick to think of it, though Emily could sense a kind of pride or excitement in her personal link to the news.

"It could happen to anyone," Arlene said. "Look at that Duquesne student last week, stabbed on Forbes in broad daylight. It's not just the bad neighborhoods anymore. Highland Park's a perfect example. There are some blocks back there behind Negley that are like the Wild West. You can hear the gunshots at night."

She wasn't completely exaggerating. Emily had seen the neighbors complaining on the news after another shooting, mothers clutching their babies on the sidewalk, and once or twice she'd been startled by a single, distant report, the abrupt *pock!* carrying over the rooftops like a balloon, though now that she recalled it, the last time had been during the day and might have been a starter's pistol kicking off a road race in the park.

"Have you been through Friendship lately?" Arlene asked. "Along Penn there by the cemetery? I thought that strip was supposed to be turning around, but everything's closed."

"I know, it's a ghost town." Emily wondered if she'd been there to see

Henry, and felt guilty. She really needed to visit him. She needed to visit her parents too, and Louise, but when would she find the time?

"You heard about the home invasion right here in Edgewood."

"I thought that was Wilkinsburg."

"That was right here." Arlene jerked a thumb at the parking lot. "It was one of those row houses on Pennwood, up by Hampton, not ten blocks from here. Two men forced their way in, held this other man against the wall and shot him."

"Awful," Emily said, and stole a look at the buffet. There was no line.

"Apparently he owed these characters money and couldn't pay them."

"It's always drugs, isn't it?"

"So they killed him. Just like that."

"You have to wonder," Emily said.

"I know."

"Well, I'm ready for something to eat. How about you?"

Later they agreed the A chef must not have been on duty. The hash was salty, to Emily's taste, the pancakes dry. Next time she'd try the waffles.

As they crossed the parking lot to her Subaru, Emily eyed a scruffy ring of black men—not teenagers either—by the doors of the Giant Eagle. They weren't panhandlers, they didn't carry your bags to your car for a dollar, yet they were there every day, rain or shine, smoking and talking on their cell phones, and the police didn't seem to bother them.

After she dropped off Arlene, as she was waiting for the light at Braddock, she locked her doors. She always did, no matter where she was, though she couldn't deny she was extra vigilant as she made her way through East Liberty.

At home Rufus didn't come downstairs to greet her. She found him in her bedroom. He barely lifted his head, regarding her blearily, his eyes bloody, as if he'd risen from the depths.

"What if I were a burglar? Would you just let me waltz in and take whatever I wanted?"

He let his head drop and puffed out a sigh.

"Don't let me disturb your beauty sleep."

She didn't blame Arlene for her hysteria. What was more vulnerable than an old lady living alone? The city had always been a dangerous place. The world was. At least part of the fault, Emily thought, lay with the *Post-Gazette*, giving these horror stories so much coverage. What she resented was how easily she'd been infected, how quickly these groundless fears turned her cowardly. She spent the rest of the day in the garden, planting her summer bulbs, glad to be getting it done, and yet she kept looking up from her work, spade in hand, and glancing around, as if someone might be sneaking up on her.

LOVE, EMILY

She didn't want anything for Mother's Day, other than her children's happiness. The arrangement Kenneth sent was nice—Emily set it on the coffee table, where Rufus sniffed the pink asters as if they might be edible—but meant less to her than his call.

She didn't have to wait for it. Like every Sunday, she'd come back from coffee hour and was plowing through the *Times* when the phone rang. His reliability was a gift in itself, and if this eagerness to please could make him timid, and distant when he felt he'd failed, he was also like his father in that he would never purposely hurt anyone, a trait Emily, not blessed with an even temperament, respected and envied.

"Happy Mother's Day, Mom."

"Now it is." She thanked him for the flowers.

"Not my doing."

"Still, they're very nice. So, what's new in New England?"

Not a lot. Everyone was doing okay. After much discussion, Sam was registering for summer semester.

"That's wonderful," Emily said.

"We'll see."

"You don't sound convinced."

"I don't know how to say this. He and school just don't mix."

"I gather, but what's the alternative?"

"Exactly."

"All you can do is keep encouraging him. I'd love for Margaret to talk to him."

"It's an idea," he said, one of Henry's favorite evasions.

"In any case, please tell him I'm rooting for him."

"I will."

"Ah! Important question: will it interfere with him coming to Chautauqua?"

"I knew you'd ask that. His finals are the third week of July."

"Perfect."

From there they branched off to more general topics, giving her a chance to share how tired she was of the election, and the desperate state of the world. He'd have to ask Arlene about the Pirates, she was done with their shenanigans. The weather was wet, but her garden was coming along. Rufus was still hanging in there. The Millers' was still for sale. As always, she felt she had no news to report, as if her life had reached a kind of stasis.

"All righty," he said, and "I love you, Mom," and "Happy Mother's Day" again before saying goodbye. She'd turned down the stereo to talk, and when she set the phone back in its charger, the house went quiet around her.

Margaret would call when she called. Emily had learned long ago there was no profit in trying to anticipate her, and dialed up the volume again and went back to the arts section, continuing with a review of the Emerson Quartet she'd been enjoying, but instead of imagining herself in the balcony at Lincoln Center, she found herself fretting about Sam, and then about Sarah, who'd lost her job in Chicago. The worst thing in the world for Sarah would be to move back in with Margaret—for both of them—and Emily wondered if she should offer to help, or whether, like so many of her overtures, it would be taken the wrong way.

As a mother, she couldn't say she'd done her best with Margaret, but she'd tried beyond the point where others might have reasonably given up. Henry had, worn down by the cycle of promises that turned out to be lies, the brief clean periods between treatment and relapse, the lost jobs and credit card debt. Though she understood it perfectly, his withdrawal from their daughter was perhaps the greatest sorrow in Emily's life. Through everything, she'd always included Margaret in their plans, knowing, often, in those terrible years, that her invitations would be ignored or flatly rejected, and when accepted, the results would be disastrous. For Emily,

Margaret's absence was a sadness; for the rest of the family, a relief. Kenneth, like Henry, was embarrassed by her, as were Sarah and Justin, who seemed to have taken her cautionary example to heart, feeding themselves and getting good grades so they could escape to a more orderly life—but that was the past, Margaret would insist. She'd been sober nearly four years now. She liked to talk about a blank slate, and in some ways their relationship had changed, but in others it felt like the same struggle they'd waged since Margaret turned thirteen. While she was more open and affectionate—showily at times, as if in her gratitude she could no longer control her emotions—Emily suspected it wasn't entirely genuine. Likewise her constant references to making amends and surrendering to a higher power, when more than anything Emily wanted her to take responsibility for her life, past and present. The money troubles, the parade of boyfriends, the inability to follow through on all but the most immediate plans—these were the same problems that had plagued her forever.

Dismayed at the arc of her thoughts—today of all days—she folded the paper and took her cup and saucer into the kitchen for a refill. Gazing out the back door at the dripping trees as she waited for the kettle to warm, she wondered at the whole chain of continuity running back through her mother to her Grandmother Benton before her and down through Margaret to Sarah. Had her mother been as unhappy with her? Because they battled just as often and hard. In her later years she complained that Emily never visited, that they always had to visit Pittsburgh to see the grandchildren, an accusation Emily disputed bitterly, since it seemed she was always driving to Kersey. Always, never—their positions were absolute. The old house was a bungalow, and when she and Henry visited, they stayed in Emily's room, the rose-patterned wallpaper untouched since the Depression, the ceilings water-stained, and by the second day she was ready to leave. How many times did she have to win her freedom, and wasn't it unnatural to feel this way? Because she did love her mother. It was grueling, this confusion. She wished she could express this to Margaret—as if, just by being mothers and daughters, they were all caught in something larger, something ultimately not their fault.

She returned to Henry's chair, arranged the afghan over her lap and pulled the lamp closer so she could work on the puzzle, the bulb warming her, but within minutes pushed it aside, threw off the afghan and stood, waking Rufus. He watched her as she passed, headed upstairs, but didn't follow, and she was grateful. For what she was about to do, she needed privacy.

She climbed toward the second floor deliberately, head bowed, her eyes on the risers, certain she was making a mistake. Whether she was doing penance or indulging herself, she regularly performed this rite, pawing through her horde of treasure like a curator, knowing it would change nothing. Like Margaret with chocolate, she couldn't resist.

In her room she ceremoniously faced her dresser. It had been her mother's, salvaged from the old house and expensively refinished. The top drawer was shallow, a repository for baggage tags and travel alarms, shoehorns and passports. Her mother had kept everything, and opening it after her death, Emily had been staggered. Much of the clutter dated from Emily's girlhood. It was here that she found her birth certificate, and her silver rattle, and her father's wallet. Among these keepsakes, tied like a gift with a yellow ribbon, was a bundle of hand-drawn cards Emily had forgotten making. Browned at the edges, her penciled hearts and flowers and cakes and houses celebrated the unalloyed joy of the only child. Here, in all seasons, were the smiling stick figures under a smiling sun. The first time she'd leafed through them she'd been abashed at not just her clumsy lettering but her earnestness. *Love, Emily,* they closed, over and over, abundant proof of her goodness and innocence, and yet when she revisited them, as she did now, she felt a strange regret, as if they'd been written by someone else. Her mother hadn't saved any of her other letters, only the program from her college graduation and her wedding announcement.

As if in imitation, the other packet Emily removed was fastened with a pink ribbon—Margaret's cards to her, in crayon but graced by the same wobbly hand and free sentiments. Side by side, they seemed evidence of a mysterious bond, as if she and her mother were destined to share the same fate. *I LOVE YOU,* Margaret had scrawled. Emily lingered over the words, wondering if the feeling behind them still held true after all these years, or was it just a fossil, the promise, like the child who'd written it, gone forever?

This was precisely the danger of having too much time to herself. She retied the packet and returned it to its niche, closed the drawer and descended again. She sat with her half-done puzzle, listening to Bach and the rain, fending off unprofitable thoughts, waiting, though she knew better, for the phone to ring, and then, when it finally did, felt relief.

"Happy Mother's Day," Margaret said.

"Why, thank you, dear. Happy Mother's Day to you too."

"I'm not your mother."

"And for that," Emily said, "you should be eternally grateful."

THE START OF THE SEASON

For Emily, the real start of summer was marked not by Memorial Day and its poppies and parades, but the opening of her day lilies. They sprang up with the heat, their long stalks tilting over the driveway, their pumpkin-colored blooms facing the sun, a jubilant crowd welcoming her home. Her garden was in full riot, her alliums looming like pale blue moons above her phlox and sedums and gladioli. One border of Dalmatian bellflowers hadn't quite filled in, but on the whole she was pleased. She spent hours hunched on her stool, communing with the elements, pruning and pinching in the hope of even more glorious results. The sun rejuvenated her, her skin soaking in the vitamin D, and when the phone trilled in the kitchen, she let it ring.

Lately she'd been plagued by the Special Olympics. She'd made the mistake of giving them money once, and now they called almost daily. She resolved not to let it ruin these perfect hours. She put the machine on and lowered the volume to zero, closed the back door.

Outside, time, once so agonizingly slow, lifted from her. She and the bees and the worms—even the spiders—all had their jobs to do. Left to her work, she forgot everything but the task at hand, falling into reverie. Rather than break the spell, she skipped lunch, and at the end of the day felt an enervated, quenching sense of accomplishment. Her hands ached from gripping her spade and her shears, and when she'd washed, she rubbed a generous menthol blob of Aspercreme into their bony backs. After dinner she sat on the porch, admiring the fireflies and savoring a well-earned glass of Chablis until the bugs drove her inside, then went to bed early, righteously tired, and the next morning knotted the ties of her coolie hat under her chin, flipped down her clip-on sunglasses and set to it again.

These were the days she'd waited for, the days that made the rest of her life worthwhile. Because she knew they were fleeting, she reveled in them. She guarded them like a miser, and not just from the intrusions of telephone solicitors and Marcia's random visits. Now that the semester was over, Jim Cole was home.

He spent most of his time outside, reading on their back deck or tinkering in the garage, where he kept his bicycle. Midafternoon, in the heat of the day, costumed in fingerless gloves and scandalously tight racing shorts, he strapped on a turtle-shaped helmet and went for a ride by himself, stopping to chat through the fence with Emily on his way out and then again on his return. He said nothing of import, merely pleasantries about the weather and glosses on current events like the Bore to the Shore, and Emily wanted to tell him that while she understood he felt obligated and probably thought he was doing her a great kindness, she would be just as happy not to talk to him right now, thank you. Instead she kept working, figuring he might recognize her continued industry as a lack of interest, but he was a man and an academic, and more than once she had to excuse herself and duck into the kitchen to escape him.

She thought it odd that Marcia didn't accompany him on his jaunts, and that he never ran with her in the mornings, and wondered if their solitary pursuits combined with her moonlit vision of Marcia presaged the unraveling of their marriage. They were a strange pair—Betty agreed, if Arlene didn't—and now instead of ignoring them, as was her wont, Emily began to watch for signs of rupture. Whenever either of them appeared—watering their window boxes or setting out a saucer for Buster—she read their expressions as if they were characters in a portentous French film. Despite all of Marcia's huffing and puffing, she was still plump. It was Jim who seemed thinner, his face drawn, his neck stringy. While Emily ate her dinner, she peered at them sitting on their deck, Marcia tipping a wineglass, Jim with a nonalcoholic beer, and wondered if they were discussing, in a resigned, civilized way, their insurmountable differences.

More than the Coles or the Special Olympics, her own compulsiveness distracted her, charging her with errands she'd actively put off. The Subaru was past overdue for an oil change. It definitely had to have one before

Chautauqua. She needed to buy dog treats, and a lemon, and milk, which she'd forgotten to put on the list. She meant to call the city again and find out what was going on with the sidewalk. She should have a plumber come and take a look at the faucet in her bathroom. And she still hadn't been to see Henry or her parents.

Arlene, meanwhile, was making noise about the Arts Festival, opening that weekend. They both enjoyed the event, despite its sprawl and the inconvenience of parking downtown. It was the one time a year they made it to the Point, which never failed to impress, jutting like a prow into the choppy confluence. Neither of them cared for the carnival food or loud music designed to draw the younger crowd. Their pleasure was wandering along the midway, visiting the tents and looking over the artists' wares, some of which were remarkably well done and some so ludicrous they defied explanation. It was a game on the way home to choose their favorite abomination, teasing each other that they'd go back tomorrow and buy it to give as a Christmas present.

"Imagine her face!"

"What would she do with it?"

Emily couldn't put her off forever. The best she could do was check the Weather Channel and pick a day when the forecast was iffy. Thursday they were calling for scattered thunderstorms.

"Friday's supposed to be nicer," Arlene said.

"They're only saying thirty percent. I think we'll be fine."

She resented being put in this position. She felt calculating and stingy, when all she wanted was to close her eyes and lift her face to the sun. It reminded her of the afternoons her mother banished her to her room, where she was supposed to contemplate her sins like a prisoner but instead spent the time sharpening her arguments—pointless, since her father wasn't interested in them when he got home, only in a proper apology. She'd had to learn to be a dutiful daughter, and thought not much had changed. She still sulked like a child when she didn't get her way.

She'd chosen wisely, it seemed. Thursday when she picked up Arlene the sky was undecided. By the time they found parking, the banners along Stanwix Street were belling like sails. The wind came straight up the Ohio, blowing spray from the fountain across the plaza, darkening the concrete.

"I don't like the looks of that," Arlene said, pointing to the scrim of clouds sliding behind Mount Washington.

"They said scattered," Emily said. "This could all blow over by lunchtime."

They'd paid an outrageous sum for parking, so there was no question of retreat. Despite the wind it was warm out, and the midway was teeming. They strolled along the stalls, browsing the cluttered tables. Washed-out watercolors and coat-hanger sculptures, twig baskets and wreaths and tray after tray of clumsily done jewelry. It was like a flea market without bargains. Surrounded by so many glaring examples, they joined in a running discussion of what was art, what was craft, and what was simply bad. The pies looked nice though, made from organic apples and whole wheat flour, and a deal compared with the Amish at Chautauqua. In front of the Hilton a jazz trio played tastefully, a welcome improvement on the usual tuneless folk music, and they stopped for crêpes and a glass of wine, watching a tug with its load of coal push upriver, a sight that always reassured her of Pittsburgh's and therefore her place in the world. After lunch, as she'd so blithely predicted, the sun came out, and while part of her still wished she were at home, she and Arlene found some very nice sandstone coasters and some truly priceless Iron City beer can lamps they somehow resisted. All in all, she had to admit, she had a good time, and for her immortal soul's sake, she was glad it hadn't rained.

The next day, of course, it poured.

TUBBY TATERS

Just as for years Emily had been steadily losing weight, at her own mortal peril, Rufus had been steadily gaining it. He'd always been voracious, a beggar and a scrounger, a connoisseur of garbage. Emily thought it only natural that as his metabolism slowed he'd thickened, since he did nothing but sleep all day. Mornings he stationed himself at the far end of the dining room, taking the sun by the French doors. He lay stretched on his side in a rhombus of light, perfectly serene. She was busy planting annuals, bustling in and out with muddy flats, and his boneless contentment provoked her. "Hey, Tubby," she called on her way past. "You still with us?"

She had a dozen names she teased him with. Big Boy. Le Grand Elephant. Mr. Toofus McBoofus. He'd always been a clown, and now that he was old and grumpy, he was an easy target.

Lately, though, she'd begun to worry about him. Betty noticed it. She wasn't joking: over the last few weeks he seemed to have gotten bigger. His stiff hips were padded with fat, his rear end broad as a hassock. On their walks, before they even reached the corner of Sheridan, he was panting, and at night, beached on his side, he gurgled as if his lungs were full of fluid. His chest was heavy, and felt lumpier to Emily, though Dr. Magnuson said the hard nodes under his coat were just fatty cysts typical of a springer his age. When she called him in from outside, he no longer raced for the door and spun around for a treat, just waddled across the yard like a bear, his head down, his shoulders rolling.

"Betty's right," she said. "You are a mess."

His back left leg was weak. Climbing the stairs, he had trouble gaining traction on the polished wood, and sometimes stopped halfway as if he were stuck.

"Keep going," she said behind him, ready to intervene. "You can do it. Come on, one more. Good boy."

He wasn't much better going down, frog-hopping his back feet to the next step, and then the next.

Still he tried to shadow her around the house like he used to, unable to break their routine. After breakfast he liked to follow her up and lie across her feet while she brushed her teeth.

"No, Boo-Boo, you stay here," she said. "I'm coming right back."

Kenneth suggested stick-on carpet treads, Margaret a baby gate.

"I don't know what I'm going to do when he can't get up and down the stairs."

"How about one of those chairs on a rail?" Margaret said.

"I'm serious."

"Can't you just put his bed downstairs?"

"He wouldn't be happy," Emily said. "I wouldn't be happy."

"He's had a good life."

"He has."

"All you can do is make him comfortable."

"I know," Emily said, aware that on some plane they were talking about her.

She worried that he was in pain and she was being selfish. Ever since Margaret was a toddler they'd had a dog, usually two, and to contemplate life with no companion of any sort was awful.

She gave him his fish-oil pills like she was supposed to, though they did nothing. More than ever, he reminded her of Duchess near the end. He had trouble getting up, his paws slipping and scrabbling, his back end collapsing several times before she could cross the room and lift him.

"I know, pal," she said. "It's not easy."

For all his problems, he was still interested in his food. He could still catch his treats, he still slopped water from his dish all over the kitchen floor. On hot days he still liked to go outside and lie on the cool concrete of the back porch. He slept with the thin tip of his tongue protruding as if he were dead—something he'd never done before, and which upset her deeply. In the midst of her work, she stopped and peered at his rib cage to make sure he was still breathing. What would she do if he wasn't?

He had a checkup scheduled for next Tuesday, but during their morning walk on Friday he lay down on the sidewalk in front of the Millers' and wouldn't get up. She called the vet to see if she could bring him in. They said yes, by all means. She had to ask Jim Cole to lift him into the back of the Subaru, and then had to help.

On the way there she realized that unlike the end of Duchess, there was no one to appeal to, that the responsibility was hers alone. If she had to put him down, she would, regardless of whether she was ready.

At the vet's, Michael and an assistant lifted him out, slinging him between them like a sack.

In February he'd weighed sixty-six pounds. Now, four months later, he was just over ninety-two.

"Oh, buddy," Michael crooned, "what is going on with you?"

"So I'm not being alarmist."

"I'd be alarmed too. A dog his size shouldn't be this big."

While the assistant held the leash, Dr. Magnuson had Rufus sit and then stand. "Thank you. I appreciate you being so patient with me." The doctor ran his big hands over his haunches, cupped his paw and extended his weak leg. Rufus looked back and growled low in his throat.

"I understand," the doctor said, patting him. "I wouldn't be happy either if I were you."

"Could it be from when he fell?" Emily asked.

"I seriously doubt it. Anything structural would have presented right away. The real problem is his weight, because now everything has to work that much harder. Anytime you see a rapid weight gain like this, there's usually something else going on. I'd like to run some tests, but from everything you've told me, I suspect his thyroid isn't producing like it should be. It's relatively common in the breed, and again, at his age things break down. The good news is that if this is what I think it is, we write him a prescription, we put him on a diet, and he feels better in a month or so."

His thyroid. Like Aunt June with her iodine pills. She was so sure he was dying that, while she was grateful for this possibility, at first she didn't believe the diagnosis. It only sank in on the way home, and then she felt horrible for not realizing he was sick. She announced the news to the children as if his life had been spared.

All weekend she prayed the doctor was right, and was grateful when the tests confirmed it. A normal thyroid level was around thirty. His was two. She quoted the results to Betty and Arlene and Marcia as if it were a miracle he was alive. It was. She certainly hadn't earned this reprieve.

From then on she monitored his progress like a nurse, coating his pills with fat-free cream cheese and spending extra for the senior formula in cans. Instead of Milk-Bones and Liv-R-Snaps, she gave him celery sticks, which he crunched as if they were treats. Morning and evening she walked him up and down Grafton, regardless of the weather, encouraging him at every step. She was sure the neighbors thought she was senile, a crazy old lady out talking to her dog in the pouring rain.

She praised him for eating, for pooping, for lying there quietly. "Yes," she said, "you're a good boy," and scratched behind his ears, ruffled his chest, rubbed his belly. She wiped his rheumy eyes and made him sit still while she cleaned his ears with a Q-tip. She bent and pressed her nose to the top of his head, taking in his scent. She was aware that she was doting on him, but didn't care.

Betty thought he looked better, and while he still had trouble with the stairs, little by little his wind returned. One morning when Emily let him in from outside he gamboled across the kitchen, spun around and huffed, his plume of a tail wagging.

"Look at you," she said. "Someone's feeling better."

Mr. Feisty, she called him, Mr. Excitable, and ultimately, when he was back to his normal size, Mr. Pork Pie, and Chubbers McBubbers, but lovingly. When she came home from buying him canned food and found he'd pooped in the living room, she cleaned it up without rancor, and when he barked at the mailman, or the doorbell, or nothing at all, she was more amused than cross.

"Rufus Jamison Maxwell," she said, "what in the world am I going to do with you?"

CYD CHARISSE

She was wrong about the Millers'. The Tuesday after Father's Day, as Emily watched from her living room window, the realtor pulled up in her Mercedes, and with the fussiness of a decorator, centering the placard and then standing back to admire her work, crowned the Howard Hanna sign with a smaller one that announced a sale was pending.

Emily had had more than fair warning that this could happen, so it wasn't a shock, and yet, as depressing as the house sitting empty was, in some way this was worse, being both sudden and final, as if, like Henry and then Louise, it too had been taken from her.

As with any upsetting piece of news, her first instinct was to share it with those closest to her, except Kenneth and Margaret were both at work. She hesitated to call Arlene, thinking her sympathies wouldn't run as deep, but when she knocked on the Coles' door there was no answer, and she needed to tell someone of her discovery while it was still fresh.

"That's so funny," Arlene said. "I was about to call you. I just heard on the radio: Cyd Charisse died."

"Cyd Charisse."

"The dancer."

"I know Cyd Charisse."

"Remember her in *Singing in the Rain*, with Gene Kelly? I *loved* the way they danced together. And *Silk Stockings*? I must have seen that a dozen times. She was so elegant and mysterious. I wanted to be just like her."

Stymied, Emily wanted to say that at no time in her life had Arlene been anything like Cyd Charisse, and yet, despite herself, Emily recalled watching Cyd Charisse and Fred Astaire from the balcony of the Penn

Royal and wishing that someday she would be that much in love, and that beautiful, and if the mystery now seemed as canned and schmaltzy as the old Tin Pan Alley songs they moved to, it did nothing to diminish the romance of sitting in the dark and wanting to be up on the screen, living another, infinitely richer life. She didn't want to be Cyd Charisse, she just wanted to believe the feelings she was feeling were true, and would be waiting for her when she found the man she loved, because outside of the Penn Royal she'd never felt them.

"I always wanted to be Gene Tierney," Emily said.

"She was lovely. What was the one with what's-his-name? Dana Andrews. Where he was a detective."

"You mean *Laura*."

"Yes! Remember the theme song? *Doo* do-do dooo."

"I do," Emily said, "thank you."

"Sorry. I've been listening to this tribute and getting all misty. What did you want to tell me?"

"I was calling," Emily said as preface, "to let you know the Millers' sold."

"Good," Arlene said. "It's about time, right?"

"I suppose so."

"I wonder what they got for it."

"I'm sure it'll be in the paper."

"What was it listed for?"

She went on to speculate, but Emily had lost interest, and wondered, once she got off, how she'd ever let herself get caught up in Arlene's ramblings. She had her own losses to mourn without Cyd Charisse. She'd been in love as deeply as anyone, and if Henry wasn't exactly dashing, he was honest and kind and smart, and besides, what good was it now to compare her life to the movies? The whole idea was inane. Phone in hand, she circled the coffee table, finally stopping by the window, where she could see the sign. On a flyer she tried Kenneth, and then didn't leave a message.

IMPROVEMENTS

In retrospect, she was foolish to think they might hold off until she'd made her getaway, but why did they have to choose the height of July? She was so close to leaving, so tired of the stifling weather. She didn't need this mess on top of everything else.

The Millers were lucky to sell when they did. The letter notifying her arrived on Friday, and by Tuesday the place was a war zone, dump trucks idling outside, making the windows shake. Rufus barked as if they were being attacked. To replace an ancient terra-cotta sewer line, the water company was taking up a swath of street and sidewalk all the way down to Highland, including the tongue of her driveway. She felt surrounded, the house an island. They suggested affected residents park on Sheridan or Farragut, meaning Emily would have to leave the Subaru not just at the mercy of the elements but where she couldn't see it. Her other option was to lock it in the garage and depend on Arlene, the prospect of which felt like a trap. They gave her no timetable—it was possible they'd be there all summer—and so she found a spot on Sheridan not too close to the stop sign but far enough from the big sycamores so they wouldn't shed directly on it, and then, thinking of the Olds, spent several minutes trying to tuck it into the curb, scraping one rim in the process.

There was no escape from the noise, even with the house sealed against the heat. They had to break up the street, and all day long the saws whined, biting through the asphalt, opening seams for jackhammers and backhoes and finally workmen who climbed down into the trenches and squared them off with shovels. The trucks kicked up dust which settled on her hedges, powdering the porch rail and the mailbox like white pollen. She went out to water the garden, but ducked right back in again, fearing for her lungs.

It was too hot anyway. It was the muggy heart of summer, when the air upstairs was as thick as their old attic, and she emptied the dehumidifier twice a day. At night she opened her windows and turned on her table fan, but it just made noise, and she lay there sweltering in the sheets, wishing she could sleep. These were the moments she missed Chautauqua the most, with its cool evenings. When the children were little, she spent the entire month at the cottage, Henry driving up on Friday after work and back down Sunday night. The week itself was quiet, a time to read on the dock while the children frolicked. They lounged around the screen porch, played croquet in the shade of the big oak. Late afternoon, as the heat deepened, clouds massed to the north, thunderheads piling skyward until they could hold no more and storms banged down the lake, bringing relief. After dinner the children needed their sweatshirts. By bedtime some nights they'd have a fire going, and while the new place wasn't the same—a cramped and charmless rental just above the Institute, set well back from the water—dusk still fell like the dusk she and Henry had paddled out into that very first summer after the war. In two weeks she would be back there, and happy. Until then she just had to make the best of things.

By law they couldn't start before eight in the morning. She was naturally awake at five, and used these free hours to walk Rufus and water her garden. The first few days she holed up inside, as if she could wait them out, all the while chafing at her confinement. She felt as if she were under house arrest, though she realized it was mostly self-imposed. She was free to leave, but really, where was she supposed to go?

Kersey, to see her parents one last time. With the new car she had no excuse not to.

The answer hurt, and directly she dismissed it, offering up a concession. She would go see Henry—Louise too. What she'd do with the rest of the day she had no idea. She wasn't going to hang out at the library like a homeless person, despite their air-conditioning.

Henry was less than ten minutes away, Louise just another five. Emily was overdue for a visit, and still, day after day, she put it off, as if by stalling she might wriggle out of it somehow. She'd go after she came back from Chautauqua. Surely it wouldn't make any difference to them. As logical as that sounded, Emily recognized it for a lie. In the evenings the bulldozers and backhoes sat idle by the curb, drawing out the curious, and each night as she watched the neighborhood children and their fathers circle the stilled machines, she scolded herself for wasting another day, yet the next morning, overrun once more, she found herself resisting, and finally it was only by writing his name down on the calendar as if they had a date that she made herself go.

HARD TO KILL

She needed something that could take the heat. The Maxwells' plot lay on the southern face of a knoll overlooking a large ornamental pond crowned with lily pads, and while the view was desirable, and serene, besides a few flowering pear trees the slope was bare. Even in the beginning, when she'd visited faithfully, no matter how often she watered, the sun burned up the geraniums she planted, the wilted petals reminding her, every Sunday, of their shared helplessness before the elements. She understood there was nothing she could do short of being there daily, yet even now, as a gardener, she couldn't resign herself to the sacrifice. At the same time she couldn't very well show up empty-handed. After much consultation with Mike Hornek at the nursery, she settled on a potted cosmos, one each for Henry and Louise. If it rained at all while she was away at Chautauqua, at least they'd have a fighting chance.

To get to the cemetery she had to drive through Garfield, a neighborhood she avoided on principle. The cheap Italian restaurants she and Henry haunted in college were gone, reduced to nail salons and storefront churches, the sidewalks dotted with litter. From her speakers, Albinoni purled on incongruously.

She should have asked Arlene to come. The thought had been nagging at her since she'd made up her mind to go, and while she was utterly justified—of all her errands, this was the most private—in the past year they'd grown so yoked that she couldn't rid herself of the feeling that she was somehow cheating Arlene.

It was nearly ten, by the clock on the dash. She'd timed her arrival to coincide with the gates opening, and as she eased from light to light through the ravaged main drag, she was surprised to find, besides a few hefty women clumped at bus stops, the usual ne'er-do-wells loitering in doorways, waiting for earlybirds. She kept her eyes front, and was relieved to finally turn in at the pillars and leave behind the world of the living.

Inside, the orderly past reigned. The slate-roofed Gothic chapel with its rosette window and verdigris-streaked downspouts might have been shipped stone by stone from the high moors of Yorkshire. The lawns were groomed smooth as fairways, each tree and shrub lovingly tended, their shadows dark and sharp in the clear morning light. There was no one around, the only motion a bright cardinal flitting across the road and lighting on a snowball tree, which she took as a good sign.

She didn't need to stop at the office. Though she'd long forgotten his section number, she knew the way by heart, angling off as the drive wound through the terraced hills and woody nooks, splitting and then splitting again. She envied their spearlike poplars and torturous Japanese maples, dark as port. The grounds ran on and on, deep and wide as a park, an endless English garden in summer's full, blowzy bloom, nature half tamed for the strolling patron's contemplation. She passed lichened mausoleums and obelisks, nodding at favorites like the kneeling, harp-winged angel and Mr. Vandergrift's absurdly heroic Corinthian pillar. The rough-hewn boulders and cracked marble sarcophagi, the ornate bas-reliefs—the grand permanence of it would always impress her. Here was Pittsburgh's history in vaulted crypts and bronze war monuments, the industrialists and artists, the actresses and architects. Coming from Kersey, she'd thought it would be an honor to be buried here, and still did. As morbid as it sounded, she'd be proud, one day, to lie beside Henry.

She knew it was an illusion, the idea that he was here. Henry wasn't one to linger. His spirit or soul had flown, off to happily tackle whatever work was needed. And yet, as she turned the last gentle curve and slowed, pulling to the side, she felt a flutter of anticipation comprised equally of excitement and dread, as if he might chastise her for being late.

Her door unlocked automatically—the one thing she didn't like about the car. She was alone, and stepped out of the air-conditioning into a suffocating stillness. The pond, several rings below, was carpeted with lily pads. In the trees cicadas whined, a shrill, simmering thread. From a distance, like a passing train, came the low, shifting rush of the city.

She popped the back, the metal of the hatch searing her palm, making her snatch her hand away. She'd brought a watering can, along with her gardening basket. Neither was heavy, but with the cosmos, she'd have to make two trips. Against her instincts, she left the hatch open, thinking she'd be right back.

Three white marble steps flanked by urns led her up onto the lawn—a lush green despite the lack of rain. The section dated from the mid-nineteenth century, when Henry's great-grandfather had secured the family plot with oil money. As far as she could see, nothing had changed since her last visit. The stones she passed were older, the names raised rather than graven, letters edged with soot. CHALFANT, KNAPP, ATWATER—families lost to history, as she and Henry would be, ultimately. The idea made her bite her lip. Why, here, surrounded by its symbols, did she doubt the promise of eternity?

The slope was steeper than it appeared, and shadeless. Wanting to look nice for him, she'd worn the wrong shoes, and had to be careful, taking little mincing steps, carrying the cosmos out before her with both hands as if it were a hot casserole. As she neared the Maxwells' plot, even before she could read his name, she saw the flag on Henry's grave. It was her doing, indirectly, having let them know he was a veteran, and yet its presence stung. She thought it was wrong that someone else had visited him when she hadn't.

Beside him, his parents' graves were naked, and she wished she'd thought to bring something for them. She was a poor guest, her mother would say. The Maxwells had taken her in when she was just a raw girl from the sticks. For a moment she stood there shielding her eyes from the glare, recalling holidays they'd spent together, Lillian in her pearls and apron flitting about her kitchen with a tumbler of gin, waving away Emily's offers of help. "I know it doesn't look like it, but I've got my own system." It might have been last Christmas, yet—could that be right?—she'd been dead nearly thirty years. She was so much what Emily had wanted to be, cultured and unflappable. Without her, what would Emily have become? It seemed too great a debt to ever repay, and here she'd brought her nothing.

Lillian and Gerald's headstones were matching, cut from a single block of Vermont granite. When Henry had died, Emily had done her best to find the same stone but it was impossible, and the slight difference in color bugged her like a flubbed note. She'd included the bill of sale in the folder with her will so the children would know where to go for hers. She could rely on Kenneth. She'd reminded him of it several times over the phone, and while he wasn't as responsive as she might have wished, he knew it was important to her.

Why? When was the last time they'd come to see Henry? After her funeral, when would they ever come back to Pittsburgh? It wouldn't matter to her then, so why did it matter now?

Because, like the stone, it did. The problem, she thought, was that she couldn't draw a solid line between life and death, or, approaching that line herself, hopefully refused to. She was sure it was selfish, and ungrateful, given the eternal peace she prayed would be granted her, but she didn't want to leave. All she'd ever wanted was a quiet, dignified life. She thought she might finally achieve that here.

She would be on his right, replicating the way they slept, Arlene in the very next plot. Even here, Emily couldn't escape her.

Though she knew it was foolish, rather than tread on their graves, she detoured around the edges, walking an imaginary aisle between the plots, as if they could hear her tromping around above them. She stopped at the head of Henry's, resting one hand on the arched top of his stone as if it were his shoulder, then, bracing herself, bent over, the motion squeezing out her breath for a second, and set the pot on the grass. She hoped he didn't mind the pink.

"I'll be right back," she said, but then, as she gingerly picked her way down to the car, felt silly. When she'd first come, she could still hear his voice in her head, and indulged in conversations they might have had at home. "I don't know what to do about Margaret," she'd say, and hear him answer, "She's an adult, you don't have to do anything about her." Now she heard only herself, and she sounded doting and maudlin, neither of which Henry had any patience for, even before he fell ill. "Don't talk to me like I'm an idiot," he once scolded her from his hospital bed. "I'm dying, not stupid." She understood him exactly. She was as practical as he was, and as angry, or had been then. She feared that the years alone had warped her, turned her sentimental, as they'd done her mother, staying on in the old place, growing stranger and stranger each time they visited, talking about people who were long dead as if that morning she'd run into them at the IGA. The danger was just this, retreating into the netherworld of the past, but what else was there?

Even with the back open, the car was an oven. She had to set the basket and the watering can down to close the hatch, then climbed the three steps again and trudged uphill. The weather was wrong—it wasn't lunchtime and it was already hotter than they said. She imagined how bad Grafton Street was, with the noise and the dust, and was grateful she was here.

"Here we are," she said like a nurse.

She hadn't brought her stool, and stiffly folded herself down on the grass, falling backward the last few inches, her outstretched hand tipping the basket, spilling a jumble of gloves.

"Very graceful, Emily."

Somewhere beyond the pond a mower sputtered to life, then throttled up, buzzing. She straightened her visor and tugged on her gloves, chose a spot in the center and got to work with her spade. Under the grass the ground was baked hard. She chipped at it, taking little divots.

Why did she think it would be easy?

There was a spigot behind the Spruill crypt, and she carried the watering can over and filled it halfway. She could barely lift it with both hands, and had to stop on the way back to flex her fingers.

She emptied the can over the beginnings of the hole. Rather than soak in, the water pooled and ran like quicksilver through the grass.

"Honestly now."

She tried the spade for a while, then went and got more water, stopping twice this time. The water seemed to soak in, yet when she settled herself and started digging, the ground refused to yield. She rested, catching her breath. The sun was higher now. She was sweating and her gloves were muddy, and she was tempted to just pack it in and come back tomorrow with a shovel.

To stand, she had to first get on her hands and knees, lean back and free one foot so it was flat on the ground, then brace a hand against Henry's stone and half pull, half push herself upright. She was tired and hot, and it was an effort, though, as Dr. Sayid always said, she weighed almost nothing. She was not quite all the way up, remarking on how little strength she had—what few reserves a person her age possessed—when a wave of dizziness struck her. Her vision dimmed, a shadow passing between her and the world. With both hands she held on to the stone, afraid she'd pitch backward and hit her head. She clung to it, hoping the spell would lift, seeing, as she waited, Arlene at the Eat 'n Park.

She thought, wildly, that if she was going to die, she was glad it would be here.

Did she really believe that? Because she didn't want to die at all. She wanted to go to Chautauqua. She wanted to see the children. She was just being dramatic, as her mother so often accused.

She waited, stock-still, suffering the rush, and gradually her senses returned, like blood filling a sleeping limb. She touched a hand to her throat. Her pulse was fine. She'd just stood up too quickly.

"Slow down, leadfoot," she said, as if she were talking to Rufus. "It's not a race."

She heeded her own advice, taking a break before she lugged the can over to the spigot, and then filling it only a quarter of the way. She made four trips, thoroughly saturating the ground before sitting down again. It seemed to help. Slowly but surely she was making progress. She dug and rested, dug and rested, switching the spade from hand to hand. She leaned in over the hole, chopping at the sides, scooping out the muck. She was sure that anyone watching would think she was a crazy woman, stabbing at Henry's grave in her get-up. She didn't care. There was no guarantee the cosmos would last the week, let alone the winter, but she was already a mess, and this was what she'd come to do. She wasn't leaving until she was done.

OLD HOME DAYS

There was nothing like crossing things off her list to raise her spirits, and her sights. Days after visiting Henry, fortified by her success and spurred by the rapidly dwindling calendar, she loaded a pair of cosmos into the Subaru and set off for Kersey.

She left early in the morning, before the workmen arrived, taking the shortcut through the zoo. The sun over the reservoir was blinding. Already there was traffic backed up at the bridge. Once she was across the river and headed north on 28, it dissipated, and soon, except for the occasional school bus or coal truck, she was alone on the road, the windshield filled with blue sky.

It had been a good ten years since she'd been back, and Henry had driven then. She couldn't recall the last time she'd made the drive by herself, though she'd done it enough when the children were little, piling their sleeping bags and pillows into the station wagon. 28 had been a winding two-lane then, snaking over the hills and through the hollows, slowing for every crossroads hamlet. Now the lower half was practically an interstate, bypassing places like Slate Lick and Ford City, whose drive-ins and billboards they'd ticked off like mileposts. To pass the time they played games. "I spy with my little eye" was Kenneth's favorite. How disappointed he'd be. On both sides the woods ran unbroken, a grassy strip down the middle. There was nothing to distract the driver, and while it made the trip that much faster, she thought it was a loss, and was glad when, outside Kittanning, the two lanes became one, funneling her into a bumpy chute that led to a stoplight she remembered once being new.

From there on, the road was familiar, each curve and dip an old friend. Junkyards and Christmas tree farms, hunting camps and log cabin taverns.

It was like going back in time. She was pleased to see the Twin Pines was still going strong, and tickled that the black barn advertising Mail Pouch tobacco was still standing, the sign faded yet legible: TREAT YOURSELF TO THE BEST.

"Yes," Emily said, "why not?"

She was happy to be out of the city and on her own, going somewhere, a foretaste of Chautauqua, mere days away. From Spaces Corners to Distant, she knew the lonely houses and windbreaks and cornfields, the dusty lanes that led off into the hills. In New Bethlehem the few changes she noticed were on a large scale—a huge addition to the high school, and right past that a hideous commercial strip with a Wal-Mart and a sprawling gas plaza. The train tracks they used to have to slow for to save the car's shocks were paved over, weeds sprouting between the ties, but outside of town the Shannon Dell looked ready for business, the giant cone on top freshly painted. The old round-shouldered gas pumps by the butcher shop, the dollhouse-sized church on a pole that marked the turn for a real one— she reveled in each rediscovery, as if these treasures had been preserved for her. It was a mystery. She'd been driving this road her whole life, fleeing or returning, her every passage fraught with guilt. It was only natural that the landscape would hold some residual tinge, yet, rather than feeling pursued by those old ghosts, she felt welcome, as if, imperceptibly, over the intervening years, there'd been a shift within her.

"I'm sorry you don't like coming back here," her mother often said, to cap whatever petty dust-up they'd had. How could Emily explain: it wasn't her mother or Kersey she'd disowned, but her earlier self, that strange, ungrateful girl who strove to be first at everything and threw tantrums when she failed. From the moment she left home, Emily had tried to distance herself from that child, taking on the calm mantle of privilege and sophistication, an impersonation impossible to sustain there, where everyone knew her as a teacher's pet and a crybaby. Perhaps Emily had finally forgiven her. Or it might be, she thought, having lived long enough, she'd come to think of everyone close to her with a helpless tenderness, accepting that life was hard and people did their best. Certainly it was true of her mother. Was it a sin to extend that pity to herself?

She wondered, less charitably, if her good mood had anything to do with the fact that this could be the last time she made the drive—as if she might be free of these questions once and for all. The idea troubled her, and she cleared her throat and refocused on the road.

Near Brookville, where 28 met I-80, she poked along the busy strip of truck stops and fast-food boxes, afraid she'd miss her turn. The interstate would always be new to her, an intruder from the future. In the sixties when it was being built, the chamber of commerce imagined it would fuel a boom, belatedly bringing industry to Kersey. All that was needed was another interstate running north-south, which, as her father enjoyed pointing out, no one but the chamber of commerce had ever imagined. "If wishes were horses," he loved to say, "beggars would ride." Since I-80 went in, Kersey, like all the towns around it, had only grown smaller. Henry called the cluster of gas stations around the interchange the last bastion of civilization. "Everybody wave," he told the children, a joke she didn't appreciate, dreading, as she did, sleeping in her old room.

She slowed to read the green signs. "East," she said to double-check, and swung up the ramp.

At the top she had to merge, but didn't see a gap, and waited, stopped, as several pairs of tractor-trailers whipped past, neck and neck, rocking her car. A big SUV rolled up behind her, and though she pulled out as soon as she saw an opening, before she was fully in her lane the other driver slid wide and roared past as if, like Arlene, she were going too slow. She checked her speedometer and was even more annoyed. She was already going the limit.

She stayed on the interstate for just one exit. Technically she'd never left 28; it was a jog to let through-traffic skip downtown Brookville, which she didn't miss at all. She stuck to the right lane and, getting off, was happy to leave 80 to the truckers and speed demons.

After the turn for Munderf, the road climbed into the rugged hill country, winding through deep woods, the asphalt humped and rutted by logging trucks, muddy turnouts for trailheads and deer-crossing signs everywhere. By a shuttered ranger station, Smokey the Bear stood guard with his shovel, holding her solely responsible for stopping forest fires. She was close now, another twenty minutes at most, and congratulated herself for making it this far. There was still time to turn back—but why would she think that? She hadn't come just for them, out of strictly filial obligation. She was here for herself as well.

Brockway was the last big town, pallets of different-colored bricks stacked high beside the old glass factory, and then she was out in the sticks again. Toby Creek ran alongside the road, looping wide in oxbows, then cutting back underneath. Mile by mile she was following it, like her life, upstream to its source. As she passed through Crenshaw and Brockport and Challenge with their consignment shops and bait ponds and used car lots, she thought that this was all hers, all home. She wanted to apologize to her mother, and wondered if it was too late.

The cemetery was on Skyline Drive, just over the line from Dagus Mines. In high school it had been the big make-out spot, the view supposedly an aphrodisiac (she would never know). As she crested the hill, all of Kersey spread before her in miniature, glinting in the sun: Main Street and the courthouse dome, to the west the roof of the new school and its giant parking lot, the blocks beyond dotted with cheap swimming pools. Her house was down there beneath the shade trees on Taylor Street, and as she neared the entrance she had the urge to go see the old place first, and just as quickly vetoed the idea as cowardly. She'd have time later. First things first.

DOGS MUST BE ON LEASH AT ALL TIMES, a sign welcomed her. Inside the listing iron fence, the grass was burnt yellow and badly mowed, tufts sticking up everywhere, the drive narrow and crumbling at its edges. Having just visited Henry, she couldn't help but compare the two cemeteries. There were no heroic columns or pillared crypts, no obelisks or angels, just row on row of modest stones. No one famous was buried here. Like Kersey, it was homely and remote. You'd only find it if you already knew the way.

She parked and turned off the car, popped the hatch and stepped out, expecting silence, but was met instead by the rhythmic clanking of a piledriver rising from town. Between blows an engine chuffed—twice, three times, gathering steam—and then the hammer banged down again. She supposed it was good: someone was building something. Her father would be pleased.

As glad as she was to be distracted, there was no putting off the inevitable. She didn't have to climb any precious marble steps. There was no pretense of this being the Elysian Fields or the royal gardens, just gently sloping pasture with a pleasant view. Take away the graves, and a herd of cows would be right at home.

Instead, here were her parents, like the farmer in the old joke, out standing in a field. Like Henry's, their headstones would always look strange to her, as if there were some mistake she was incapable of fixing. Inert and adamant, they did such a poor job of representing her mother and father. While for her own stone Emily coveted the clean simplicity of names and dates, she could see why the Egyptians topped their sarcophagi with carved likenesses, and why the Japanese put photos on their markers. A visit wasn't simply a tribute but a way of feeling closer to a loved one, and while Emily did feel a slight vertigo, facing them, she knew, as she did with Henry, that her parents weren't really here, and while it only made sense, in some way it was also disappointing, as if, after such a long journey, she'd arrived, finally, in the wrong place.

Why did she always want more, when this was all there was? "I'm sorry, Emmy," her mother would say, with her teacher's maddening patience, "but that's not how the world works."

She knew that now, and it still didn't matter. Like a child, she refused to surrender to the world. She stood at the foot of their graves a moment longer, saying a prayer, then went back to the car for the watering can and a shovel.

It was just as hot as the other day, and she was careful not to overtax herself. After she dug the first hole, she took a break, sitting in the dappled shade of a honey locust and sipping iced tea from her thermos. A gray haze had settled on the far hills like fog. There was no wind, not a breath. The pile-driver was becoming annoying, making her think of Grafton Street, and Rufus, probably sacked out in her room, dead to the racket outside. She'd already started packing for Chautauqua. If she'd known they were going to tear up the whole street, she would have booked the cottage for the month. There was no reason to be in the city. From where she sat she could see Irishtown Road stretching north through the state forest toward Saint Marys, and imagined hopping in the car and following it. She could just hear herself asking Arlene to swing by and pick up Rufus.

The idea of going back home tired her. If she let herself, she could sit here all day, maybe even sleep, curled at the foot of the trunk like the fool in a tarot deck.

"Up and at 'em," she said flatly, and slowly rose, her knees creaky.

Why was she so uninspired? It had been a good day—ideal, really. The drive had been surprisingly easy. The view of Kersey was perfect. There was no one to intrude on her solitude, and yet she felt let down, or was it natural here, that sadness? Her parents had been gone a long time; so had she. Why did she expect, after all these years, to suddenly come to some new understanding? As much as you might want to, you couldn't change the past.

As she dug the second hole, she thought that was right. She would be judged by how she'd lived her life, not how she wished it had been. She accepted that completely. She was painfully aware of her failings. Every Sunday she confessed them, and while by no means clear, her conscience was no heavier than most, or so she hoped.

"Be a good girl and get me my sewing," her mother asked. "Be a good girl and bring the sheets in."

Had she been good?

She wanted to think so.

Could she have been better?

Yes.

Of everyone, she'd treated Henry the best, and even on that account she had her regrets. She and her father got along, but in the end he did her mother's bidding, a betrayal Emily couldn't forgive at that age, the same betrayals her own children held against her: making them do their homework before they could go out and play, refusing to let them wear ripped blue jeans to school, grounding them for sneaking beer from the basement fridge. She was sure she was even more unreasonable than Margaret as a child. She recalled sitting on the edge of her bed and screaming at her closed door, not words, just screaming to protest this latest punishment, and yet, when the children asked her mother what Emily had been like, all her mother would say was, "She had her moments."

Her mother was a better person than she was. Not all people could say that, or admit it, but Emily knew it to be true, just as Henry was a better person than she was. They'd done their best to save her from herself. It was no revelation, and yet she'd never thought of them together until now.

"Funny," she said, and looked out over the town, biting her lip as if the idea might lead somewhere. It didn't have to. This was why she'd come, and rather than humbled she felt lucky, and grateful.

She finished digging and set her mother's cosmos in the hole, tamped down the loose dirt with her toe, careful of the stem, then watered them both again. She didn't give them much chance up here, unprotected, but for now they looked nice, a cheery burst of color. There was nothing more to do, yet she didn't want to leave, and stood there for several minutes, drinking her iced tea while the pile-driver kept time, before she lay a hand on each stone—her father's first, then her mother's—and lugged everything back to the car. It took two trips, giving her ample time to say goodbye.

Downtown, little had changed since her last visit. The courthouse stood stolid in its shady square, the front walk flanked by cannons. The Clarion Hotel was long gone, and the Penn Royal, and the Woolworth's where each spring her mother took her to choose among the new dress patterns. Once she'd known every shop on Main Street, down to the pool hall at the far end her father called the Bucket of Blood. Now the only place that looked halfway familiar was a coffee shop called the Busy Bee, and it was closed. Even the Sheetz at the stoplight where the old Sinclair used to be had turned over and was now a Get'n'Go. And yet the shape and scale—the feel—of everything was the same, including the almost total absence of people, though it was just past lunchtime.

A block into the quiet side streets, nothing had changed. Grace Methodist and the free library and the post office were all as she remembered them, and the gloomy Gothic revivals on Court Street she'd thought were haunted, hurrying by at dusk with her freshly checked-out books hugged to her chest. At Center she turned right. She realized that she was recreating the way she walked home. It wasn't subconscious: there were only so many streets.

Seeing the old place was a tradition. The last time she'd been back, she discovered that the new owners, with no regard for the neighbors, had painted the bungalow sky-blue with lavender trim. Emily guessed it was supposed to be whimsical and different, but it came off as showy and obnoxious, a color-blind crime against the house and the town. Instantly she'd wanted to go get a can and a brush and cover it up.

As she turned her corner, she expected to see this pastel monstrosity and was puzzled, momentarily, when it didn't leap out at her. Instead, she found that—as if they'd known she was coming—whoever owned the place now had restored it to its original white with forest-green shutters.

She pulled up in front and leaned across the passenger seat to see better, leaving the car running. Her mother's hydrangeas were in bloom, and the porch rail was lined with window boxes full of lush petunias. At one end a white wicker glider hung from the ceiling, recalling the wooden one she and her mother shared those lazy summer afternoons, shelling peas or snapping beans as they waited for her father to come home. The roof had been redone, the chimney repointed. Emily had to quash the urge to jump out and ring the bell and thank the new owners profusely.

The idea that the house had magically returned to its natural state was like something from a fairy tale. She wished she'd brought a camera, though of course—besides Arlene, possibly—there was no one to show it to. Emily was so mesmerized that it was only when she swung into the Volkers' driveway to turn around that she noticed the Lowerys', a bungalow nearly identical to theirs, right across the street, was for sale.

Immediately—insanely—she wanted it. The strength of her hunger shocked her. She had no desire to live here again, yet the first thought that flashed through her mind was that if she sold the house on Grafton Street she could buy the Lowerys' outright and still put away a couple hundred thousand.

What would she do here? She hardly knew a soul. There was no classical radio, and compared to Pittsburgh, the library was a joke. Plus, she argued belatedly, what would Arlene do without her?

She had no answers for these questions, yet the temptation lingered well after she took her last look at the house and made her way through downtown and out Skyline Drive. As she passed the cemetery, she glanced over to check on the cosmos, taking in the long view beyond, then broke off to concentrate on the road. Seconds later the sign for Dagus Mines slid by, and she was across the town line, gone. Outside of Challenge, Toby Creek ran sparkling beside her, dropped frothing off ledges, and as she followed it downstream—like the water itself, headed for the Allegheny and Pittsburgh—she thought of how strange her visit had been, how different from what she would have predicted, and couldn't quite say why, though the effect was clear, and startling. Normally she was glad to leave Kersey behind. Now she was happy to think she might be back.

EXIT, STAGE LEFT

Chautauqua. The very word was a promise. All year she clung to the idea of return. Now, mercifully, it was here. She'd completed her errands. She was ready for her reward.

The car was packed, it was time to go, but as she went through the upstairs a final time, Emily couldn't shake the feeling—with her more often than not now—that she was forgetting something important, something she'd specifically reminded herself not to forget. She'd taken the car in for an oil change and gotten gas, so that wasn't it. She had cash and her checkbook, her credit cards and her triple-A card, just in case. Wednesday when Betty came they'd cleaned the fridge and put out all the garbage and recyclables. She'd done laundry yesterday, and the breakfast dishes were running. Marcia would water her garden, Jim would mow the lawn. She'd turned off the mail and called the paper. What else could it be, and what could it matter? She'd only be gone a week.

She thought it must be something small and essential, like toiletries, but her toothbrush holder was empty, her toothpaste missing, gaps in the shelves of the medicine cabinet where she kept her prescriptions and deodorant. She knew she had her hairbrush (she'd forgotten it too many times in the past). Shampoo, conditioner, body wash. Whatever it was, it wasn't in here.

Rufus was waiting for her in the hallway, sitting at attention. Since yesterday he'd stuck close, hovering, afraid he might get left behind. On the stairs he crowded her going down, his shoulder bumping her knee. She pulled up, making him stop.

"Cool it," she said, "or I *will* leave you here."

He knew it was a bluff. Once she was done lecturing him, he scurried down, spinning at the foot of the stairs to face her, his tail slapping the back of the sofa.

She had his food, his bowls, his treats, his pills, his bed, even an old army blanket of Henry's for the chilly nights.

It wasn't anything in the fridge. Marcia had already lugged the half-filled cooler out to the car for her. Once they got there they'd have to hit the Lighthouse anyway.

She did a last, unnecessary check of the kitchen, Rufus tagging after her. She'd already turned off the computer in Henry's office and made sure the answering machine was on. She'd locked all the windows and put the chain on the back door.

As she was testing the French doors, the grandfather clock struck the quarter hour, meaning she needed to get going. She said she'd be there at nine, and unlike Arlene, she wasn't in the habit of making people wait.

"All right, Mr. Nervous-in-the-Service," she said, and he bolted for the front hall.

Keys, sunglasses, gum. She clipped on his leash, and with her hand on the knob, scanned the living room as if something might come to her, then closed the door.

It was Saturday, so no one was working. Down past Farragut the bulldozers and backhoes stood idle, abandoned like toys in a sandbox. They were still tearing things up, as if they had to destroy the entire street before they could begin rebuilding any part of it. They'd be lucky to be done by fall.

It was easier to stick Rufus in the backseat. She spread Henry's army blanket across it to protect the leather. "Upsy-daisy," she said, and he reared, bracing his front paws on the edge of the seat. On good days he could get in by himself, but today he balked. "Hang on, Tubby." She set her pocketbook on the sidewalk and lifted his hind end, and he flopped in awkwardly, rolling on his shoulder. "Get comfy. It's going to be a long one."

The morning was still and overcast, the trees laden. The radio was calling for thunderstorms; they'd probably run into some on the way up. Going over to Regent Square there was almost no traffic, only some firemen at Penn and Braddock trying to extort money from people at the light. Rufus did his job, barking as if they were carjackers.

"Good boy," she said.

She arrived right on time, and then had to climb the stairs and ring the bell. Arlene apologized, she was running a little behind. Emily didn't bother to ask why, just stood in the entryway while she fed the fish.

"I'm afraid I'm having one of those days," Arlene said, as they brought her bags down. "I don't know what it is, I keep thinking I'm forgetting something."

"Something important."

"Like my glasses, but I've got them."

"Something you told yourself not to forget."

Arlene gawked at her as if she'd read her mind.

"Me too," Emily confessed. "It's been driving me crazy all morning."

"So it's not just me. That's a relief."

"Is it?"

"Yes. Okay, no, not really."

They stowed her bags in the way-back and buckled up.

"It's going to be strange," Arlene said. "I'm so used to driving."

"You can navigate."

"Go straight till you hit Hutchinson—"

"Thank you," Emily stopped her, turning the key.

"—then take a left."

"Enough."

Arlene was fiddling with her vanity mirror, and suddenly it came to Emily: her visor.

"Dammit."

She wanted it so she could sit on the dock and read without being blinded. Last night she'd washed it in the basement sink and hung it up to dry. She could picture it down there, waiting for her in the darkness beyond Henry's workbench.

"Do you want to go back and get it?" Arlene asked.

"No."

"We can."

"I'll find one up there," Emily said, resigned.

"I still don't know what I'm missing," Arlene said, as if to comfort her.

Emily leaned in and reset the trip odometer to zero. With both hands she put the car in gear, then checked over her shoulder and pulled out.

"And we're off!" Arlene said.

"Yes," Emily said. "We most certainly are."

AVAILABLE FROM PENGUIN

Songs for the Missing
A Novel

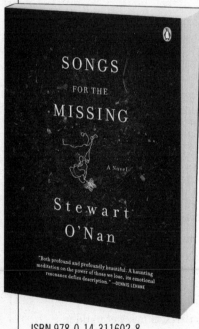

ISBN 978-0-14-311602-8

Returning again to the theme of working-class people and their wrenching concerns, *Songs for the Missing* begins with the suspenseful pace of a thriller, following an Ohio community's efforts to locate a young woman who has gone missing. It soon deepens into an affecting portrait of a family trying desperately to hold onto itself and the memory of a daughter whose return becomes increasingly unlikely. Stark and honest, this is an intimate account of what happens behind the headlines of a very American tragedy.

PENGUIN
BOOKS

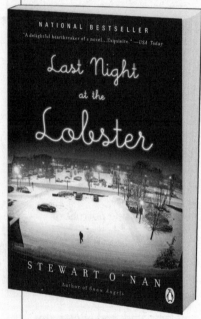